THE SHAM

A Novel

NICOLE

BARRELL

THE
SHAM

NICOLE BARRELL

Woodhall Press | Norwalk, CT

woodhall press

Woodhall Press, 81 Old Saugatuck Road, Norwalk, CT 06855
WoodhallPress.com

Cover design: Jessica Dionne
Layout artist: L.J. Mucci

Library of Congress Cataloging-in-Publication Data available

ISBN 978-1-954907-72-0   (paper: alk paper)
ISBN 978-1-954907-73-7   (electronic)

First Edition
Distributed by Independent Publishers Group
(800) 888-4741

Printed in the United States of America

For my parents, whose art and intellect and stubbornness made me, me.
I miss you every day.

One need not be a Chamber—to be Haunted—
One need not be a House—
The Brain has Corridors—surpassing
Material Place—

Far safer, of a Midnight Meeting
External Ghost
Than its interior Confronting—
That Cooler Host.

—Emily Dickinson

PART I

1

Margo

Last January, on impulse, I'd bought a tall, skinny little house on East 8th. It was a foreclosure, the only reason I could afford it. Then I realized I couldn't *actually* afford it, not after discovering the faulty plumbing, the insurance, the mold. But I'd been so blinded by the need to prove that I could do something on my own that I convinced myself I could "make it work." This was stupid; I know this now.

By the time summer rolled around there was no getting around it: to keep the house I'd need a roommate. It would have to be a stranger. Someone who wouldn't pry and wheedle her way into my life—or worse, my past. I knew I would not find someone like this on the SouthieRentals app or on RoomCare.com. Those people liked to go to brunch. They expected granite countertops. They'd want to *talk*.

Craigslist was more my speed, I decided, more anonymous. This, as it turned out, was also very, *very* stupid.

August

When I got back to the kitchen after cleaning the upstairs, I realized I'd left the bills right out on the counter. Not only that, you could see the mold over by the fridge. The house was a dump, but I had to at least try to mask this before the first candidate arrived, in fifteen minutes.

For the mold, at least, I'd found a solution: hide it with a big-ass plant.

The pot was massive, up to my knees, and inside was a raggedy, browning bamboo plant. I'd picked it up at an estate sale earlier that morning and had managed to heave the hulking thing into the kitchen, where it now sat on top of the mold.

But right now, it was still peeking out, that black rot. I squatted and hugged the pot, sliding it to the right. There.

Next, the mail.

As I swept the pile into the drawer, the name inside the clear envelope window of one envelope caught my eye, turning my stomach.

Maggie Nevins
19 Punkhorn Lane
Marshside, MA

Mags, Dad would call me. Or Mom, sometimes, through her wine-stained veneers, *Maggie the Mood*.

The person to whom these bills were addressed no longer existed. Unfortunately, I, Margo Sharpe, was still responsible for the balances, the late fees, the ruined credit. And not to mention, the shame.

* * *

Carmen Kangaroo came right on time. She was short, round-faced, and beautiful, with long dark hair to her mid-back. She wouldn't make eye contact or shake my hand, or answer me when I asked about her unusual last name. She just bobbed on her heels and said, "I have to pee."

I tossed my head back. "Third door on the left."

Carmen left the bathroom door cracked, more than cracked, practically open, her piss stream violent against the sides of the bowl. She shouted over the peeing, "Some people call me Roo. Not everyone. Just my friends. You can call me Carmen."

I refused to talk over her piss, so I waited for her to come out before responding. There didn't seem to be a flush coming, though. Just more questions.

"Do you go out in Southie a lot? I heard last-call is at one. Is that true? That's so *early*."

Then, the doorbell rang. I jumped, both from the noise—it was more of a prison buzzer than a ringer—and because this was not an open house. I'd created buffers for each appointment, and not only that, I'd masked the address on the listing. I'd been *careful*.

At the door was a wimpy, nebbish-looking thing with floppy brown hair and pointy elbows. He wore a nasty look on his face.

I said, "Who are you?" but before he could respond, a yell from Carmen came down the hallway.

"Dude. You're *late*."

"Sorry, babe," he said, stepping past me.

The two of them stood nose to nose in the hallway, whispering. I strained to hear what they were saying, but all I could make out was, "small...old...weird."

I turned to shut the door. Except now, there was someone *else* standing on the stoop: a tall, skinny blonde with a horrid haircut. This was turning into some sort of circus, exactly what I didn't want.

"And who are *you*?" I said.

The blonde's smile collapsed and a look of bewilderment crossed her face.

3

"I'm Lucy. Lucy Somers? Sorry, I know I'm a little late—"

She was the teacher. That's all I could remember. That, and she was early.

"Aren't you supposed to be here at noon?" I asked.

Lucy's face reddened. She tapped her phone, which had been clutched in her hand, and dragged her finger down. Then she looked up at me, eyes wide.

"Oh my gosh. You're right. Noon. I had ten on the brain, for some reason."

I wiped my damp forehead, then made sure to finger-comb my bangs as far down as they would go.

"All right. I'd say you could join the tour now, but I can't give you my full attention, so it might be best—"

"Sure," Lucy said brightly, cutting me off. "I'll join now. Since I'm here."

Reluctantly, I opened the door wider and Lucy stepped inside, her eyes darting first to the narrow stairway straight ahead and then down the hallway, which was also narrow. I could sense what she was thinking: The place was stifling. Claustrophobic.

Lucy looked to the right, to the living room, which was small and spare. It had a scratched-up coffee table and a pilling yellow couch, its back against the bay window. I followed her gaze out that window, to the new building across the street with the fancy wreath on the door, central air-conditioning, and occupants—with their expensive blonde highlights and social lives and doting parents who visited on the weekends—who were nothing like me. Not anymore.

* * *

"Appliances aren't updated," Carmen said, dragging her finger along the stove.

"And no granite," squeaked the boyfriend.

I turned to Lucy, who waited obediently for my instruction. Her long, thin arms were crossed over her chest, like she was hugging herself. She might have been trying to hide her massive pit stains, which I wanted to tell her was a lost cause.

"This is the back deck," I said, pointing to the glass slider. I was hoping I could distract them from how run-down and outdated the rest of the kitchen was—the ancient stove, the peeling tiles. But as I tried to nudge the rubber lock with my thumb, it wouldn't budge.

"Gets a little sticky with the humidity," I mumbled.

Thankfully, after another push of my thumb, the door gave way.

Carmen crossed her arms. "I was hoping to see the water? Not, like, other people's decks and their gross little yards."

It was true. Any distant view of the harbor was obstructed by the backs of other buildings. And directly below were chicken-wire fences and tiny tomato gardens and clotheslines of neighbors I'd never met.

But I'd been careful not to embellish the listing description, and hadn't bothered to filter any of the photos. In fact, I'd included a picture of the very scene they were taking in right now. I had tried not to mislead anyone. Well, any more than I already was.

Thankfully, Lucy piped up.

"You were very thorough in your listing, Margo. I appreciated all the information up-front. You laid everything out so nicely."

Carmen let out a little snort, rolled her eyes, and then she and the boyfriend stepped back inside.

Lucy went to follow them, but before she did, our eyes met. Hers were gray and shining, and her mouth betrayed a smile—a joyful, incredulous smile—and I became so infected with it that I, too, smiled, and between us grew the seed of an understanding: that sometimes, people were just off their fucking rockers.

5

* * *

There was only one room left to show, the upstairs spare bedroom. I soldiered ahead down the short hallway, bracing myself for what Carmen and the boyfriend would have to say about it (Too small! That is *not* a closet!) when out of the corner of my eye I saw Lucy about to enter my own bedroom, which was the first door on the left.

"Wait," I called out. "That's off-limits."

Lucy halted. But Carmen ignored me and burrowed her way inside.

By the time I caught up to her she was at my dresser, holding up an old picture of Brad. In this one he was in his front yard, about to kick a soccer ball with his leg suspended in the air behind him, his dark hair falling into his intense, dark eyes. His skin, tanned from the summer, practically glowed against his white shirt.

"Is this your brother?" Carmen asked, eyes bugged. "And is he single? Because if so, I'll sign the lease right now."

The boyfriend flinched at this, and rightly so.

"It's not my brother," I said. "It's my boyfriend, Brad."

"Interesting," Carmen said, giving me an exaggerated once-over.

I could have said the same about her little rodent, but I held my tongue.

She reached for another framed picture. This one was taken more recently, Brad with his arm around me at Delaney's, our—or, if I was being honest, *his*—favorite bar.

"Look, Roo," the boyfriend called out, "she used to be blonde...and hot."

He'd somehow skittered over to the windowsill, where I kept my family photos, and was holding an old picture of me on the boat with my mom and dad. (Why hadn't I remembered to put these *away*?)

Carmen curled her lip. "Please. Not *that* hot."

That's it, I thought. I stalked up to the boyfriend and wrenched the photo out of his hands and then turned and did the same to Carmen.

6

"I *said* this room is off-limits. Now *get out!*"

The last two words were so loud and ferocious they bounced off the walls and sent Carmen and the boyfriend clear out of the room.

In the mirror I saw my cheeks were brick-red, my whole face and neck beaded with sweat. I was afraid to meet Lucy's eyes, to get her reaction, and too flustered, thinking only of getting these two out of my house, immediately. I would rather live with a live porcupine. Carmen Kangaroo? Please. It sounded like a fake name. And I would know.

* * *

Back in the living room Carmen said, "You know what? This place isn't *so* bad, for the price. When are you making your decision?"

I gaped at her, speechless. After all that! I should have just told her right then to leave, but it was so much easier to avoid confrontation and let her down over text, so I said, "Soon."

"What does that mean?" Carmen asked.

At first, I thought she was prodding for a specific date and time, but then realized she was looking past my head, at a lone sign on the wall, oversized, hung by a long metal wire, that said INCONCEIVABLE!

"Oh, that."

I waved my hand at it, like it was nothing. Like it didn't matter.

"It means, like, *unbelievable.*"

The sign had been a gift from Dad to Mom—a quote from her favorite movie—and it had hung by their bed. Miraculously, it had been spared from all the blood. If it hadn't meant so much to them, I'd have burned it.

Carmen regarded me with her wide, dark eyes. "You look so... *familiar,*" she said, turning to the boyfriend. "Doesn't she?"

"It was nice to meet you guys," I said, herding them quickly toward the door, my forehead slick with renewed sweat. "I'll call you as *soon* as I decide."

* * *

I'd almost forgotten about Lucy. She'd missed all that, thankfully, since she'd hung back to check out the spare bedroom.

I listened for sounds, wondering what she was doing. For a while I heard nothing.

Then, to my relief, I heard the toilet being flushed, followed by the sound of the sink turning on, then off, and finally, Lucy's slow, creaking steps down the stairs.

When she joined me in the living room, her eyes climbed to the wall behind my head, to the INCONCEIVABLE! sign.

"*Princess Bride*," Lucy said softly. "Right?"

I nodded.

"Love that movie."

I didn't dare say anything in return or else I'd start to weep in this poor girl's face. Grief and shame were weird like that. I'd be perfectly fine and then, *wham*—waterworks.

Lucy stood opposite me, awkwardly, expectantly.

I had so many questions, but I was too afraid to ask. Did she like the place? Or was she just being nice, oohing and ahhing over everything?

And did I want to choose her by default, just because Carmen was so awful?

I motioned toward the couch.

Lucy sat, coiling her hair with thumb and index finger over her ear, greasing the strands. Around and tuck, around and tuck, one swirly vortex. But the strands wouldn't catch; her hair wasn't long enough. It was an odd length, a little past her ears, like a cut gone wrong. Plus, it was too frizzy and poufy to lay flat. As for the rest of her, she was rail-thin, gangly, her shoulders bony and visible under her T-shirt.

I sat in the armchair across from her and watched as her eyes darted all around the room and then back to me again. I braced myself for the get-to-know-you questions I could feel coming. But we continued in silence, and the questions didn't come.

Someone had to say *something*; we couldn't just sit here like this forever. I supposed it was up to me to begin.

I cleared my throat. "Where'd you say you went to school, Lucy?"

"Local community college," she said, smiling shyly. "Really small. You've never heard of it, I'm sure."

I couldn't even remember where Lucy had said she was from; I kept getting her application confused with Carmen's. The Midwest somewhere? Or the South? Somewhere far away. It's what made them both so attractive.

"Probably not," I said.

I shifted in my seat, waiting for her to ask where I went to college (nowhere, I was too much of a mess, and no money anyway) or where I grew up (on Cape Cod, in a little town called Marshside, a place I never wanted to see again).

She didn't ask these things. Instead she leaned forward and said, "Do you know you have mice?"

"Mice?" I sat up straight in my chair. I hadn't heard the scratching in the walls in months. It wasn't possible. They were gone. "No, I don't have mice. I'd know."

"Sorry," Lucy said sheepishly, then held out her phone. "I took a picture. It was, like, in the corner, near the window? In the spare bedroom."

Sure enough, there were black, rice-sized pellets.

My face grew hot. I'd run out of time this morning and hadn't really cleaned the second bedroom as thoroughly as I should have; otherwise, I'd have seen that.

The way she was looking at me made me want to melt into the floor, and this felt strange—like the ball had bounced out of my court, and suddenly, my fate was being decided by a stranger, and not the other way around. Like it wasn't my choice for her to live here, but hers.

I found myself asking, shyly, "Is this...a deal-breaker for you?"

"Not at all," Lucy said. "As long as you get an exterminator. Can I be transparent, though?"

"Sure," I said.

She stared down at her feet. "I have a couple more apartments to look at. Depending on how it goes..." She looked back up. "Maybe I could come back tomorrow, for one last look?"

I forced a smile and said, "Sure."

As I walked her to the door I felt my shoulders tighten, feeling equal parts devastated—I could lose her; she was the best option, wasn't she?—and terrified. Because for all I knew, she could be the worst.

2

Her

It was a little before eight, and it was getting dark. The oppressive heat from the day had lifted, and the armpits on her thin white T-shirt were dank.

She was sitting inside a beat-up glass bus shelter on a metal bench. She had on a baseball cap, into which she'd tucked her hair so it looked as if she didn't have any. Two other people stood waiting for the bus, on their phones, paying her no mind. She felt safe, unseen.

A bus came squealing down the street. The two others got on the bus. She did not. She stayed.

She'd been sitting there for the better part of the day, other than bathroom breaks, and was beginning to give up and accept that Margo didn't leave her damn house. This was a colossal waste of time.

The house itself was tall and narrow and pointy, like a pencil, wedged between two double-deckers and separated by alleyways, just wide enough to stow trash and recycling bins and not much else. The first floor had one bay window—that was the living room, according to the childishly drawn floor plan on Craigslist—and one small window above the front door. At night, you could see the stairwell through it.

In person, the shit condition was no surprise. The house looked just like it had on Google Earth, and just like it had that time her father, Gary, had driven her up from Pennsylvania, worried about her taking the bus by herself, and just like those times soon after when she'd told her parents she was checking out grad programs and instead took the bus—*by her fucking self*—and went straight here, to 509 East 8th Street, South Boston.

South Boston. *Southie*. Home to Castle Island and *how 'bout dem apple*s. Home to Whitey Bulger's victims buried toothless in dirt basements.

And home, most importantly, to Margo Sharpe.

Normally, these trips would be timed during work hours, so she could get a proper look at the place without Margo there. But today was a Saturday. Today was The Big Day. Margo was likely considering whom to choose, though the answer was obvious, at least in her estimation. At the thought of Margo's options—oh, she almost laughed.

A welcome breeze brought a brief respite from the heat, along with the smell of trash. Cities were disgusting. Why anyone chose to live in them was beyond her.

But then, movement, in the window.

Seconds later, Margo appeared at the door.

Finally.

Margo walked slowly down her steps, head down, absorbed in her phone, then took a left and disappeared around the corner.

Unsticking her sweaty ass from the bench, she stood and followed Margo from a safe distance.

It seemed Margo was headed toward an unmarked building that had one cloudy front window, inside of which was a faintly lit green sign.

THE SHAM   PUB

The "ROCK" part of the sign was broken, unlit.

Margo slowed her pace and bit that stupid lip of hers. It appeared to be some sort of nervous habit, same as tugging down those horrid black bangs over her signpost forehead as if that would hide how big it was. As if it would hide *who* she was.

Margo stopped in front of the door, checked her phone, and then cupped her hands to peer into the cloudy window. She stood up straight, took a deep breath, and entered through the heavy mahogany door, into the dark.

Peeking through the window—even going inside and sitting incognito in some dark corner—was tempting, but not an option. Talk about obvious.

Plus, that wasn't part of the plan. This was still strictly the research phase.

There was another bus stop, further down the street. She went there instead, sat, and opened her small notebook. Her little sister, Savannah, had bought it for her in Vermont, at a shop somewhere near that gross hippie college she went to. The cardboard cover was labeled "Decomposition Notebook." It was literally made of shit.

"Happy Birthday," her sister had said, very earnestly, and it had taken everything she had not to throw it back in her sister's face. But her parents were standing right there, nervously watching, so she'd smiled and said, "Thanks, Savvy."

Now she turned to the next blank page, midway in, and wrote, "8 p.m., Tuesday. Goes to dumpy bar called The Sham."

13

She closed the notebook, stood, and walked in the direction of her car, a beige shitbox she'd gotten from some grandma on West 4th who was losing her sight and couldn't drive any longer. As she walked, she ignored the constant buzzing of her phone.

Her parents: *Are you okay? Are you safe? Where did you sleep last night? CALL US!*

Minutes later, one from Savvy: *You can't be mad at them forever.*

Once she'd settled into her car, pillow and blanket crumpled in the backseat, she replied to her sister: *Yes, I can.*

3

Margo

Aunt Izzie had been calling me a million times a day.

"After all that's happened to our family, Margo. Strangers, off the Internet—*really*? Isn't there a friend, or a coworker, someone you already know?"

(Translation: Margo, are you a gigantic loser?)

Every time, I told her, "Iz, I'm broke. I have no other option." And she knew that it was true, so it always ended there.

As for the stranger part, I didn't have to say why I didn't try to live with a friend. She knew full well I didn't have any.

It was my fault for riling her up, anyway. Early on I'd sent her some doozies, like the message I got from some "accountant" named Betsey S: *"Hi. Wut is your policy on drug use? Will be very tidey and throw needles away in trash."* And another from someone named Benny:

"Hi! I understand you don't want a male roommate, but I assure you, I'm a stand-up guy. As in, I stand up while you bend over."

I was trying to be funny, making light of the outrageous people you can find in the dark corners of the Internet, but it made Izzie so nervous that one day she drove up two hours from the Cape, leaving Uncle Steve to watch Ray and Damon, my young nephews, which she *never* did, to help me vet the candidates. That's how I'd landed on Carmen and Lucy—the most "normal" of the hundreds of responses I'd received.

But were they normal? Carmen certainly didn't seem like it. And in a way, neither did Lucy. Why, during the tour, had she been staring at me like that? And not just in moments of commiseration, but small moments, watching my every move? Or was this just my imagination?

Now, I climbed into bed and pulled the covers up to my chin, preparing to cope with a difficult situation the only way I knew how: a midday marathon nap. It was a sign of depression, Izzie always said, the excessive sleeping.

As I lay there, Carmen Kangaroo texted six times; she apologized for the boyfriend coming unannounced, she was going to break up with that stupid loser anyway, and not to be rude, but had I given any more thought to upgrading the appliances, or...?

I imagined myself sitting on my parents' basement stairs, perched on the bottom step.

"Dad, be honest. Is Carmen *that* bad?"

He would have rolled his chair to the doorway of his home office, brown eyes twinkling with irreverence. "Good God, Mags, yes. She's *obnoxious*. You can do better than that."

Then Mom's voice, calling down the steps: "Agreed. But that Lucy character—what was the matter with her hair? It looks like someone took a weed whacker to it. It's a called a *comb*."

Now, there was no one to ask. No basement steps to sit on. I had to rely on my own instincts. Instincts that had steered me so wrong in the past.

Four little words kept me from texting Carmen back.

"You look so...*familiar.*"

* * *

"Is that the lease?" Lucy pointed to a pile of papers on the coffee table.

It was the next day. Lucy, as promised, had returned.

I changed the subject. I wasn't ready. "Did you look at any other apartments?"

Lucy twisted her head to look around the living room. "I did. But nothing really compares to here. The price, the outdoor space... and," she turned to face me, "you seem really nice. Not like some of the other girls I interviewed with. They say Boston people are rough around the edges, and I can see the truth in that..." Lucy trailed off.

I scratched my arm. Bit my lip. I figured I should ask if she had any more questions about the apartment itself, or about the financials, when to my shock Lucy stepped forward and said, "So should I sign the lease or what?"

Gone was the diffidence, the softness, from yesterday. Her voice, even, seemed deeper. Rougher. Or maybe I was imagining all this. Maybe it was just my nerves.

"The lease—right," I said.

I wiped my wet palms on my shorts. What would I do if I *didn't* offer Lucy the apartment? Explore other options? And if so, *what* options? Needles-in-the-trash Betsey? Bend-over Benny?

I found myself walking to the coffee table, gathering up the stack of papers, and handing it to Lucy. It was only nerves. I was being ridiculous.

"Pen?"

"Right."

I turned and fished through the drawer of the coffee table, coming up with a black ballpoint pen.

Lucy took it and kneeled, laying the papers flat against the rough surface and pressing the pen on the highlighted spots where she was to initial.

I tried to ignore the thrumming in my head, that piercing sense of fear that refused to go away despite Lucy being exactly what I'd set out to find, exactly what I'd *asked* for right there in the listing: *Not a social arrangement. Would like someone who keeps to themselves and respects privacy.* Her response: "I live out of state but will go home often on weekends. I'm very close to my family. I keep to myself."

She sounded perfect. So why did I still feel so unsettled?

I stared down at Lucy now, head bent over the lease. Was it that she looked so ordinary, but at the same time, like she was from another planet?

Lucy looked up. "Everything all right?"

I realized I'd been looming over the table—too close—and chewing my lip.

I stepped back. "Sorry."

Lucy looked back down. "One more spot to initial." She flipped to the back and etched an "LS" onto the final line. "Guess it's official now," she said, smiling and standing up.

It was official. I was doing this. I was sharing my space with a stranger. And that's what she'll have to remain, I told myself. Don't *ever* forget that.

I held out my hand. "Welcome to 509 East Eighth."

* * *

When I talked to Brad after Lucy left, he was happy for me, but he wanted to be sure Lucy paid the rent, so he gave me the third degree about her background.

"She's a teacher," I said. I made sure to keep my voice cheerful. "I checked her references and they all said the same thing. A little quiet, but reliable. Although, it's funny, now that I've met her, I can't picture her commanding a classroom. She's super shy. Or something. Maybe timid is a better word. Except today, she was a bit more..."

I stopped. I was always babbling to Brad, since I didn't really talk to anyone else, besides Izzie.

Silence.

I continued. "She seems easygoing. She didn't ask a lot of questions."

"You like it when people don't ask you questions," he said.

"I do," I said, suddenly annoyed. I loved him, but hated how he could see through me.

"And when she gets curious about you?" he pressed. "About everything? Someone in such close quarters, wondering why you're hiding yourself away?"

I told Brad I had to go.

* * *

The Sham's bartender was a redhead with an Irish brogue and a missing front tooth. It had taken a few solid minutes of me standing at the bar before he ambled over, carrying a couple bottles of Bud in the crook of his arm.

"What'll ya have?"

"One of those, please."

He set one down.

"Menu?" I asked.

He nodded to a white sheet of paper with curled corners stuffed between the ketchup and the salt and walked off.

He didn't seem to recognize me from yesterday, my first time trying The Sham. I'm not surprised. I'd only stopped in briefly, for a beer. I'd been so distraught after the tour that I failed to make eye contact with anyone, choosing to sit in the farthest corner table, facing the wall.

At least I was in a better mood today. No more perseverating, no more plaguing over whom to choose. It was a done deal. Best of all, I could finally make a dent in my bills with Lucy's rent money. I could afford meals out sometimes. Like now, here, at The Sham, a place my boss, Corinne, had urged me to try for months.

When Corinne first mentioned it, we'd all been in a team meeting in the conference room, where one of the "team-building" icebreakers projected onto the whiteboard was *Share one thing you're proud of!* Normally I revealed nothing about myself at work—not where I lived or what I did for fun, nothing. But I'd just bought my place, and though I wasn't proud of much in my life, this—this I'd done on my own.

When it was my turn, I spoke quickly about my new small, pointy house in Southie. Corinne asked what neighborhood, and I told her, conscious of everyone watching me, conscious of their curiosity.

Corinne clapped her hands together and said, "Oh, you *gotta* try this place down the street." She was standing by the projector, looking down at our ten-person events marketing team sitting around the oval conference-room table. She explained, "I'd go there all day Sunday with Debbie, back when we pretended we were 'just friends'..."

Titters around the table. They were now married.

"Anyway, I may be in my thirties now, and lame, living in the burbs. But let's just say we enjoyed lots of *beverages* at The Sham."

Everyone laughed. We all loved Corinne.

"It's a total dive," she said to me, smiling. "But I think you'll love it."

That's when my least favorite coworker, Astrid, quietly—so only I could hear—said, "You *would* love it. Because no one goes to that dump except Southie *trash*."

I ignored her, like I always do.

Soon they moved on from me—someone got a puppy, another person won a trip to Mexico—but after the meeting, Corinne took me aside and gave me a hug.

"I'm so, so proud of you."

I said thank you, and then immediately rushed to the bathroom, shut myself in a stall, and cried. I didn't deserve her kindness.

Because Corinne believed I was someone else.

Here was the truth: I'd started out as an office cleaner. A GED didn't get you far at one of the top tech firms in Boston, so one night I fudged my résumé and left it on Corinne's desk—she'd always been nice to me, always granting me a big smile, saying thank you when I emptied her trash. I told her I was an orphan, along with a tiny white lie: that I was homeless. I was renting an even worse dump at the time, but this additional fib seemed necessary. Some people have dead parents. Big deal. I needed a gut-punch.

She fell for it. Corinne immediately took me under her wing, and over time told me about her own tough childhood in the Dorchester projects. Every day I walked into that office, filled with guilt and shame, and thought of coming clean. But every day I thought better of it. I couldn't afford to lose my job.

The bartender had returned. "You decide?"

I scanned the menu again quickly. It was stained and the options were limited. Seven items, in total, and at the bottom it stated NO SUBSTITUTIONS. I wasn't surprised; The Sham had piss-poor online reviews, no Wi-Fi, and no air-conditioning, and, according to SParkLYEats12 on Yelp, *You can essentially buy a better sandwich using the discount deli meats at Stop & Shop. In fact, I believe that's what they use.*

21

I happened to like Stop & Shop deli meats. I ordered a ham sandwich, then found a table along the opposite wall.

Mindlessly, I checked a slow-loading Instagram for Brad's profile. Right now, he was volunteering with his Little Brother, Corey; on his story, he'd posted a photo of two hands, one large, hairy, tanned, and one small, fair-skinned, holding ice-cream cones.

I smiled. For all the suck in my life, I reminded myself, at least I have him.

* * *

After a while I looked over and saw a plate sitting on the bar that appeared to be mine.

When I went over to get it, I noticed the slip said CUSTOMER: GIRL.

But when I stepped back, a loud yelp rang out.

"Oh, buddy, I'm so sorry!" I said, realizing I'd stepped on a large black paw.

A husky, middle-aged man on the stool beside me tugged at the leash of the massive black dog lying at his feet.

"He's fine, ain't ya, Bearie?" he said, in a thick Boston accent.

I could hardly make out the name when he said it, but the dog's collar confirmed his name was Bearie MacDonald.

The full view of the dog pricked my heart. He looked just like Sunny. Thick black fur, dark brown eyes, and massive strings of drool dragging to the floor.

"Newfie," I blurted out, and the man nodded. I added, "I had one, once. They're great dogs."

"He's a good boy."

The man's gaze strayed back to the Red Sox game, playing on the wall-mounted TV.

I nuzzled my face into the dog's fur, stroking his back, *a little much*, as my mom used to say, embarrassed about my effusive dog-petting whenever I came across one.

"I can walk him for you, if you want," I said. "Anytime. Day or night. Just ask."

As soon as I'd said it, I was stunned; I didn't know what had come over me. Nostalgia, that's what it was. I missed Sunny. Missed cuddling up with her on the sunroom floor while Mom did her yoga, perfect ass in the air, urging me to join: "Mags, come on—you won't get those shin splints at field hockey after a session with me, I promise…"

"Are you serious?" the man said, looking at me.

"Oh. Yes, I'm serious. I'd walk him. For free."

He told me where he lived and asked if I was close.

"I'm right around the corner," I said. "Five-oh-nine."

"Coulda sworn you were gonna say it was one of those new fancy jobs up Broadway," he said, wagging his head toward that direction, with the trace of a scowl, "but 509—that was my buddy Richie Vito's place, before he rented to this messed-up couple who wrecked it. Mold, plumbing issues—tell me you got it gutted."

"No, not yet—but I just got a roommate," I said, "so hopefully I'll get help with the mortgage and then do some work on it. She moves in next week."

"Congrats. A friend?"

"No, Craigslist."

"Ah. Be careful with scammers, yeah? Used to be a cop. Saw too much of that."

I nodded. "Thanks. I did a background check and all that."

"Good. I'm Owen, by the way."

"Margo."

We shook hands and he handed me a business card.

"That's got my cell on it. You can text me your number and I'll be in touch about Bearie."

I nodded and looked down at the card. In neat lettering at the top it said, "Owen MacDonald, Private Security Services."

He hopped off the stool, leaned down, and lifted Bearie's paw to wave it. "Say bye to our new friend."

And they were gone.

I grabbed my plate from the counter. The ham sandwich came on a fresh, soft sub roll, contained fist-thick honey ham and mustard sauce that was simply unbelievable. It was the best ham sandwich I'd ever had.

* * *

"Excuse me?"

I eyed Lucy over the top of my laptop. I was sitting on the couch pretending to work, keeping an eye on things while Lucy moved in. But right now she was grimacing, like she was afraid to ask me something.

"Yeah?" I said.

"So sorry. But, umm, do you mind helping me with something? It's the last thing in the truck. And it's a little heavy."

The moving men, several of them, were standing around on their phones. I looked at them, then at Lucy, but she seemed not to notice. I followed Lucy outside.

Lucy gestured at the lone item that remained in the moving truck: a large, black trunk. It looked like pirate treasure or something, with gold clasps and a tattered exterior.

We heaved the thing up the two front steps and then inside. We made it midway up the stairs when I couldn't take it anymore.

"Let it down," I gasped. "I can't."

Lucy, who was on top, looking down, said nothing, and let it rest against the step.

"Can't they help?" I wagged my head, my face drenched in sweat, down at the movers. Through the slats of the banister I could see the men exchanging concerned glances.

"It's too valuable," Lucy said, lowering her voice. "Vintage."

"But you're paying them to—"

"I don't trust them with it, okay?" Her tone was clipped. She patted her pocket, inside of which her phone had begun to buzz. "Dad's trying to FaceTime," she explained, rolling her eyes and smiling. "*Again*. I'll let it go to voicemail."

"How many times has he called?" I asked, trying to keep the irritation out of my voice. She'd been FaceTiming for hours, by my count, showing her father all the rooms, taking decorating advice from her mother.

"A million," she answered. "He feels bad he had to work and couldn't be here. He's trying to make up for it. I love him, but seriously, he's so annoying." She paused. "Are you close with your dad?"

"No," I said. I knew what I was supposed to say next, what I had trained myself to say, but it hurt to say it out loud. "We're...estranged."

"Oh, that's so *awful*. I don't know what I'd do without my dad." Lucy thought a moment. "Like, imagine one day you marry Brad"— she paused—"that's his name, right? And say one day, not soon, but *one day*, you get married. Wouldn't it be so sad not having your dad walk you down the aisle?"

I took up my end of the trunk. "Can we actually get moving? I have a ton of work to do."

"Sure," Lucy said, and she looked a little guilty, like she wanted to say something else, but she didn't.

When I maneuvered to the next stair my grip slipped a little, and I imagined falling headlong into the coatrack, impaling myself.

"Mind spotting us?" I shouted down to a mover.

He came up quickly and ended up practically carrying the whole thing. He plopped the monstrosity in the center of Lucy's room, causing the gold clasps to rattle.

"Careful!" Lucy gasped.

I guess she did have a point about them not taking too much care with her things. One of the clasps had come loose. Lucy caught me looking at it and quickly pressed it back down.

He left, and I followed him out.

"Hey," Lucy called after me.

I turned.

"Thanks for your help. And I'm sorry about prying earlier. About your dad. I feel like I upset you, and it's really none of my business."

I was about to mumble something like, *It's fine, no big deal,* but then stopped myself. Because no, it was *not* okay. I had to set a precedent here. This was day one, for God's sake.

"You're right," I said, looking her right in the eye. "It's not your business at all."

4

Her

Today she took a break from watching boring Margo. Instead she meandered over to M Street, checking the building numbers against what she'd written in the Decomposition Notebook. *Corner of M and East 5th*. She couldn't tell whether the blue dot on her phone's map was sending her in the correct direction, so she kept walking, head down, as the blue dot inched forward—and then it became clear it was taking her away from her destination, not toward it.

She turned fast and bumped into something. A large man, walking a very large black dog.

"Watch where you're going," he said.

"Oh, fuck off," she said, and kept walking.

She could sense the man's gaze searing into the back of her head. She didn't care. What was he, anyway, some loser mall cop? All dogs were disgusting, but that beast took the cake. That *drool*.

Minutes later, she rounded the corner. There it was; his building.

Instead of going there she went to the coffee shop directly across the street. An outdoor table offered a perfect view of his front door, which was elevated by a few steps. The facade of the triple-decker was brick, with flower pots. It looked nice. She wondered how he could afford it. His LinkedIn indicated he was a bit of a job-hopper; he didn't seem to stay long at any company. But he was always in some sort of finance position, described in dry jargon she didn't understand.

The time on her phone said 6:20. He should be home from work by now, she thought. His Instagram story, from an hour ago, had taken place on the Seven bus, stuffed with twentysomethings, chronicling an argument that had broken out between two females. Hair pulling and purse smacking and everything. He'd captioned it, "Cat Fight."

That was the bus he took home. He wouldn't have gone to meet up with Margo, yet, would he? She supposed there was only one way to find out.

Wait, and watch.

Margo

I listened for sounds of Lucy in her bedroom and heard nothing. It was odd, sharing a wall with someone, after all these years. I hadn't shared one since Aunt Izzie took me in, after my parents died. In those days, when all I did was sleep and cry, through Izzie's guest-room wall I'd hear her on the phone with the police, the *Dateline* producers—oh, how she screamed at them—and the home insurance reps. Who knew you had to fight for victim's comp and the removal of body decomposition, and bodily fluids? Not Izzie, and sure as hell not me.

I shook my head and squeezed my eyes shut. I'd trained myself not to think about all this, at least consciously. Clearly, I still needed to work on that.

I turned my attention to the four different outfits laid across my bed, eventually landing on a baggy T-shirt and a pair of Mom's old jeans.

My uniform these days. Brad wouldn't care either way, I knew this. He understood my need to be incognito. He understood everything.

Still, thoughts of Mom snaked their way back as I surveyed myself in the mirror. I imagined what she'd say if she saw me now. *You're too young to let yourself go. Here, for God's sake. Put on some of my foundation.*

Aunt Izzie was nicer about it, but she still considered my new appearance, or *dis*appearance, a travesty. I suspected Izzie's disappointment was over me no longer looking like her sister. My resemblance to the beautiful Patty Nevins had died right along with her. I'd even shirked my given name, Maggie Nevins. The old me. The name even *sounded* nicer, happier. Margo Sharpe sounded harsh and mean. Troubled.

I checked my phone. It was ten to seven. Plenty of time to get to Delaney's.

Then came the sound of the front door opening and closing, the sound of Lucy dropping her work bag at the base of the stairs, with the ringing of its metal buckles, and finally her climbing the stairs. I tried to shut the door before Lucy reached the top, where if she turned to the right she could view right inside my room.

And this she did. I was too late.

"Going somewhere?" Lucy called to my slowly closing door. "Is this your date night with Brad?"

As the door shut, I called out, "No."

6

Her

She watched the two of them through the bar window. All she could see was the back of Margo's raggedy-ass head (had she even bothered to brush her *mop?*) while Brad looked straight ahead, or rather, down, into his phone. Margo was doing the same. How romantic. Real lovebirds.

"You in line?"

A portly guy with a long beard, around her age, gestured to the empty space in front of her, the gap.

"You go ahead."

"You sure?"

"I'm sure."

She glanced back at the window. Brad's head was turned now to the right, to a guy next to him on the barstool, and they were comparing something on their phones and laughing.

Margo, pathetically, was trying to see what they were looking at, without being too obvious, although it was.

But she didn't care about Margo. Not right now. She cared about him.

She squinted through the window, her face so close her breath was causing it to fog a little. Turn a little more, Brad, she thought. Just a little...

And then he did.

She almost gasped aloud. Brad was...devastating. There was no other word for it. She wasn't sure she'd ever seen someone so gorgeous. He was much handsomer than the pictures she'd found online. And the other pictures, the ones that had been mailed to her, were *really* old. Older, certainly, than the photos on Margo's dresser.

Her heart raced as she watched Brad tilt his head back, laughing at something. He had an incredible smile. It's like there was an aura around him. The female bartender, for her part, was pretending not to sneak glances at him as she dried a glass, thrusting her chest out so that her tits looked bigger than they were.

Someone else tapped her shoulder and asked if she was in line. A rush of irritation coursed through her.

"No," she snapped, jerking her shoulder away from their touch, her gaze still glued to Brad.

After staring for a little while longer, she breathed out and whispered aloud, "Wow." The wonderment wasn't simply due to Brad's beauty as a human being. What was most stunning was the *resemblance*.

Urgency cleaved her chest. She had to find a way to talk to him. To see him. To tell him everything. *She had to find a way.* And soon.

7

Margo

"Hi, sweetie," Izzie said, as soon as I picked up. "I've been trying you for days. So...?"

"So, she moved in."

"Oh, how wonderful!"

"I guess."

"What do you mean, you *guess*?"

"I—"

I stopped, my ears pricked to a noise I thought I heard. I waited. I was never certain whether Lucy was holed up in her room or not home at all. It was a Saturday, and I had no idea how she filled her days. I noticed she hadn't "gone home, out of state," yet, like she'd claimed in her application.

"Margo? Did I lose you?"

"No, I'm here," I said, keeping my voice low, just in case.

"So, what's the issue?" Izzie asked. "I remember you saying after the interview that you thought she was nice. Sweet, kept to herself. Sounds like just what you wanted."

"She's nice and all, but she, like, *stares* at me a lot," I said. "It's weird. And in the kitchen, in the morning? I'll be making coffee and she's sitting there, *staring.* Then she tries to talk and stuff, but I told her I'm not a morning person, so at least she's stopped *that.*

"Also, she's got weird habits. She labels everything with her initials. She labeled a salt shaker. A *salt* shaker. And get this—she's on FaceTime with her parents twenty-four/seven. It's absurd. She's, like, twenty-five. I think."

On second thought, had Lucy ever said how old she was? Maybe I was confusing her with Carmen Kangaroo.

"Either way," I said, "grow up, you know?"

Aunt Izzie laughed.

"Oh, Margo. This is what having a roommate is *like.* You need to share your space. And just a warning—you might even get into a few arguments here and there. God, the fights I'd have with my girlfriends in college over the dumbest stuff. And when your mother and I shared a room, it was like World War..." She trailed off, sighing. "My advice? If something bothers you, just nip it in the bud. Don't get worked up over trivial things."

Izzie was out of breath. The three of us, me, Izzie, and Mom, had always been similar in the way we spoke. Once we got going, the words trilled out fast, urgent; we barely took a breath.

"And honey," Izzie continued, "I know the stuff with her parents makes you upset. But don't hold it against her."

I stayed quiet a moment. Then I said, "I know. You're right. I'm being stupid."

"Think of it this way. She's not as bad as that Kangaroo person, is she?" Izzie said.

"God, no," I said, a smile creeping onto my face. "Not even close."

"Good," she said. "Despite all this, I will say, you sound better. You sound more...animated. More alive. I'm really happy you have stuff going on. That you're getting things back on track. Maybe this means you'll come visit me soon? That you feel okay enough?"

"I don't know about that," I said, though really, I wanted to say, "The answer is a still a big fat *no*."

It was unbelievable to me that Izzie had stuck around, having to contend with the rumors about Mom. It must have been torture.

Just a few weeks ago I'd checked online, and sure enough, seven years running, came the annual mention of my parents' deaths on Marshside Moms Community Forum—"Where Cape Cod Locals Can Vent!"

The "Remembering Patty and Andrew on this day" posts would quickly devolve into revived gossip and rumors, all nested in the comments: *Not to sound awful, but our beloved Party Patty WAS quite the flirt. What was with all those parties, anyway? All that drinking? One can't help but think that if they'd toned that down a little...*

And always, the same question went unanswered, marked by crying emojis: *How could this have happened in our happy little seaside town?* Topped off by a *#RIPPattyandAndrew*, of course.

"You have to be relieved," Izzie said now, "to have found someone?"

"I won't be so broke," I sighed into the phone, "that's for sure."

"Well, yes, but—you'll have a companion. Someone to do things with, if you allow it. Once you're comfortable, of course."

Izzie's tone was so hopeful, it broke my heart.

She continued on: "Maybe you'll have a social life again?"

"Maybe," I said, but I didn't mean it.

* * *

After I hung up with Izzie, I turned to check the positioning of the plant next to the fridge. The thirsty plant was dying a slow death, but at least the rot was still hidden. When would I be able to afford a mold guy to come in and take care of that? Lucy would have to live here three years or something, to make a dent in my bills. I wasn't sure how long it would take, exactly; I was horrible at math. I just knew it would be a long time.

The bills were relentless. They were divvied into two stacks on the counter, for Christ's sake, so they wouldn't topple over.

At least I had a new source of cash—even if it was just a few extra bucks a week: Bearie. Owen had called, asking if I was still interested, and I'd immediately said yes. Today I took Bearie on our first stroll around Castle Island—the first of many, I hoped. Afterward, when I dropped him off, Owen tried to slip me a twenty.

I shook my head and said, "It was nothing. Gets me into the fresh air. It's a favor to *me*. I can't take that."

"Nonsense. I'll put it your mailbox if you don't take it now."

I took it and walked home. And when I got there, on the kitchen counter was a package, a rectangular box two feet in length, long and narrow. Lucy must have brought it inside at some point.

With relief, I saw it was addressed to Margo Sharpe, at this address in South Boston. I'd been adamant with the post office that any bills forwarded from my parents' house on Punkhorn Lane, addressed to Maggie Nevins, needed to be held at the post office before September 1, when Lucy moved in. I couldn't have her stumbling upon them and asking questions.

I poked the box with my finger. It was light, sliding easily across the counter. The mailing label had been generated by the post office.

I traced my finger along the clear tape sealing the box. It spanned almost the entire cardboard surface, layer upon layer of thick, impenetrable tape.

"Looks like you need help."

I turned. Lucy was behind me, holding up scissors, or rather, they looked like garden shears. I didn't have time to decline.

Lucy wedged herself beside me and poked the tip of the blade into the tape. There was a sharp pop as it broke through. She started to drag it along the perimeter.

"It's okay," I said, trying to pull the box away, and in doing so, Lucy sliced not the box but my arm. "Ow!" I shouted, pulling my arm to my chest.

"Sorry!" Lucy said, eyes widening at the short, thin line of vermillion blooming against my pale skin.

Lucy tossed the scissors into the sink and pulled a wad of paper towels off the roll, attempting to stanch the wound with the too-thick fistful. All I could do was stand there, in shock, as Lucy dabbed—or rather, shoved—the towels into the cut and smooshed it around.

"You can stop now," I said, finally, withdrawing my arm and cradling it with the other. "It's not even that bad."

It wasn't. Once the blood was wiped away, a tiny scrape was revealed.

Lucy held the bloody paper towels to her chest, her lips slightly parted, then ducked her head to the bottom row of cabinets, opening, closing each door. "Where's the trash, again?"

I showed her, for the umpteenth time, and Lucy stuffed them in, toppling an already too-full trash can. She stood back up and stared at the package. "You're not gonna see what it is?"

Feeling Lucy's eyes on me, I pulled the box open. Inside was another box. Inside that was a neat bouquet of flowers with a card from "Jackie's Flower Shop." The message inside: "Love you, Margo. Brad."

"He gets me flowers sometimes, just because," I said, feeling myself smiling.

"Well, tell him to stop."

My head jerked up. Whenever I mentioned Brad, Lucy got all corny and mawkish, begging to meet him, asking me to retell the story of how we'd met, and then dropping not-so-subtle hints to set her up with one of his friends.

But not now. Now, her tone now was clipped. Angry.

"What do you mean, 'Tell him to stop'?" I asked.

"Because I'm *allergic*. I said it on my application. Flowers, dogs, everything."

"You did?" I said. The hundreds of responses from all those months of searching were crowding my memory.

Lucy itched her neck. A small red hive had formed. Then, two more.

"All right," I said, disappointed. The flowers were so beautiful, so delicate. A small, tasteful bouquet. My favorite. He knew not to send lilies, or anything that smelled like a funeral.

Lucy crossed her arms, and her words came out like a bark. "Seriously, you need to bring that outside. To the trash."

"The *trash*? I'll just bring them up to my room—"

"Which is *right* next to mine and this place has, like, zero air circulation. It needs to go outside. *Now*."

Talk about an overreaction. So, she had the sniffles and a little red hickey thing on her neck. Did that mean I couldn't enjoy the few things in life that made me happy?

I scooped up the box, fighting an urge—an alarming, hysterical urge of my own—to throw it in her face.

"Thanks," Lucy said sweetly, her face transforming in the blink of an eye. She was smiling now. Beaming, even.

In the alleyway, I dumped the fresh—expensive—flowers in the trash bin. What a waste.

Before closing the lid, I spotted something. Underneath some coffee grounds was an unopened envelope addressed to Margo Sharpe, from the exterminator, some guy Owen had recommended the last time I saw him at The Sham. I'd had to interrupt his conversation with a bunch of his friends—the Pats were on, I guess (I no longer paid any attention to sports, with Dad gone)—but he'd happily shouted across the bar, "Hey Murph—you got the number of that guy?" and in less than two minutes I was kindly sent away with the contact of someone half the price of what I'd found on my Google search.

I shook off the envelope and opened it. It was the initial rodent report—I'd been meaning to call to request an update. The report featured a graph that revealed each room had been checked. The box next to the column "Evidence of Rodents" was blank, for every room. There was a note at the end. *No mice or other rodents detected. Do not recommend follow-up.*

8

Lucy

Lucy went upstairs to her bedroom and shut the door. She put her ear to it, listening. There was the sound of the front door opening, and then the little wrought-iron gate that separated the alleyway from this house and the next. And finally, the trash bin, the lid lifted, the bag of trash landing at the bottom in a thump. There was the sound of rustling plastic, and a couple minutes later, the lid dropping onto the bin, closing it. Finally, Margo's footsteps as she hopped up the front steps and reentered the house.

You could hear everything through the thin walls of this slum. Everything.

Lucy retreated from her door and began to pace, thoughts racing.

Flowers, for *no reason*? What was that about? How was he even *into* her?

Margo wasn't pretty or interesting. She was bland and oily, mousy and edgy—and not the good kind of edgy, the kind that gave someone mystique. No. Margo was a boring pile of *trash*.

The only comfort Lucy could find in the moment was allowing herself a fantasy: stuffing Margo's head into the trash bin, where it belonged, alongside that bouquet. Just grabbing her by the hair and smooshing her ugly mug into the thorns, the sharp little spikes tearing at her greasy flesh. Pacing the tiny bedroom—so fucking small!—Lucy tugged at the ends of her hair.

Brad was not only solar systems out of Margo's league, but how could he not have figured out who she *was*? Margo had been hiding in plain sight for seven years. Was he *daft*? Did he not have Google? Lucy had found her in a matter of days. All she had to do was track down Izzie Sharpe, that stupid fat aunt of hers, and go through her trash and her mailbox. God. It was so fucking easy.

How could he not recognize Margo for who she was? Presumably, he saw her naked—how disgusting—or after a shower, those bangs plastered back, revealing that forehead, her *face*...

Lucy had so many questions for Brad. Better yet, she had so many *secrets* to spill, revelations that would make him run far, far away from Margo Sharpe—fake name—Maggie Nevins. Brad needed to know Maggie was responsible for it *all*. That he was due sweet, sweet revenge.

Suddenly, Lucy looked down. A tuft of wiry blonde hair had appeared in her hand, accompanied by a slight sting at the back of her scalp. She tossed the hair in the trash and continued to pace.

Lucy just knew, once Brad met *her*, that they'd have an instant connection. Instant.

The thrill of it flared up within her. She felt alive, for the first time in...a very long while. Maybe ever.

She just had to get started. Really started. It was time.

She sat on her bed, and from her knapsack took out her phone and her Decomposition Notebook. And then, she went to work.

PART II

9

Margo

I drove up and down every one-way, up I Street, down H Street. But it was street-cleaning day, so only one side of the road was available. Every time I crept up to a potential parking place, it turned out to be a fire hydrant, or a handicapped spot, or, in one strange case, an elderly woman holding a Red Sox balloon. Finally I gave up and headed down by the water, nearly two miles away, and found a spot there.

Locking up the car, I caught a glimpse of myself in the car window and saw my face was drawn into a scowl. *Maggie the Mood*. It had been a long, long day. A day of dirty looks from Astrid and mistakes on the master spreadsheet and Corinne telling me for the fifth time I needed to pay more attention to the details, and also, Wendy has mono, so we need you to come to Chicago with the team—it'll be *fun*!

Turning the corner, the first thing I saw was Lucy's beige sedan, parked right out front.

Another surge of irritation.

I missed coming home to an empty house. I missed being *alone*.

Inside, the TV had been left on, and in the kitchen, it looked like a bomb had gone off: open cracker boxes, dirty cutting boards, half blocks of cheese. In the sink, egg-caked pans from Lucy's breakfast—yesterday's. Also, sitting at the center of the table, an empty bottle of red wine.

Lucy was out on the deck, reclined in one of the white plastic lounge chairs, her back to me.

I slid open the glass door. Lucy smiled up at me absently but then immediately went back to swiping on her phone.

I found myself frozen, unable to speak. How do you tell a stranger they're a colossal fucking slob? And I still needed to mention the exterminator report, which was fishy in and of itself. Although maybe those droppings she'd seen were just really old?

The real issue was why she would have thrown out my mail. Wasn't that a federal offense? Lucy seemed to throw nothing *else* out. Her trash was always left on counters, her tissues beside, not in, the bathroom trash, her junk *everywhere*—

Lucy looked up again. "Margo! Sit. Have some wine." She pointed to the side table, on which sat an extra glass beside a bottle of red.

"Thanks," I said.

I poured myself a glass and took a sip, settling in beside Lucy on the other lounger, the crappier one with every other slat missing. It was a miracle it didn't collapse under my weight.

I took another sip, a big one.

"Rough day at work?" Lucy asked.

"Why do you say that?"

"You look tired."

"Yes. Rough day." Another sip, and then a deep breath. "So, Lucy. The stuff in the kitchen—"

Lucy interrupted, leaning forward. "*Why* was it rough?

46

Another sip. This was going to my head. Fast.

Lucy watched me expectantly.

I supposed I could chitchat a bit, ease into things first.

"Well," I said, shifting a little in my seat to face her, "my boss, Corinne—she's normally awesome. But we're short-staffed, and she told me today that I have to travel to one of our trade shows in Chicago next week. First of all, I hate traveling with them. I'd much rather stay back in the office and—"

"Stay back and do what?" Lucy said. "Sorry. I don't understand what you do, exactly. Don't think you've ever said."

"Oh, umm, I work in corporate events. Analytics coordinator. I pull numbers and stats, basically. Anyway, I've only traveled to a couple events, and they're just so...social. But the worst part? Tickets for the flight are astronomical, because it's so last-minute. Since I don't have a corporate card, they make me pay up front. Last time, I submitted my receipts the very next day, but it took them months to reimburse me. It really screwed me up financially. I don't come from money like some of the others girls on the team. As you know, I'm...on my own."

Lucy shook her head. "You poor thing. This is why it's *so* sad you're not speaking to your parents. I'm sure they'd bail you out if you asked. At the very least, you should demand a corporate card."

I took another sip—more like a swig—and swallowed. I decided to ignore the comment about my parents.

"I *did* demand a corporate card. Well, I asked for one. Politely. Then, Astrid"—I paused, thinking of Astrid's pinched face and pig nose and smug attitude and then went on, the wine fueling a volubility I didn't know I still possessed—"says, *right* in front of Corinne, that people who don't attend events regularly shouldn't get a corporate card. Corinne agreed and said, 'I suppose you're right, Astrid.' Then, when Corinne wasn't looking, Astrid gave me this smirk."

Lucy's eyes were wide. "What's *her* problem?"

47

I shrugged, as if I didn't know *precisely* why Astrid hated my fucking guts, but that was a story for another day, a story for a real friend, and Lucy was not a friend, I reminded myself.

I stared into my near-empty glass. What was I doing?

Lucy became absorbed in her phone again, and I was glad for the silence. It was okay to sit out here with her. Harmless. And it was even okay to vent once in a while. In fact, it felt good.

I watched the lights and shadows of the neighbors, listening to the Red Sox announcers and newscasts, a low hum. I wondered if these neighbors had secrets, like mine. I wondered if they went to bed every night and woke up every morning feeling shame and dread and disgust. I wondered if their parents were alive and if they loved them, if they missed them. My eyes began to water and I blinked them back. Stop, I told myself. Stop doing this to yourself—

"Check this out," Lucy said, suddenly. She flashed her phone. "Bryson T, Dorchester. Likes to fish and loves the Red Sox."

I'd almost forgot she was beside me. I looked at her screen and raised my eyebrows. "Original."

"I know," Lucy said. She pulled the phone back and squinted. "He's kind of cute, at least." She looked up, smiled, and swiped her finger across the screen. "*Oops!*"

I was so glad I wasn't on those apps and that I had Brad. It seemed to take up so much *energy*. Swiping and checking and waiting. Exhausting.

A few moments later she shrieked, waving her phone. "He responded. He's at Delaney's. Wanna go?"

Delaney's. Brad's favorite bar. Not to mention probing eyes, unknowns.

Plus, it was clear I'd had too much to drink. Brad couldn't see me like this.

I realized I hadn't noticed Lucy pouring me another glass, and now we'd started on a new bottle, the provenance of said bottle unknown.

I looked at the time on my phone, shocked that I'd been out here for over half an hour. Where had the time gone? And how was I so drunk?

"Thanks," I said, "but I think I'll go to bed. It's late, and I'm beat. And kind of drunk." I forced a giggle and shrugged.

She sat back, frowning, her giddiness from before, gone. "You've got to be kidding me. You're making me go *alone*?"

"I don't like bars," I said. I found myself sneering back at her. "I feel like I've mentioned that."

"But you like Delaney's. And that dump bar, whatever it's called." She paused. "The Sham."

I stared back, unblinking, suddenly feeling as if the world was rotating faster and faster.

"Fine," Lucy said, after several seconds of silence. "I'll go alone."

With that, she got up, puttered around in the bathroom for a couple minutes, and then left, slamming the front door.

I stayed outside, feeling dazed, uneven, staring at the two empty wine bottles and two glasses, left on the floor of the deck, between our lounge chairs. Lucy hadn't finished hers; it was practically full.

I stumbled to bed, questions swarming in my head.

What was her problem? Why was she...

And then, as my head was hitting the pillow, one last question, faint:

How does she know where I go?

49

10

Lucy

Lucy knew she'd ruined it. She'd moved too quickly, revealed too much, been too aggressive.

She looked up, shivering. It was a cool night, and she hadn't grabbed a jacket.

Margo was drunk, anyway, Lucy reasoned, as she clomped down the sidewalk in her heels. She won't remember I said that about The Sham. Or Delaney's.

But she might.

Lucy's phone buzzed in her hand. She looked down at it and clicked decline. She waited for the voicemail. She knew there would be a voicemail.

When it came through, she played it.

"Honey, talk to us. We got an envelope, from Boston College? And we opened it."

Lucy halted on the street, feet from the entrance to Delaney's. Shouts and music flooded out of the door.

"You said you got in?" continued her mother's voice. "But you didn't. And you don't have a job. We opened up your bank statements—we're sorry, but we were *worried*—and there are no direct deposits coming from anywhere. No income. Naturally, Lucy, your father and I are beside ourselves. What in God's name are you doing?"

Margo

"I don't feel safe."

It was Lucy.

I'd woken with a start to my phone rattling on the nightstand, the name LUCY SOMERS on the display. I looked at the time. Not even thirty minutes had gone by since I'd gone to bed.

Lucy was saying something else now but her voice was competing with crowd noise, music. Yelling. Eventually I managed to make out, "...catfished...feel like I'm in danger," followed by a hiccup. It sounded like she was crying.

"Why don't you leave?" I said, rubbing my eyes and yawning.

"He'll follow me. Please. Can you come here? Walk me home? *Please*?" There was a hitch in her voice—fear, or desperation.

I sat up, and against my better judgment, said, "Fine."

In a dizzying blur—I felt more drunk now than when I'd gone to sleep, the alcohol having hit me like a Mack truck—I walked to Delaney's, texted that I was there, and waited by the curb. Two minutes. Four minutes. No Lucy.

To pass the time I thought of texting Brad to tell him I was here, but didn't. I knew he wouldn't be here on a Thursday; that wasn't his night. Monday was his night. *Our* night.

I was about to go inside and battle the crowd of drunks to try to find her when I got a text: "Give me another minute."

More waiting. I texted Aunt Izzie, even though she was probably sleeping. She'd wake up to a bunch of texts, which wasn't unusual. I got a little maudlin at night, especially if I allowed myself even one drink. No wonder I didn't do this shit anymore.

"Lucy made me get out of bed and come get her at the bar. So annoying." When I texted the word "Lucy," I hit a key by mistake. It autocorrected to "Lunacy."

It began to drizzle, and then, pour.

I went over to the black awning with its big cursive D and looked inside, at the shoulder-to-shoulder throng of people my age with parents who were surely helping to pay for the $14 craft beers and the astronomical rents in those luxury condos I heard Owen griping about once, the ones that were ruining the character of South Boston and driving the locals out.

Through the window, I recognized a couple of the girls sitting at the nearest high-top. They rode the Seven bus, too, though they made it clear they were "slumming it" every time they stepped on as they gripped the grimy pole, complaining there weren't enough Ubers.

"Margo!"

Lucy.

She clenched her hand around my upper arm, hard, and wrenched me inside. I didn't want to make a scene, so I let Lucy pull me like a trolley through the swarm of bodies. There was a small clearing, and Lucy and I stationed ourselves at the bar, where two shots awaited us.

"Where's...what's-his-face?" I shouted, but Lucy didn't answer. Instead, she thrust a shot glass into one of my hands and a wedge of lime into the other. "On me. *Roomies!*"

I looked around and saw a mishmash of elbows and blonde hair vying for our coveted spot at the bar. Then, not believing what I was doing, I slammed the shot, wincing at the acrid taste.

I hadn't had a shot since...sophomore year. Erin Jenkins's house. I'd been with Jessie Davis, my best friend, dancing on the table, jungle juice sloshing in the red Solo cup, Jessie's braids swaying as she moved.

Lucy handed me another drink. I shook my head, but Lucy shoved it into my chest, causing it to spill. She was then commandeered by a short male, who began yelling in Lucy's ear. I shook his shoulder. "Are you the catfisher?"

Lucy gaped at me. "What? No!" and then turned to the guy and laughed, shaking her head in apparent disbelief.

"But where is—"

I stopped. It didn't matter what I said; every word was swallowed by the music. It was eighties night, and the bar had just erupted into a Whitney Houston singalong.

After a while, another shot materialized, and soon, I found myself singing along, too.

Things went hazy. Lucy fell off a stool. I helped her up, the two of us wheezing, gasping in laughter. Lucy clutched her shin—tears from hilarious embarrassment, she said, not real pain—she didn't even feel it—falling down her cheeks.

At one point I thought I saw Carmen Kangaroo glaring at me from the far corner, but then I lost sight of her. I'd blocked her number, I thought vaguely. No wonder she wouldn't be happy with me. I should have at least given her a reply. When would I be a nice person again?

For a millisecond, my eyes shot over to the opposite corner. I thought I saw Brad. I tried to move closer, to see past some tall guy blocking the view, but then it turned out to be someone else. Of course. Brad wouldn't be here, I told myself.

I took a sip of my drink—what it was or where I'd gotten it, I wasn't certain. I squeezed my eyes shut and opened them, feeling myself sway, and steadied myself against the wall.

Thursday is not Brad's night to come here, was one of my last cogent thoughts. I'd snagged on the idea of Brad like a fishhook.

It's not his night. It's not his night. It's not his—

And then, everything went black.

12

Lucy

Lucy watched Margo fumble with her key in the lock and didn't help her, despite having her own key in her jacket pocket, and the sober wherewithal to open the fucking door in half the time. But she waited on the stoop, watching Margo. Plotting.

Margo finally stumbled inside, kicking off her shoes. One hit the ceiling. She was saying something about being hungry, slurring her words, like her tongue was stuck to the back of her teeth. Lucy stoically endured her yelling in the kitchen about making her famous buffalo mac and cheese and babbling about nothing. She stood close by, watching, pretending to laugh whenever Margo's lazy eyes lifted to look at her.

Finally, what Lucy had been waiting for happened: Margo set her phone down. Too busy making the mac and cheese—banging pans, spraying the orange powder everywhere—Margo didn't notice

57

Lucy scooping the phone from the counter and sliding it into her pocket, but first clicking it on, keeping the screen awake, so that the auto-lock wouldn't activate.

"Be right back," Lucy said, and slipped off to the bathroom.

When Lucy came back, Margo seemed unaware of the passage of time, swaying against the counter and singing the song that was on at the bar right before last call. Something about a *psycho killer*. Something about having to *run far away*. The mac and cheese began to burn. Margo shrieked, "*Burning down the house!*" and started babbling about how her mom *loved* the Talking Heads.

Lucy set Margo's phone down where she'd found it and shut off the burner.

"Oh, what was your mom like?"

As soon as the words escaped her lips she wanted to kick herself. According to Margo they were "estranged." She should have said *is*.

Luckily Margo didn't seem to be picking up on anything: not the phone, not Lucy's disdain, and certainly not Lucy's latest little slip-up in verb tense regarding Margo's mom, Patty "The Whore" Nevins. Even in a compromised state, Margo had trained herself to keep such topics quiet, and it didn't look like tonight was the night Margo would spill her guts.

On the contrary; at the mention of her mother, Margo stopped singing and talking altogether. She sat very still at the kitchen table, staring down into her lap.

"You okay?" Lucy asked, putting her hand on Margo's back.

"I miss her."

"I'm sure you do miss her."

Margo looked up at her blankly, and waited a beat. Then, she said, "I'm hungry."

Lucy turned her head so Margo wouldn't see her pursed lips as she spooned the burnt noodles into two bowls, shaking some salt on Margo's with the shaker labeled "LS."

This, Margo commented on. "You're so weird. You label everything."

Lucy laughed humorlessly, handing Margo her bowl.

Margo dug in, slopping the orange sauce all around her mouth, spilling it onto her awful, baggy T-shirt, reminding Lucy how embarrassing it was to have been seen earlier at the bar with such a frumpy, gross-out mess. How embarrassing the whole night was, pretending to laugh, pretending to fall off the stool so that she could try—and ultimately fail—to grab Margo's phone on the way down.

But at least she'd gotten to it before the night was over. Stage One, complete.

Lucy told Margo she was eating in her room; she was tired.

When Margo stumbled off to bed, and she heard the light turn out, Lucy tiptoed to the bathroom and shut the door. Then, as quietly as she could, without slopping water everywhere and making a racket, she flushed every single noodle down the toilet.

Margo

When I woke up it was almost dawn, and my body was drenched in sweat. At some point in the night I'd peeled off my T-shirt and was now nude, save for my underwear, and still, I couldn't get cool.

A knot gnarled my stomach. I curled into the fetal position. A sudden sadness had overcome me, too. I missed my mom. I missed tea in the teapot and staying home from school on the couch while she stroked my hair. Instead, now I was alone, utterly alone, convulsing with chills, tears and sweat soaking the pillow. No one to call. No one to tell me everything would be okay, to set a glass of ginger ale on the bedside table.

Mom, I wish you were here. I'd do anything.

I'm so, so sorry.

It increasingly felt like someone was jabbing me over and over in the uterus with a knife. Then came a strong and urgent need to...*Oh, no.*

I flew out of bed, trampling over discarded clothes and stumbling into the bathroom, dropping my underwear and plopping onto the toilet just in time. The rush expelled like a breaking dam, and the relief was instant.

Fully awake now, head between my legs, elbows on knees, I breathed out a long sigh. It was over. At least, I hoped so. I twisted my torso and reached for the toilet paper. My fingers played the empty roll like a piano, as if that would produce more. I could have sworn I'd just changed the roll.

I leaned to my left, where I always kept an extra in the small toiletry basket. None there, either.

"Lucy?" I called out weakly.

I changed my mind immediately after I'd called her name. Lucy couldn't see me like this.

The hand towel was gone, along with all the bath towels. Lucy must have put them in the laundry.

My only option was to use my underwear, a flimsy pair that wouldn't do much good. So I stood up, shaking what I could into the toilet—oh, how repulsive it smelled, and looked, spatters all over the bowl, even chocolate-colored plashes that had found their way onto the seat.

Two knocks came at the door.

"Margo?" Lucy said from outside the door.

I looked around, desperately hoping I'd missed something—that a roll would magically appear. It didn't.

"Umm, can you grab some toilet paper from downstairs? I...uh, I have a situation." I tried to giggle away the mortification; it was funny, in a way. Jessie, had she seen something like this back in the day, would have *died*.

A sigh from beyond the door. "Okay. I'll look for some."

I waited for what felt like forever and then heard footsteps climbing the stairs.

"No more toilet paper," Lucy said through the door. "Not even in the downstairs bathroom."

"What happened to the rolls I just got?"

Silence.

"Okay, never mind. Umm, can you grab some paper towels, then?"

Another interminable period of waiting as Lucy went back downstairs, and then up again.

"No more of those either," Lucy said when she returned. "I'd written on the Target list that we needed both TP and PT. It's been hanging on the fridge for, like, ever."

"So why didn't you go?" I asked.

Lucy's voice was small through the door. "Because you said you didn't mind buying this kind of stuff. Back when we talked about the lease. You said you would be responsible for house expenses."

My thoughts flew. I didn't remember any such conversation.

"Maybe I meant, like, I'd pay most of the cable? This is...shared stuff, Lucy."

How disgusting and horrible I felt just now, sitting in filth, which was starting to dry.

"Look, never mind. Just...grab me a towel? There's nothing in here."

Lucy returned a moment later and knocked once again. "Found one."

I leaned as far as I could off the toilet and unlocked the door, opening it only slightly, but Lucy pushed it wide open.

"Hey!" I cried out, covering my crotch with my hands.

I thought I saw a flash, but it could have been the hallway light above Lucy's head; it all happened so fast. Lucy tossed in the towel.

"Wow," she said softly, as she backed out of the bathroom. "That is *disgusting.*"

* * *

It was nearing seven a.m. and the stomach cramps still hadn't gone away.

I called Corinne and got her voicemail. At the beep, I intended to adopt a light, breezy tone. Instead what came out was a nose-plugged, scratchy drawl. "Sorry, Corinne, I'm not feeling too hot. Migraine."

I dozed for a while until my phone dinged. The call had gone straight to voicemail. It was Corinne.

"Check your late-night outbox, Margo. No need for the charade. I'll see you whenever you're *feeling better*, and I trust this won't happen again."

My breath caught and I replayed the message, to be sure I'd heard correctly.

Outbox.

I scrambled to check. There were a few work-related emails I'd sent before going to bed, around ten p.m. But then...*Oh, no.*

> I've got a hell of a stomach bug. I won't be in tomorrow. It's relentless.
> Apologies!
> Margo

The second was longer, causing me to moan as the words blurred before my eyes:

> Dear C,
> I am hoping to talk to you about a corporate card. As you know, you don't pay me a lot. I shouldn't be expected to pay for the plain myself, that's BS. I also do not enjoy attending events because Asturd is a btch. I hope you'll reconsider having me travel with the "team."
> Thank you,
> Margo

The last, and worst:

> Corinne!!!!!!
> Oops, I've had a few drinks. I think maybe you can tellllllll!!!!! ☺
> Maybe we could go to Sham sometime, cuz I have something to tell you?
> Sincerely,
> Margo

* * *

An hour later I watched from the kitchen table as Lucy opened and closed the cabinets, looking for something. She was in an apparent rush to get to work, her knapsack slung over her shoulder and not zipped all the way; I could see notebooks and boxes of red pens inside.

Lucy rose from a bottom cabinet, holding one of my mugs.

"Can I just say something? You make a mean Buffalo mac and cheese. I may not remember much, but I *do* remember that."

She smiled and nodded at the pan in the sink, the dirty dishes, the hardened noodles and smears of electric-orange muck.

"I don't remember making that," I murmured, shifting in my seat. All that remained in my memory after the bar was a dull, colorless void. I pointed down at my phone, resting on the table in front of me. "But I do know one thing. I *never* would have sent emails like that. I know how to *spell*."

"Wait," Lucy said, laughing, ignoring my torment, "I also remember you singing. Lots of Talking Heads."

My heart hammered in my chest and I shook my head, furious with myself, for my stupidity. Why did I drink so much? What did I *say*? I felt feverish and sick and anxious and...despondent. All I wanted to do was soak in a bath and then sleep for days.

65

I glanced at the fridge. The note Lucy said had been tacked onto it, about TP and PT, dangled there by a small magnet, yet I could have sworn I'd never seen it before. I would have noticed it. Wouldn't I have?

I got up from the table without a word. Lucy was no help piecing together the night, and there was an unnamed irritation burbling in my chest and stomach. If Lucy hadn't dragged me there...

I'd gotten halfway to the stairs when I heard, "Hey, Margo?"

I stopped and turned.

Lucy had appeared at the other end of the hallway. "You talk to Brad yet?"

I looked down at my phone. I'd checked my outgoing texts, the last ones sent right before Lucy dragged me into the bar. We had not spoken last night, at all.

"No," I said. "Why?"

"Well, after what we saw, I thought you would." Lucy leaned against the wall, inspecting her fingernails.

"What do you mean—what did we see?"

Lucy looked up and raised her eyebrows.

"Oh, my God, you don't remember? We saw *Brad*. He was with some girl. Had his arm around her. I wanted to confront him, but you were crying and wanted to leave. You were so upset..." She shook her head sadly. "If I were you, I'd dump that asshole."

14

Margo

Later that day I took Bearie on a long, long walk. When I'd offered to take him for a few hours, Owen was grateful. He was working a late security shift at the bank downtown, and his girlfriend, Tawna, a haughty, Marlboro-smoking sourpuss I'd only met briefly, at The Sham, had a twelve-hour nursing shift at Boston Medical.

More than anything I needed to get some fresh air. I needed to think.

We walked, slowly, around Castle Island, Bearie's jowls and drool flapping in the wind, and on the way back I led him down M Street. To Brad's.

The blinds were drawn. I half expected to see some idiot blonde coming down his steps, stinking of sex and shame, dressed in an outfit from the night before. But this didn't happen.

I opened my phone to text him. "Why did you—" Delete. "How could you—" Delete.

I slipped my phone back in my jacket pocket.

* * *

The following day I went back to work and immediately, Corinne called me into her office. I sat with my notepad dumbly in my lap, as if preparing to take notes on my own insubordination. Ready, possibly, to be fired.

Corinne often did five things at once, and she was making me wait. She tapped at the keys, eyes on the desktop screen, pausing briefly to jot something on a legal pad. Finally, she clicked the mouse once and looked up.

"So."

I sat very still.

"If you had a problem with buying a plane ticket, you should have said something."

"Of course. I'm so sorry—"

"And if there are certain members of the team you have issues with, we will need to get HR involved. Is this something you want me to do?"

I shook my head, cheeks flushed. I wanted to say, *I didn't send that*. But I wasn't certain.

In the end Corinne gave me a strike one disciplinary warning. Disappointment dripped from her. The brown eyes behind her tortoiseshell frames were painfully exacting, watching me as if she'd never seen me before. As if she regretted ever taking this orphan under her wing.

After I was dismissed, it took fifteen minutes for me to get my act together in the handicap stall.

Later, tears dried, I found myself neck-deep in work. The pre-event frenzy was under way for the whole events marketing team, and no one was more stressed than Astrid. When I offered her help, Astrid sneered.

"It's bad enough you played hooky yesterday, leaving us with all the shit from Tacit," she said, referring to one of our sponsors. It was my job to pull attendee stats for them; they were obsessed with numbers and analytics, which was my whole job.

"Sorry," I said, once again near tears. Had my email gotten back to Astrid? That would be the icing on the cake.

Astrid waved me off, her pinched face screwed close to her screen. "You've done enough."

* * *

The following night, I thought I heard a noise coming from downstairs. The whole tall, narrow house would often sway at the slightest trace of wind, and night noises within the thin walls were abundant, so I dismissed the noise and drifted back to sleep. But an hour later I awoke again with a start, heart pounding. A nightmare. I'd dreamed of him. His hot breath on my neck, and that familiar odor—sweat mixed with dirt, rain...

This time, I got up, wide awake and thirsty. Tiptoeing down the hall, I put my ear to Lucy's closed door and heard faint snoring.

Downstairs I grabbed a glass and filled it from the tap; Lucy had left the Brita nearly empty, per usual. As I returned the Brita canister to the fridge, I stepped on something with my bare foot. Something gritty. I reasoned it could be sand from my walk with Bearie the day before, as we'd walked down to M Street Beach before returning home.

Flipping the light on next to the stove, I inspected the sole of my foot. It wasn't sand, but dark soil. Potting soil.

My eyes flew to the potted plant beside the fridge. It was slightly askew, pushed out a bit from the wall. The mold was completely visible now, peppered with dirt, and I noticed something else, something new: a linoleum tile peeled at its edge.

I squatted down and tried peeling the edge further with my fingertips, to see how loose it was, but I couldn't get it to budge. The stench I'd assumed was coming from the fridge—Lucy's rotting leftovers; I'd almost grown used to it—had gotten stronger as I squatted, my face close to the floor.

I grabbed a knife from the block and pried up the corner easily, revealing a dark hole beneath. The noxious odor assaulted me immediately. I had to pull my T-shirt up and over my nose. Using my cell-phone flashlight to see better, I peered inside and gasped. *Fur.*

I tightened the shirt around my nose and leaned down to view it more closely. It was a dead rat of alarming bulk, with a coiled tail and blood caking its brown fur. Upon closer inspection, I saw not one but *two* rats, crammed together. And a *lot* of blood.

After bagging the rats—the size and heft of them were ungodly; I'd never seen anything like it—I placed them in the trash bin outside, gagging the whole while.

Back inside, I attempted to find an entryway, some explanation for how they'd gotten there. Nothing.

Almost as if someone had put them there.

* * *

From: Izzie Sharpe Paine (izntshelovely@email.com)

To: MargoSharpe@email.com

Subject: Punkhorn House

    Hon, I have some news about your parents' house. Sigrid is sorry, but she's got a full load and is passing us along to a new realtor. Says the house is in severe disrepair and will never sell unless we do something about it, even in the hot market right now, with all those rich New Yorkers snatching up their third homes, driving us locals to the poorhouse with nowhere to live (insert eye roll!). Plus, you know—the history of the place. It spooks people. We can't do anything about that, of course, but it would be worth fixing some things up. The new realtor wants us to meet Saturday to discuss possible improve-ments. I said we could—Steve can watch the boys. You'd be back from your work trip Friday, right? I know you hate coming back here, honey, but as you're the official executor of the estate...

I'd seen the subject line the other day and purposely ignored the email, wishing it would just go away. But with my flight to Chicago in two hours and me running on almost zero sleep, unable to go back to bed after the rat debacle, I'd pulled out my phone and checked my personal email.

And here it was, something from which I could never escape: my unsellable childhood home. The Punkhorn House.

It was bad enough I had one dump to deal with, here in Boston, but my parents' house just sat there, needing heat in the winter so the pipes wouldn't freeze. My parents had owed an exorbitant amount on the mortgage, having chosen to refinance and borrow from their 401(k)s to pay for their stupid boat and memberships at the club, maxing out their credit cards so they could throw their precious parties. They were a textbook keeping-up-with-the-Joneses couple, mired in horrific debt when they died.

And lucky me, the one who had to pay for it all.

In more ways than one.

Lucy

That morning, Lucy woke up to a call from Margo, from the airport.

Margo had left the house earlier in a tizzy, cursing about missing her flight as she ran in and out of the bathroom. Finally, she'd clomped downstairs with her suitcase and jumped in an Uber.

Lucy had crossed her fingers that Margo would miss her flight, but from the sound of it now, on the phone, she hadn't.

Lucy listened for a moment to what Margo was saying.

"*Rats,* Margo? That's disgusting. You'll have to call an exterminator again. Did you ever even call one the *first* time—?"

She half listened to Margo's whiny rebuttals, something about finding an envelope in the trash from the exterminator. Something about how Margo didn't want to sound *paranoid*, but the rats looked like they'd been planted there.

"*Planted* there?" Lucy said. "That's preposterous, Margo. You clearly have a vermin problem. I saw you were trying to hide the mold with that plant. This is getting to be kind of gross. I don't want to feel like I live in some type of slum."

This really got Margo going, and Lucy had to pinch her nose to keep from guffawing right into the receiver. She finally forced her smile to disappear and put on a grave face.

"Just call the exterminator, 'kay?" Lucy said, adding, "And, PS? Don't expect me to pay for any of it." Whatever Margo said next went unheard, as Lucy had already hung up.

Margo

The flight to Chicago was hell. I couldn't stop thinking about Lucy. Had she really put the rats there? Why would she do that? The mere idea was outrageous.

I heard snickering from across the aisle.

I could see Astrid leaning forward, whispering to another logistics associate, Shanna, through their seats.

"You're so bad," Shanna whispered back.

Astrid's profile shifted so she was looking at me. I locked eyes with her until she turned away and sat back in her seat, smirking.

I wondered how I would tolerate Astrid over the next two days at the event.

Five minutes into meeting her, you knew she went to Dartmouth. She also talked a lot about her doorman, about her ski vacations in Switzerland, her sister's bachelorette party in Bali. She made me sick.

75

But Astrid was up for a promotion, and Corinne loved her. So, I had to play nice in the office, and I would have to play nice as we worked side by side for the next two days, grueling twelve-hour shifts setting up and managing the trade show, from six a.m. vendor breakfasts to the party-till-midnight networking events.

It wouldn't be easy staying out of Astrid's way. I'd learned this the hard way.

It happened a little over a year ago, when I was still part of the custodial staff. I was the person who replaced the toilet-paper rolls in the bathroom on the Events floor, and emptied everyone's trash bins, the little ones tucked under everyone's desks.

It was during one of these late evenings that the basis of Astrid's hatred for me formed.

Astrid was the only one left in the office that night, hunched over her computer at her desk, furiously biting her nails, earbuds in. I was doing my rounds, quietly emptying the bins. At one point, I happened to look up and see Astrid take a jar out of her desk. It was a small glass mason jar with a lid, filled with white flakes of some sort. Astrid took a moment to hold the jar to the edge of the desk and then sweep what turned out to be a smattering of freshly bitten fingernails into the jar. It was at that moment I bumped into one of the cubicle walls.

Startled, Astrid swiveled her head and the jar spilled onto the floor. The white flakes that had filled two-thirds of the jar now blanketed the carpet beside Astrid's chair, like mounds of shredded coconut.

The two of us froze, looking at one another.

It was gross, but to me, not that big of a deal. You see everything as a janitor in an office building. Jizz stains, vomit, everything. So I tried acting casual, and stepped forward.

"I'll get that."

"No," Astrid said, sharply, her face a deep brick red, as she tried rolling her chair over the pile.

"But—" I said, weakly. I was nervous about leaving it there; I had a strict checklist from the head custodian.

"Fuck off, maid," Astrid said. "Leave. *Now*."

I did leave, but revisited the spot two hours later, when I was done with the remainder of the floor. Both Astrid and the pile were gone.

It was a couple weeks later that Corinne hired me on to the events marketing team as a junior associate, based off the résumé that said I had a college degree. I'd expected that working alongside Astrid would pose an issue, that she was a little embarrassed—I noticed she avoided all eye contact with me at meetings, and she made a couple of snide comments about me—but I had no idea how *much* of an issue.

One day, Astrid came out of a stall in the bathroom while I was at the sink. I wanted to clear the air, figuring if we just addressed it, we could squash the whole thing. I watched her in the mirror and spoke softly, kindly, as she washed her hands.

"Hey, umm, please know that I'd never tell anyone."

Astrid glowered at me in the mirror. "Tell anyone...what?"

"About...that night. The jar."

"I don't know what you're talking about, *maid*."

With that, she stomped out of the bathroom, and she'd been gunning for me ever since. I suspected her endgame was to make me so miserable that I'd quit.

Fat chance, bitch, I wanted to say. Too bad I've seen horrors far worse than you. And I reminded myself of this whenever Astrid undermined me in a meeting, or exposed small mistakes on my spreadsheets.

Far, far worse.

17

Lucy

That night Lucy sat out on Margo's deck swiping through her phone, enjoying the freedom of being home alone. She couldn't believe she'd been here over two months already. It felt interminable in some ways, but in others—it was flying. She really was having a lot of fun. Behind her, through the slider door and in the kitchen, was a sink full of crusty pans, and beneath it, an overflowing trash can. Here, outside, Lucy spilled several splashes of wine on the lounge chair and smooshed bleu cheese from her salad into the slats. Stinkier the better, was her motto.

Lucy looked up from her phone to watch the flies land on her wineglass from the night before, which still sat precariously on the deck railing.

The phone vibrated on her lap and she looked down. When she saw the notification, she grinned. "*Jackpot.*"

She got to typing what she needed, and when she finished, she stood up and stretched, yawning as she said aloud, "This is just too easy."

Then she walked up to the wineglass on the railing and flicked it off with her pointer finger. It sailed down to the barren wasteland that was the small backyard, which sloped steeply downward, and landed with a smash.

She turned and went inside, giddy with anticipation. She had to pick out what to wear tomorrow. She had to look her best.

Stage Two. It was finally happening.

Margo

I thanked the cab driver and tipped him, waited for my receipt, and then trudged into the house, dropping my small suitcase by the coatrack and hanging my jacket. The house was quiet, and it reeked. A popcorn bowl, grease and kernels stuck to the side, sat on the coffee table, one wineglass, half full, beside it. In the kitchen, fruit flies hovered in the air above the rotting bananas in the bowl—all Lucy's—and over the dirty dishes stacked high in the sink.

I didn't have the energy to find out where Lucy was and confront her, tell her to clean up her filth and that this *couldn't keep happening*. That I couldn't live like this. I knew I had to say something eventually—knew there was a larger conversation that had to take place. But now wasn't the time. I was simply too tired.

The conference had been a nonstop shit show from the moment we arrived at the labyrinthine hotel (I couldn't wait to tally the complaints: "Who chose that hotel? Could it be any more of a MAZE?") until event breakdown just hours before. Then, I'd snoozed the entire flight home, and again in the cab while sitting in rush-hour traffic. Now, it was nearly eight p.m., and the rumbling in my stomach was all I could think about.

I considered The Sham, but I didn't want to wear out my welcome there; the bartender, and, of course, Owen, had warmed to me, but I sensed others found me a nuisance. Young, and a female. And not a desirable female. A greasy, weird one.

Pizza it was. I called in an order for a large pie, then texted Owen to see if Bearie would be up for a nighttime walk—"Been cooped up all day." Owen texted back: "He'd love it."

I'd chosen my favorite pizza place, one of the better ones, but it was a little under a mile down Broadway. Luckily the night was cool and the air fresh, and Bearie's happy sniffs made the walk worth it.

Outside the pizza place, I tied Bearie to a pole outside. He lay down obediently, head on his paws. I patted his head. "Good boy."

I reached for the door handle, but when I looked through the glass and saw her, I stopped in my tracks. There was Lucy, facing the counter with her hands on her hips. Her jeans were tight and she wore a crop top, unusual for the chilly fall weather, and unusual for her typical style, which tended toward schoolmarm. It seemed she had on makeup, too—dark kohl around her eyes, and deep red lipstick.

Beside Lucy was a tall, dark-haired male, dressed in a light jacket and jeans. He shuffled a little to the left, closer to Lucy, who looked up, smiled, and said something to him. Then he shifted his head, just slightly, to the left.

No, I thought. *No, no, no.*

I stumbled back a couple steps, almost trampling Bearie, and dry-heaved into a sidewalk grate.

19

Lucy

Lucy floated home. They'd ended with a hug and a kiss on the cheek, and Brad's enthusiastic request to meet up again, this week. The place closed at ten o'clock, and he had a volunteer shift early in the morning with his Little Brother, Corey, but he'd agreed they had *so* much more to talk about.

Indeed they did. She hadn't even gotten into *half* of it! She'd forced herself to bide her time; she didn't want to overwhelm him. She didn't want to scare him off.

When Lucy neared the house, she noticed the lights were on in the living room.

"Margo?" she called, when she got inside.

No answer. But when she got to the kitchen, Margo was sitting at the table. To Lucy's delight, it was like *Lord of the Flies* in there, tiny black dots swarming around Margo's beastly, pig-on-a-stick head.

Lucy smiled, buoyant from her date, buoyant at the fact that Margo had to sit in this filth for however long, the flies buzzing around her like a saw.

"How was the work trip?" Lucy asked sweetly.

Margo said nothing. She looked even uglier. A complete sourpuss. Lucy couldn't have loved it more, but outwardly she put on her best frown.

"Everything all right?"

"Where were you just now?"

She knows, Lucy thought, with a start. She didn't know how the hell this could be, but she was certain of it, and specious excuses and lies flew through her head. What should she say?

Don't ruin everything, Lucy.

Don't lose your cool. Be smart about this...

She clamped her mouth shut before she blurted out something incriminating before she needed to. Maybe Margo didn't know. Maybe she was just annoyed about the filth. Either way, Lucy was a bit surprised at Margo's straightforwardness. It was almost as if Margo was acting as the aggressor. Up until this point, Margo had relied on her whiny edict: *not a social arrangement*. This had allowed Margo to avoid any and all confrontation, no matter how hard Lucy tried to rile her up. Even when Lucy was openly behaving like a disgusting asshole, Margo hadn't let out a peep of complaint. It was *no fun*.

But not now. Margo appeared ready to fight. At this prospect, Lucy thought, *Bring it on, bitch*. She waited, keeping her expression a mixture of concern, care, and innocent confusion.

"I saw you," Margo said, still glaring. "With *him*."

Lucy leaned against the counter and crossed her arms, eyeing Margo warily.

"With who?"

"Don't play stupid with me. With Brad. How'd you find him? A dating app?"

84

"Oh, Margo...I'm sorry you had to see that. But you see, the thing is...well, how do I put this—"

"Get to the point," Margo snapped.

"You know what, you don't have to jump down my throat, okay? Let me speak." She paused, waited a beat. "You need to know that I went there for *you*."

Margo narrowed her eyes. "For *me*?"

"I was swiping the other day, and there he was. 'Brad, twenty-six, Southie, loves to volunteer. *Single*.' Same guy from the photos in your room. Same guy we saw with that girl at Delaney's that night. I was furious for you, and wanted to give him a piece of my mind. I didn't want to bother you during your work trip. I made it *seem* like a date, but it was just to get him to meet up with me. I did it for *you*. He shouldn't be cheating on you like this. So blatantly. That must be so mortifying for you."

Margo looked at her, leery.

"If that's true, why'd you come in here all giddy and happy? Why wouldn't you mention *immediately* where you'd been?"

"Well, first, I didn't have a chance—you attacked me the second I walked in. And second, I planned on telling you, but it's a little awkward, because..." Lucy stared at Margo, fixing her gaze. "Look, I wasn't giddy. I was *nervous*. Brad told me something, and now I don't know *what* to believe." Lucy put on her most sympathetic face. "And you must know what he said," Lucy said, laying on more faux sympathy, keeping her voice soft and sweet. "You must."

Margo remained silent.

When it became clear Margo wasn't going to respond, Lucy said, "Margo. He said he had no *idea* who you were."

* * *

The silence in the room must have been oppressive—for Margo, at least. Lucy felt like she could float right out of the room, she was so happy. Of course this psycho made everything up. She should have known. Someone like Brad, with someone like Margo? It was an absolute *joke*.

"He's lying," Margo said, finally. But she was looking down at the table.

You're lying, Lucy thought, with glee. *You're* lying, and I should have known.

"I showed him your picture," Lucy said, shrugging her shoulders, giving her a sad, exasperated look, "and I gave him your name. But when he denied knowing you, and started asking questions about you, like, where you went to high school, or where you grew up, your hometown, I realized that I know *nothing* about you." She waited for Margo's reply. She didn't get one, just like she'd expected. "Like, I think you said something about the Cape once, where your...aunt lives?"

"He's lying," Margo said again. "Probably to get you to sleep with him. I don't broadcast this, and I'm not proud, but...we have an open relationship. It's a little unorthodox."

The way she said it, Lucy was almost convinced. Especially since she didn't know what "unorthodox" meant. But Lucy had to give it to Margo: The girl could lie. And well.

"Right now, we're on a break," Margo went on. "After the whole thing at the bar, you know. I was upset, so...I know he's on dating apps. It's not a surprise to me. It upsets me, of course, but it's not a surprise."

"Oh," said Lucy, finally. "I *guess* that makes sense."

"Are you seeing him again?" Margo asked, her eyes shooting up.

"No way. He got so mad. Especially when I accused him of lying. And when he realized I'd tricked him into a date. He called me a catfisher and acted like I was a *psycho*." Lucy made an exaggerated pouty face and pulled her hair behind her ear. Finally, it was almost long enough to tuck back—even if there were still self-inflicted bald spots everywhere, although she thought she did a pretty good job of hiding those.

"Well, don't worry," Margo said, visibly relieved. "I'm ending things. For good, now."

"Oh, I'm so glad," Lucy said. "You deserve so much better, Margo. Really. You're a catch. And so pretty."

Margo narrowed her eyes at Lucy and cocked her head, a renewed look of suspicion across her face.

Shit, Lucy thought. Once again, she'd taken it too far. No one on God's green earth would ever find her attractive, and Margo knew that more than anyone. *Quit while you're ahead.*

Margo rose from the table, pushing the kitchen chair back so hard it almost toppled over. "By the way, you need to fucking clean this up. There are flies everywhere. It's *disgusting.*"

After Margo stomped upstairs and slammed her bedroom door, Lucy finally allowed a breath of relief to escape. Next time, she needed to be more detail-oriented. She'd known when Margo's flight was scheduled to arrive, knew she should have checked the flight status— and yet she'd gotten too cocky. Too excited.

She couldn't afford to get ahead of herself, to let her excitement over Brad cloud her judgment ever again.

20

Margo

The following morning I made good on my promise to go to the Cape to meet Izzie and the new realtor for the Punkhorn house. It was also an excellent excuse to get away from my house. Away from Lucy.

Who *does* that? I thought, as I put my blinker on and turned off onto the exit. Who lures someone on a date, just to chastise them? And on behalf of someone who is not even a *friend*!

I'd reached the Marshside exit quickly, too quickly, after a smooth ride down the two-lane stretch of Route 6 known to locals as "Suicide Alley," the name of which I'd always hated—even more after what happened to Mom and Dad. It being early November, there was no standstill summer traffic, but fully present were my nerves.

The first thing I saw as I crossed over the town line was Mom's old hair salon, a FOR LEASE sign on the door. Beside it, the shop where Jessie and I had scooped ice cream for two months before the owner fired us for eating "mess-up" sundaes in the back. I could almost feel my heartbeat in my ears.

Bearie's panting drew closer. His massive body was sprawled across the backseat, his head out the window, but now he'd come forward and was sniffing my hair.

I reached back to pet his head. "You okay, buddy?"

He rested his head on my shoulder, like he was asking me the same.

My former family home at 19 Punkhorn Lane was located off a dirt road, and technically part of a large swath of conservation land, also called the Punkhorn. But I was not headed there; not yet, thankfully. The first stop was Aunt Izzie's. I took the scenic route to her house, down 6A and through the historic cobblestoned village, which fronted the marsh, and beyond that, the ocean. Izzie's street was part of a network of small, interconnected neighborhoods.

I pulled into the paved driveway of Izzie's two-story saltbox and saw that she was waiting at the front door. In her mid-forties, Izzie was striking, with light brown hair, olive skin, and a smile that I believed could melt away any frown. Although she was a registered dietician, she happened to be a bit plump. I wondered if people looked at her and thought, "What do *you* know?" Mom would practically say it to her face. She could be a total bitch sometimes.

A small blond head poked through Izzie's legs.

I was about to say, "Hi Ray," when I realized, quickly calculating the years that had passed, that it couldn't be Ray, the older one. This was Damon.

"Who is that?" he said.

Izzie ruffled his hair. "Damon, honey, it's your cousin, Margo. Say hi."

He scrunched up his face and disappeared behind his mother.

I winced. "I should make more of an effort. They don't know me. Ray must be so big now."

"He's enormous. You'll freak when you see him. Turns six next month."

"*Six*," I said, "so that means Damon's like..."

"Three," Izzie finished for me, smiling. "You know you're always welcome to visit more. But seriously, don't sweat it right now, honey. Come say hi quick to Steve, then we gotta go."

She led me to the kitchen, kicking aside toy trucks and Legos to clear the path.

"Mind if we take your car?" she said. "Mine's a mess. Car seats, crap everywhere..."

"Sure," I said, relieved I wouldn't have to move Bearie, who was waiting patiently in the backseat.

Uncle Steve sat on a stool at the kitchen island, chomping on peanuts. I noticed he had more grays around the temples since I'd last seen him. I tried to calculate when that was, and realized it was when I'd first moved to the Southie house. He'd come with Izzie once more at the end of the summer, so he could look over the lease, since he was an attorney. Before that, it must have been at the funeral.

After a hug and some pleasantries, he said, "What's new? You gotta boyfriend, Maggie?"

"No, not right now."

"Got plenty of prospects at the firm..."

Izzie checked her watch. "I don't mean to disrupt Uncle Steve's matchmaking, but we're a little late. I don't want to keep the new realtor waiting."

Outside, upon seeing Bearie's head hanging out the window, Izzie squealed, "What! You got a dog?"

I explained that I'd made some friends at The Sham, one of whom owned Bearie, and that I walked him sometimes.

Izzie raised her eyebrows. "So, you'd rather be friends with some random Southie barflies than your own roommate. Interesting."

I said nothing. So far I'd kept most of Lucy's shenanigans to myself, hoping to add them to a growing body of evidence that in the end would prove my roommate was up to something. But I had to find the right time. Izzie would defend most everyone to the death, insisting on seeing the best in people. And she was already so worried about me all the time, constantly telling me I needed to get "help"—that I surely had untreated PTSD, that it was perfectly normal, but that shouldering everything alone all these years wasn't healthy, and would one day topple me. (There were many speeches Izzie would bust out when I saw her. I practically had them memorized.)

During the ride, Izzie went to work scratching and snuggling Bearie's face through the seat partition, then turned around and faced the front.

"Good to be back?"

I kept my eyes on the road. "No."

"I know it's hard, Mags, but it's been seven years. It's not as bad as it was. I wish I could tell folks where you're living, or what you're doing...even tell people your *name*. People care about you. Teachers, old friends..." Izzie trailed off, searching my face. "Honey, I wish you'd *talk* to me. Tell me what's up. How you're *really* doing."

And there it was.

I sighed and shrugged. "Iz, I'm fine."

"I suppose no one would recognize you, anyway. You look like a ragamuffin, as Grammy used to say."

I couldn't help smiling at this.

After bombing down Route 124 ("Slow *down*, Margo!"), Lamb Pond came into view on the left. It was bordered by the bike path, empty of cyclists on this balmy day.

Before turning onto the road I spotted the dock Jessie and I used to lie out on, the small private beach family friends would let us use sometimes.

I swallowed and took a right onto Punkhorn Lane.

"Jesus," I said, as we juddered across the pocked dirt, "they never filled these?"

Izzie held onto the handle above her head. "Guess not."

"When's the last time you came here?"

Izzie shrugged. "Maybe close to a year."

I shot Izzie a sidelong glance. "Looks like I'm not the only one who avoids the place. And *you* live five minutes away."

The hurt look on Izzie's face made me wish I hadn't said anything.

As we passed the first house on the left, formerly of our closest neighbor, the two of us went silent. The new owners had ripped the whole thing down, rebuilt, and demolished the professional landscaping, formerly chock-full of rosebushes and hydrangeas, hyacinths and Rose of Sharon, a lawn once bursting with color. Now, it was sanitized, all-grass, devoid of any character or beauty. I wished, for the millionth time, someone had just set fire to the whole place. Burned his house to the fucking *ground*.

Our house—the sign over the garage, crooked and faded, still read NEVINS NEST—came into view next. I stifled a gasp at the sight of it. In the yard an old yellow Adirondack chair lay askew, amid weeds and brambles. What remained of the landscaping were overgrown bushes and baby maples born from errant acorns, now over six feet tall. The yellow door, Mom's favorite part of the exterior, sorely needed a paint job.

I pulled into the driveway, in front of the garage, and turned off the car.

Tears had pooled at the corners of Izzie's almond-shaped blue eyes, but she smiled through it. "Good news is, I think you'll like this new real estate agent. I have a feeling she'll take better care of us."

The two of us sat in the car, silent.

Through the rearview I peered at the woods across the street, at the army of pines that was intersected by fire roads and deeper in, dotted by kettle ponds. Dad always used to boast to people who didn't live on the Cape: "We have the best of both worlds: right by the lake, and we've got the ocean a mile away. If this isn't the life, I don't know what is." He'd always say it with a glance at my mother, who would smile, and he'd give her a little swat on the ass.

Then there was me, always groaning when they said things like this. Embarrassed. I, personally, couldn't wait to get off that peninsula. I couldn't wait to get away from them, their parties, their selfishness.

And I got my wish.

A navy-blue sedan pulled into the driveway. I got out of the car and smoothed my sweatshirt, an old, faded Beachcomber hoodie of my mom's, and stuffed my hands in the front pocket, shivering. The door to the sedan opened, and the realtor stepped out, one long leg after the other.

When I saw who it was, I turned to Izzie. "You *knew.*"

Izzie threw up her hands in mock surrender, smiling. "Guilty."

I didn't have time to argue with her. Walking up to us, tall and regal and beautiful as ever, clad in a black blazer, form-fitting jeans, and modest heels, was Jessie Davis, former best friend to Maggie Nevins.

Margo

Jessie had the key to the front door and let us in. This was all surreal. How many times had Jessie flounced through that door without knocking ("Hiiii, Mrs. Nevins!")? How many times had we snuck *out* of it, to go to the Punkhorn to smoke and drink and laugh and talk...

But it was quickly clear, after some perfunctory pleasantries, that Jessie wasn't here to reminisce. She got right down to business, pointing at the door. "Maybe we repaint? To replace the chipped yellow." She jotted down a note on a pad, and then caught the worried look on Izzie's face. "Normally I'd just suggest buying a new door, but I understand your tight budget."

Next, Jessie—the new adult Jessie, solemn and professional—walked us through the sunroom. She suggested refreshing the trim and said we could rent some furniture for staging.

As she spoke my mind went far off, a decade away. All I could see were Mom's tennis trophies on the hutch—Patty hobnobbing with Pete Sampras at tennis galas, back in her heyday. And I could see Mom's yoga mat positioned by the window, the sun slanting in on Sunday mornings, and the yellow couch, which Sunny wasn't allowed on, but sneaked onto every night anyway...

I blinked and took in what the room was like now: nothing but dust bunnies and old, loose electrical cords.

In the aftermath, Izzie had taken care of the actual clearing of the house; I had been too bewildered, unable to help or make decisions, senses blunted and smoothed so as not to feel what brewed beneath. When I did allow myself to cry—even now, seven years later, *really* cry—it felt as if my eyes might pop right out of my head. Explode. I tried my best to avoid crying at all.

"Hon, you taking notes?" Izzie said, gesturing with her hand, waving it like a pen. "She's done a lot of work, here." She turned to Jessie. "We're so grateful. You have no idea. I think Sigrid gave up on us a long time ago."

Jessie nodded diplomatically. "Now, that's what we need to discuss. It's been on the market a very long time, and, as we all know, that's not good. It raises red flags. We're all aware of the challenge of salability, of reputation. We need to combat that somehow."

"What do people say?" I asked. "Or, like, what do *you* say when they tour the place?"

Jessie glanced at Izzie, then back at me. "Well, you know...I have to disclose that there was a death in the home."

"Two deaths," I corrected her.

"Well, technically," Jessie paused, grimacing, "there were three."

All three of us said nothing after that.

Jessie cleared her throat to break the silence and led us down the main hallway.

"Hey," Izzie said, her voice unnaturally high. "Maybe we'll skip the bedrooms today, yeah? I don't think any of us want to see them."

"I want to see," I said.

Jessie hugged the blue folder, emblazoned with the realty office logo, to her chest. "You sure?"

I nodded and stepped up to the master bedroom door and opened it.

The room was barren, unsurprisingly, and looked smaller than I'd remembered. Empty of the California King, of Mom's antique vanity over by the window ("Always do your makeup in natural light, Mags; you'll thank me for this advice one day."). Empty of the huge INCONCEIVABLE! sign, though the two nails on the wall remained.

I looked up at the exposed beam that loomed above and then tore my eyes from it; it made me too queasy.

This oversized, cavernous room had been a costly addition, one that prompted many fights between my parents. I wish I could say it was just one of them who was shitty with money, influencing or strong-arming the other, but it was both. They were painfully myopic about debt and payments and bills. Mom was into the house looking glamorous, along with her skin and her boobs and her hair. Dad was into the cars, the boats. They loved each other fiercely, but those last couple of years were strained. Making them the perfect target.

He knew. He watched, and he knew, and he pounced.

I crossed the room, footsteps echoing, and peered out the window to the side of the house that used to face nothing but undeveloped woods. I saw now that new homes had been built, saltboxes with massive additions, like this one. A thought came unbidden: *I wonder if he would have gotten away with it, had other people been around to hear their screams.*

Izzie, her face pale, hadn't crossed the threshold. She was still leaning against the doorframe, watching me. Finally she said, "I need a breather." She backed into the hallway.

Jessie gently tried to get me to follow, wagging her head toward the door, but I was rapt, casting my gaze about the room, picking up on strange things, like the dusty baseboards, and small pebbles in the windowsill. I was trying, I guess, not to acknowledge the most striking aspect of my parents' room: that it had no stains. No evidence of what had transpired that late August night. No marks on the beam where the garden hose had hung, no garden tools scattered on the floor, dripping red.

None of that. It was all gone. Wiped completely clean.

* * *

I woke up on the floor, on my back.

I turned my head to see the wide planks of yellow pine my mother had insisted on, despite the cost.

Izzie pulled me to a sitting position. "Honey, are you all right?"

"What happened?"

Jessie appeared beside Izzie; some hair had escaped her low bun, and I thought she looked really nice with her hair natural like this, but then again, Jessie would look good bald.

"You passed out," Jessie said.

"I knew we shouldn't have gone in there," Izzie said, as she and Jessie each took one of my arms to pull me up to a standing position.

I was cognizant of a throbbing at the base of my skull. I touched it.

"You hit the door handle on the way down," Jessie said, handing me an ice pack. "I keep one in the car. With the elderly population on the Cape...this has actually happened before."

I thanked her and took it. "Best to be prepared, I guess."

Jessie smiled. "Yeah."

Once I was on my feet and we made our way outside—the tour was over—Izzie turned her gaze between the two of us and clapped her hands. "What say we get some lunch?"

22

Lucy

"You listen to me, young lady—if you don't tell us what's going on, your father is driving up there and taking you *home*."

Lucy screamed her retort into the phone, holding it in front of her mouth. "He will leave me the fuck alone, and so will you."

"Have you been talking to Dr. Reynolds? Have you been following the protocol? I already know the answer. You haven't. You don't sound *well*."

"Oh, fuck off, Mom. I'm doing just fine. I'm working. I'm dating. I'm living my *best life*—" Right then Lucy's foot crunched something on the carpet, a hair clip. "Ow!" she said, shaking her foot.

"Working? *Where*?"

Lucy looked out Margo's window, at the retirement home across the street, Melrose Manor. "Melrose Middle School. It's Montessori,

99

and they don't have a website, so don't even *try* to tell me they don't exist. They're really anti–screen time and technology. Like, extreme."

Lucy began tugging at her hair. Tugging, tugging.

Calm down or they'll come.

Your work isn't done—calm down or they'll come—your work isn't done—calm down or they'll come—

"Gary?" Her mother called out suddenly. "Pick up the extension in your office. You need to hear this. Something is wrong with her. I think we need to—"

"*Ma*," Lucy said, a little softer. "Please listen to me. I'm trying to live my life. Be independent. That's part of Dr. Reynolds's protocol, isn't it?"

"*Eventually*, yes. But...you're not answering our texts or calls; it's worrying us sick. And why did you concoct that whole *story* about getting into that program at BC—"

"Because I knew you wouldn't let me alone," Lucy said. "Please. Listen. I didn't have a job yet, okay? And I was embarrassed. Savannah is little Miss Perfect, with all her internships and awards, and there I am, barely making it through community college, barely holding down a job. I wanted you to be proud of me."

She sniffled. It was dusty in Margo's room, and it served quite well as a cry-sniffle, too.

"Anyway," Lucy went on, as she fiddled with some of Margo's crap jewelry, cheap bracelets and rings gathered in a little oyster shell on her dresser, "it's all coming together and working out. I have a job, I have a place to live. Everything is fine. I figure, grad school can wait—I'll apply someplace else."

There was a faint click and the sound of her father breathing heavily.

"I haven't been answering you," Lucy went on, "because I'm busy for once. Honestly? I'm *thriving*."

Her mother *tsked* through the phone, and her father piped up. "Oh, sweetie. All of that sounds wonderful, but you can see why we're worried—you being on your own in a whole other state, five hundred miles away—"

Her mother: "Especially after what happened. You're so *fragile*—"

"You mean I'm fragile because I found out you lied to me."

Her mother's voice rose an octave. "I've told you a million times, Lucy, I was *protecting* you. I'm not getting into this right now. Your father wants to talk to you, anyway. Right, Gary? Talk to her."

Lucy scoffed.

"Honey?" he asked, his voice tinny.

"*Father*."

He started his spiel about honesty and taking care of her mental health and calling Dr. Reynolds, and how he'd pay for a bus ticket if she would just please come home, they missed her. As he talked, she busied herself by rifling through Margo's nightstand. Her fingertips came upon something rubbery, sticky.

She peered inside. It was a vibrator. *Gross*. As it rolled to the back of the drawer she saw the name written in Sharpie on the side and her lips curled into a smile.

Her mother: "Lucy, you there?"

"Yes," she said, absently. "I'll keep up my appointments with Dr. Reynolds, but only if you promise to leave me alone. Okay? Do not dare come here. Do *not*."

Margo

"I'm curious," Izzie said to me, after hailing the waitress for another water, "does Lucy know about your parents?"

I stared down at my club sandwich, which sat untouched. Then I looked up at her across the booth. "No."

Izzie glanced at Jessie, beside her. "Maybe it's not the worst idea to come clean to Lucy. She'll forgive the condition of the apartment. She'll get a more honest picture of you."

"She'll pity me, you mean."

Jessie kept quiet but nodded encouragingly at Izzie to go on.

"She won't pity you, she'll understand you," Izzie said. "Honesty is the best policy. It's corny, but it's true."

"So, I should be honest about her being a massive slob, then? And someone who legitimately gives me the creeps?"

Jessie winced. "Well, I think that's a little harsh. Be diplomatic about it, if you can."

"What about when I got sick?" I said, crossing my arms and leaning back in the booth. "I know she did something to my mac and cheese. Used old milk or something. Or worse. I don't know, and then she hid the toilet paper."

As the words escaped my mouth, I felt like a child, and they were looking at me like one. I hated that I couldn't tell them about the *worst* part, Lucy's bizarre "date" with Brad. Right now, they were only aware that Lucy was slovenly, and a little rude. I'd kept Brad my little secret. If I had told Izzie that I was still dating him—or whatever you wanted to call our arrangement—she'd freak.

"I don't know, honey," Izzie said, poking at her salad with her fork. "That's evil, if she did that."

Jessie gave a wry smile and said, "You used to make me that buffalo mac and cheese, and trust me, I spent plenty of time on the toilet. You might have made your goddamn self sick."

Izzie and Jessie started hooting at this, but I wasn't finding it funny.

"You guys. What about the emails to Corinne? I *never* would've sent those."

Izzie grimaced. "Are you *sure* you didn't? You were pretty drunk, correct?"

I wasn't sure.

Suddenly it was all too much. I needed to make them see I wasn't being paranoid. This girl was a *problem*.

"And the exterminator," I sputtered. "She threw that report away. She was making it all up. I *know* it."

Izzie stole a glance at Jessie, the side of her mouth curling into a smile.

"Margo, again, you don't know that for sure. Remember when you first moved in? You had a major mouse problem. Maybe they came back, and then left again. Or maybe, like you said, the droppings were old."

I cupped my coffee mug, shaking my head. "You guys aren't getting it. You don't pick up on her vibe. You haven't met her."

Another look passed between Izzie and Jessie. It made me realize that this little friendship of theirs—not Lucy—was bothering me most of all. Because fine, maybe they were right. Maybe what they were saying (or weren't saying, at least overtly) was true: that my fears over Lucy were unwarranted, born from trauma and paranoia. But it was clear that Izzie and Jessie had rubbed antennae prior to this day.

In fact, Izzie and Jessie seemed closer than ever. The more I saw them laughing together, talking about plans for the Punkhorn house, the more hurt I felt. Because the bald truth was this: I missed Jessie. Terribly. I had missed her for seven years, and I missed her now more than ever, as she sat right in front of me, joking around with Aunt Izzie, all while stealing confused, concerned looks at me in the process.

"You okay, Margo? We don't mean to shut you down," Izzie said, reaching for my hand.

I let her keep it there; it felt warm and comforting.

"I'm okay," I said, finally. "Just a lot to get used to, living with someone again."

Jessie and Izzie nodded and smiled at me so kindly that suddenly, I was awash with shame. Deep down I knew how stupid it was to be competing with my aunt for an old friend. Izzie wasn't trying to steal Jessie; she was trying to reunite us.

As for Jessie, she seemed genuinely concerned for me. Nevertheless, I still sensed it—the unspoken chasm between us, and I could sense that Jessie's guard was still intact.

Jessie still had no idea why I hadn't answered any of her calls or letters over the last seven years. Why I'd disappeared. I knew that to repair our friendship would require that I truly come clean, about everything. Jessie was a no-bullshit type of person. It was why I'd avoided her, why I'd cast her off, and why I didn't come right out and tell her I wanted to be friends again.

Because as much as I wanted to, if I did, she'd figure out my lies in a second.

24

Lucy

"Did you know she has a vibrator with your name on it? In purple marker. *Brad*. I told you, she's a total creep."

Lucy smiled at herself in Margo's mirror, the phone to her ear. When he finished she said, "I swear it's true. I'm looking at it right now. It was sticky, and I touched it by accident. *Blech*. I found some other stuff too, in her nightstand, that you would find interesting. I took pictures of it all."

Pause.

"Don't worry. It'll all make more sense once I tell you *everything*. I promise. And then we can get to work. Do you happen to follow the true crime podcast, *Dirty Vines*? It's my absolute favorite. The hosts are this hippie couple. Their names are Sly and Skye—so cute, right? Anyways, I was thinking—" She paused, because his sudden silence was deafening. "Umm, you know what? Never mind all that for now.

We're still on for tomorrow, right?" She waited, then said, "That's okay, I can come by after." Pause. "Oh, no I don't know where you live. That would help! Let me write that down." Pause. "Great, see you then."

She hung up and slipped her phone back in her pocket. Then she turned and let out a startled cry.

"What are you doing?" Margo snarled from the doorway.

"You scared me," Lucy said cheerfully. "I was just looking for one of these." She held up her hand. "Scrunchie."

"You can't just come into my room without asking."

"Oh, sorry," Lucy said, sheepishly. "I was only in here for a second. I borrow stuff from my sister all the time without thinking about it, so I guess I just thought—"

"This is *my* room."

"Right," Lucy said, shrugging, keeping her smile wide and bright. "But I mean, it's not a big deal or anything."

"Snooping through my things isn't a big deal?"

"I wasn't snooping. I was running in here to borrow something."

Margo shifted position and looked beyond Lucy. Lucy followed her gaze to the open nightstand drawer and the hot pink phallic wand with "Brad" scrawled on the side in faded purple marker.

Lucy chuckled. "Nothing to be embarrassed about."

"I know that," Margo spat.

"But..." Lucy trailed off.

"But what?"

"What was that picture? Of that...bald guy. Couldn't help but notice it. All scratched up, with the devil horns drawn on." She cocked her head, her gaze boring into Margo's bloodshot eyes. "Is that your...*dad*?"

"Please get out."

Lucy obliged, slithering by Margo, brushing her shoulder.

"I was just curious..." Her words trailed down the hallway, hanging in the air before she shut her bedroom door, "...because it seemed a little disturbing."

Margo

I immediately rushed to the nightstand and slid the vibrator—the least of my worries—and a couple tubes of face cream and a pen, aside, and picked up the "disturbing" Polaroid. I hadn't looked at it in a long time.

There he was, frozen in time, with drawn-on devil horns and shining hairless head and poked-out eyes, our "harmless" neighbor who had lived right beside us, on Punkhorn Lane. Dad's "best friend" and "business advisor." Mom's "landscaping expert," and unofficial shopping buddy.

Even his name still made me want to vomit, to this day. Dan.

Dan motherfucking Ellis.

* * *

Long before Dan had bludgeoned my parents to death, lifetimes before, I'd picked up on the fact that he was a creep. Not just a creep. A menace. I knew it, and Izzie knew it, but we seemed to be the only ones.

I guess my first, most vivid memory of realizing Dan was a creep was when I was around fourteen. That would make it two years before he killed them.

It was Halloween. My parents were hosting an adults-only costume party. They told me to sleep at Jessie's, but I'd lingered and watched out my bedroom window as the guests arrived, all couples. The women wore flapper costumes—sequined and feathered dresses, too short—and nurse outfits, also too short, and the men were in half-assed cop costumes with a badge tacked to their belt, or Superman T-shirts.

My parents, on the other hand, did not half-ass Halloween, ever. This was one of the many years they dressed as their favorite duo, Westley and Buttercup. Andrew donned the black mask and fake sword, and Patty, the blonde hair extensions and a long baby-blue dress with a tight bodice. Atop her head, a crown.

"Mom, your boobs!" I'd scolded her earlier, hanging around her vanity as she got ready.

"What?" she said, looking down.

"They're...out. Put them away."

Patty giggled. "You need to go to Jessie's. Let the adults have their fun."

Right then Dad, still somehow tan in October, and somehow virile in his flowy pirate shirt, came in and ruffled my hair, then walked over and plopped a kiss on Mom's head.

"You look gorgeous."

"Farm boy," Mom said, "fetch me that pitcher of margaritas. I need a *drink*."

"You guys are gross," I said, heading toward the door.

"You love us," Dad called after me as I left the room, smiling, despite myself.

Now I continued to dawdle around my bedroom, slowly packing my bag and watching out the window as more guests arrived. After a while, that song from Mr. Big began to blast through the Sonos. My mom loved that song. I could hear her laughter.

Too much laughter; she was drunk. Time to go.

I slipped my backpack on and snaked my way through the party-goers congregating in the hallway, until I hit an obstruction, someone who had widened their stance so I couldn't pass. His cold dark eyes slid over me.

"Now don't you look nice, Mags. A little Patty in training."

"Hi, Dan," I said politely, though I felt invaded. I gave him my own up-and-down glance, not bothering to disguise my confusion, disgust. "Who are you supposed to be?"

His face was red; he was sweating. He'd put on weight steadily since I'd known him, for five years now, back when he'd built the house next door. It didn't seem to dawn on him that he'd grown pudgy; everything he wore was ill-fitting.

Dan held up a gloved hand. "I'm the six-fingered man."

"That's weird," I said. "My parents chose *Princess Bride*, too. They're dressed as Westley and Buttercup."

"I know."

I wanted to ask if they'd planned it, but Mom answered this a moment later, as she weaved her way toward us.

"Dan the Man, what are you?"

He held up his hand. Her face screwed first in confusion, and then she gave a tight smile.

"Huh. How funny."

"Bye," I said, beginning to walk away.

Mom reached for my arm, pulled me close, and kissed me on the forehead.

"Bye, Maggie girl."

I shivered and walked away, but something made me turn back. I saw Dan place his hand on Mom's lower back and whisper something into her ear. She drew her head back and laughed.

"Guy gives me the creeps," I remembered telling Jessie afterward, in Jessie's bedroom. "He's so weird."

We took maybe five minutes to analyze this nobody-adult in our lives and landed on this: He was kind of lonely and pathetic; he had the hots for Patty; he was *so* jealous of my dad (Jessie: "DILF to the max."). We agreed that Dan came over too much, offering free landscaping services and flowers. I told Jessie what I knew: that Dan's crush on Mom had started in high school, when she'd had no idea who the hell he was; that it was a big joke among their friends. It wasn't until he'd built the house next door, the nearest plot out of dozens and dozens of available acreages—this was before the Marshside Conservation Commission had bought most of it up—that Patty had taken any notice of Dan Ellis.

The two of us, me and Jessie, would have this conversation a few more times over the next couple of years, our musings growing more detailed as his behavior grew more pathetic, more desperate.

Still, no one saw it coming, what he had in store for my parents. Except for me.

And I'd never forgive myself for my part in it all.

26

Lucy

Everything had gone so wrong. Lucy knew she'd been too impulsive. She hadn't thought things through.

It had started off okay. Lucy had sat down on Brad's lumpy couch, shifting her leg to avoid the questionable stains as she tried to get him up to speed. He sat in a frayed wicker chair across from her, listening.

She began with the vibrator—she didn't think her rendering over the phone had sufficed—along with a play-by-play of Margo finding out about their "date."

"Can you, like, believe her?" Lucy cawed, waiting for a response. She searched his face, but he didn't give her anything. "She said *you* were lying," she added. "Isn't that crazy?"

She hadn't even *gotten* to the picture of Dan Ellis in the drawer, to the most important part. The vital part. Maybe she was hesitating because she was a little nervous, scared to tell Brad the whole truth.

She didn't know why she was finding it so hard to come right out and tell him everything.

Well, she did know why. It was heavy, and the news would change his life immeasurably, just like it had hers. It wouldn't be easy to take. She felt badly for him. She felt badly for herself.

Unfortunately, when things got heavy, Lucy got nervous. Too nervous. That's what the doctor said, anyway. And when she got nervous, she tended to ramble nonsensically.

Brad watched, remaining silent as she blathered on, unable to help herself.

She repeated the story about coming home after their date, recounting how angry and indignant Margo had become, throwing in a couple embellishments along the way.

"She slammed the table with her hand at one point. I was so scared, Brad."

The living room smelled of sweat and old Budweiser. While Lucy was there, less than a half-hour, a pretty brunette had returned for her phone that she'd left there the night before, or perhaps that morning, followed by an awkward cheek-kiss at the door. Also, a nameless blond roommate Brad didn't bother to introduce had interrupted them as he hauled a jangling garbage bag of beer cans into the blue bin outside, saying something to Brad about a pickup game later, what sport, Lucy could not ascertain.

The whole time Brad hadn't offered her anything, not even water. It was clear her visit was a nuisance, and eating into his day. This didn't help her nerves.

Finally Brad spoke up, cutting her off.

"You've told me the same story about three times now. I'm waiting on this *bombshell* information you supposedly have, about my father? I mean, I have to admit I was curious, but I don't think you've said anything other than mean shit about your roommate. So she's, like, in love with me. I get it. Wouldn't be the first time some stalker chick was obsessed with me." He paused, holding up his hand. "And I'm not being, like, full of myself. It's just the truth."

Lucy tugged at the ends of her hair. This really wasn't working. She was getting too far ahead of herself. He didn't even know who Margo *was* yet. She hadn't laid things out very well. She'd grown too impulsive. Too excited.

"You know what, you're right," she said. "I'm being insensitive. Clearly this girl is deranged." Then, again, she couldn't control herself—it's like she was possessed. "The real fun hasn't even begun yet, anyway. Soon, she'll pay for what she did."

He looked at her in exasperation. Or, possibly, disgust. "You're making no sense. Pay for *what*?"

"Well, I have to *show* you. It's all in the trunk I told you about, which is obviously too heavy for me to drag here. That's why I wanted you to come over to *my* place, so you could look at it—"

"I'm not going over there," he said, looking at her wide-eyed. "You just told me she stalks me. That she's 'deranged'—hey. Quit doing that. You're getting hair on my floor."

She forced her hand to her lap and ignored the sting on the base of her scalp.

"Once you come over and see everything, it'll all make sense. And I think in the end you'll see that you and I..."

She trailed off, too afraid to say it. *Too soon.*

He stared at her a moment. "It's kind of like you're a stalker too. Making excuses to hang out with me or something. You probably don't have any information about my dad, anyway."

"I do have information. I have *reams* of it!" Lucy said, still pulling at her hair.

"You're hurting yourself," he said, taking her arm and pressing it to her side while at the same time pulling her up from the couch and leading her to the door. It seemed like a practiced maneuver.

"Listen," he said, "I don't know your game here. At first, I have to admit, I was curious. I thought maybe I was in danger, the way you were talking at the pizza shop on that scam of a date. And you know what? I don't *want* to know anything more about my dad. I don't even consider him my dad. Dan Ellis was a fucking *murderer*. Do you get that? You have nothing to do with him or what he did, or even with me.

"I'm sorry you live with someone who's in love with me from afar—I'm flattered, if anything. My advice is to move out and go back to wherever you came from. This isn't a true crime show or podcast or whatever. It's people's lives. So, I'm going to tell you politely: Please leave, and do not come back."

She found herself on the steps as the door was closing.

"You don't know what she did! I have to show you! You need to know that Dan was—"

But she couldn't finish. He'd slammed the door in her face.

Now, she walked briskly down the sidewalk, wiping her nose with her sleeve, then her eyes. She stuffed her hands in her coat pockets so that she wouldn't tug at the ends of her hair.

Okay, she thought. Stage Two is not going according to plan. But she had to keep moving forward. She had other ideas, anyway.

She'd let Brad cool off for a while. Once he knew what Margo had done, she just *knew* he'd be on board. He wouldn't feel so harshly about his father, either. She just knew once he heard what really happened, what Little Miss Maggot had done...

She halted on the sidewalk and pulled a pen out of her bag, along with her Decomposition Notebook. Then she jotted down the date, followed by, "Brad stuff gone wrong. Revisit when he chills out."

Then, underneath, she wrote: "Stage Two, Plan B: The enemy of my enemy is my friend."

27

Margo

"You want help installing cameras? I got a guy."

It was a Sunday at The Sham. Owen was reading the *Globe* at the bar while I perched next to him.

I set my iced tea down on a dirty coaster and sat back on the stool, rubbing my shoe over Bearie's fur, who lay beneath.

"I don't really have the spare funds."

"You at least fix your bedroom lock yet?"

I frowned. "I was quoted three hundred bucks. Is that normal?"

Owen jerked his head up. "You can get a new handle from Lowe's, twenty bucks. Guy was scamming you."

"Well, he said something about damage to the door? The wood is split, I guess from the people who lived there before. Someone maybe kicked the door in? It's all messed up now."

"I'll send over my guy, Tommy." He took out his phone and texted. "He can be there tonight. And don't even *try* to pay him."

"But—"

Owen held up a hand. "Saved a bundle on the kennel with you keepin' Bearie last weekend when you went to the Cape. I owe ya."

It was hard to pass up cash when I was so far in the hole I couldn't see out. So I said, "Okay, thank you."

* * *

Tommy came by as promised, that evening. He was twentyish, or maybe thirty; I couldn't tell. He had a long beard and crystal-clear blue eyes and he was stocky, broad-shouldered. Big, in the way I liked. He'd brought a drill and a toolbox, but after inspecting the lock, he shook his head and said, "I'll be back." He returned thirty minutes later with a whole new door.

When he was finished, we stood at the bottom of the stairs.

"I have to pay you—you bought a whole new door," I insisted. "What's your Zenpay name?"

Tommy shook his head. "My dad'll kill me if I take any money."

That's why he looked so familiar. "You're Owen's son!"

He shrugged shyly. "Yup."

"Well, I'm so thankful. For both of you. Truly."

A small smile as he lowered his voice. "He told me you have a snoopin' issue."

"Slight," I said.

"Follow his suggestion on cameras," he said. "They're not as pricey as you think."

"I'll think on it," I said as I walked him out, hugging myself in the cold as he descended the front steps. "And be sure to tell your dad thanks again."

He nodded, and then his eyes flew to the bay window. He frowned at whatever he saw. I followed his gaze, but saw nothing.

"What?"

"Think you've got more than a snooper. You've got a spy."

* * *

I walked into the living room, where Lucy sat curled up on the couch, swiping through her phone.

I hadn't realized Lucy was home. Her car wasn't parked out front. The house had been silent. She hadn't at any point made her presence known. When had she even entered the living room? How long had she been here?

"Who was that?" Lucy said, without looking up.

I stared at her. We hadn't spoken since the scrunchie episode (as Izzie had called it on the phone afterwards, after me complaining, "I told you, she's *sketchy*!").

"No one," I said now.

"He was kinda cute."

He was, I had decided, but didn't say this.

"Go out with him then," I blurted, heat climbing up my neck.

Lucy grinned, then took a sloshing swig of cranberry juice from her cup, which spilled down the side and then onto the coffee table when she set it down—next to, but not on—a coaster. "Maybe I will."

I had to leave the room before I exploded. It was the first time the word "eviction" had played seriously in my mind. The grounds for it. The plausibility. The cost.

* * *

Corinne held a surprise meeting at the end of the work day on Monday. There, she told everyone she was treating the Events team to a ski trip, the following weekend, up at Triton Mountain in New Hampshire.

"We have plenty of tickets," she said. "Bring your loved ones. The more the merrier."

"Is Debbie going?" Astrid asked.

The team was sitting around the oval table in the conference room, Astrid next to Corinne, up her ass, per usual.

Corinne chuckled. "My wife *hates* skiing. I'll be going solo."

The team passed around the pile of tickets. Some people took two, some took up to four, and some took none, citing plans that weekend. When it got to me, I stared at the still-thick pile.

"Invite your friends, Margo," Astrid said. The table wobbled a little. Shanna, beside her, was trying to keep a straight face. "And didn't you say you had a boyfriend?" Astrid asked. "Invite him, too."

I took four tickets from the stack and stared straight at Astrid. "I love skiing. Can't *wait*."

* * *

Later that evening Lucy came into the kitchen as I was heating up half of a ham sandwich from The Sham, which I had learned the other day from Sean, the bartender, was unofficially called "The Shamwich."

"I didn't know you skied?" Lucy said, pointing to the tickets on the counter.

I'd planned on bringing them upstairs with me and calling Izzie and Jessie and inviting them to come. The fourth ticket I planned to hawk. It would pay for gas and meals.

"They're for a work outing," I said.

"I see four. Who's going?"

I sighed. "I don't know yet."

"I *love* skiing," Lucy said. She waited, but when I didn't take the bait, asked, "I notice you didn't say Brad. What's going on with him, does that mean you're officially broken up? Or are you taking a break, or—"

"None of your business," I snapped, glaring at her.

Lucy scurried to the chair beside me and sat, resting her hands on the table.

"Is something the matter? Did I say something wrong?" She leaned forward. "You know what? I think we need to talk. We need to clear the air."

I set my sandwich down and wiped my mouth with a napkin, the last piece on a paper towel roll that had been full the day before. This girl went through toilet paper and paper towels like I'd never seen before.

"You want to talk," I said flatly. "But you see, this is exactly what I *don't* want. I don't want to talk. I don't want to be friends. I don't want to tell you about my love life. It's too much. You're, like, always trying to chat with me, and you've been pulling all this weird shit—"

"Weird shit?" Lucy said, hand to her mouth, looking horrified. "Like *what*?"

I searched my mind for all the affronts, and for some odd reason came up with the weakest: "Like that night you dragged me to a bar—"

"But that was one time, so long ago," she said, cutting me off. "And we had fun." Lucy's eyes were wide, innocent. "You were perfectly happy once you were there—"

I shook my head, as if to clear it. I needed to stay focused.

I hadn't been prepared to have this conversation. I knew full well how I was too mercurial for confrontations like this, how easily I could lose my cool. Lose my words. Slip up. But now, at least, some were coming.

"Let's add it all up," I said, speaking slowly. "I find you snooping in my room. And this is after you go on a bizarre date with Brad." I held up a hand so Lucy wouldn't interrupt. "Even if you had good intentions, that was crossing the line."

"I don't see it like that at all," Lucy said. "I guess I've just been trying so hard, and every time I try, I mess up. I just wanted you to like me. The thing is...I don't have any friends. I never have, and I thought I could start fresh here. I keep to myself, like I said, I really do, but I'm finding that..." A tear rolled down her cheek. "I'm really lonely."

I'd been so ready to flee up the stairs with my sandwich, but now I set my plate down.

"God, please don't cry."

I ripped off the last clean quadrant of my paper towel and handed it to her.

Lucy took it, sniffling, and wiped her nose and eyes. She did look so forlorn and pitiful sitting there, periodically tugging at the ends of her hair.

Maybe I was looking too deeply into these incidents. Maybe there *were* mice, and those rats had somehow gotten shanked by a real animal and found their way under the floorboard. I guess it was *possible*...

"I am a bit on edge," I said, choosing my words as carefully as I could. "I'm not used to living with other people."

"I'm not used to it either," Lucy said, looking up, her face brightening. "I mean, in a different way. I've told you I have a sister, right? Savannah and I are *so* close, but even still, we bicker all the time. One of us is always borrowing stuff without asking, and...I guess I just thought if I did the same thing here, it would be fine, and if I annoyed you, then it would blow over, like it does with Savvy. Clearly, that's not the case. I can tell you're *really* mad at me." She sniffled, and continued. "So anyway, I'm *really* sorry about borrowing that scrunchie and going into your room. And that was the stupidest thing, trying to get back at Brad on your behalf. So stupid."

"I guess I get lonely, too. I know how you feel." Truer words were never spoken. "And I apologize if I've been rude to you, too. But you *do* leave your stuff everywhere." I waved my hand around the kitchen. "I've reminded you about fruit flies, and I've told you a bunch of times when trash day is; it's like it all falls on deaf ears."

"I'll be better," Lucy said, earnestly. "My dad always says—" then she stopped. "Never mind. I know you're not into having conversations and stuff."

She looked down. And then, a second later, her eyes moved to the ski tickets on the counter.

"I bet you'll have a lot of fun skiing."

I fought an eye roll, but found myself saying, "If you want to snag an extra ski ticket, fine. You can come."

Stupid, stupid, stupid. I knew it immediately, but couldn't take the offer back.

"Oh, wonderful!" Lucy said, jumping up and down. "Thank you!"

She snatched the ticket off the pile and slipped it into her pocket.

And then without another word she went into the living room, leaving the kitchen a mess, and turned up the volume on the TV. Loud.

28

Margo

Izzie showed up promptly at six in the morning in her parka, propping her skis against the banister.

"Jessie texted me last night," I said, as I set her bag by the door, "and she canceled last minute. Wouldn't say why. Do you know?"

I led Izzie to the kitchen and began filling a to-go canister with coffee.

"I'll let her tell you," Izzie said, zipping up her parka. "It's a little too personal, I think, for me to relay."

"Okay," was all I said, though I wanted to say more, about how left out I'd been feeling lately. But wasn't that my fault for holing myself up all the time? For never visiting Izzie, never going to the Cape unless I absolutely had to?

"Is, umm, what's-her-face still coming?" Izzie whispered.

"Yeah. We came to a kind of...understanding the other night. Though it hasn't changed her being a slob." I nodded at the sink, full of Lucy's dishes.

There was some movement upstairs, the opening and closing of the bathroom door, the running of the sink.

"At least it sounds like she's awake." Izzie said.

I sighed at this, wishing Lucy would sleep through it, or better yet, forget about the whole thing.

It had snowed hard the day before, dumping almost a foot and leaving high drifts. I'd gotten up extra early to clean off the car and shovel around it so we could get out. I had to shovel well, as the car didn't have four-wheel drive, and the defroster was on the fritz.

Outside, as we finished packing the trunk, Lucy emerged. Standing at the top of the front steps, she called down, "You're Aunt Izzie."

"And you're Lucy."

Izzie walked around the car and held out her hand. They shook.

Lucy tossed her bag, filled with some borrowed items of mine (she'd barged into my room the night before, claiming she didn't have goggles or gloves, and so I had given her old pairs of Mom's, a bright pink pair I'd gifted her for Christmas one year). Izzie now offered Lucy the front seat, but Lucy sweetly refused.

I climbed into the driver's seat, but it was clear from the semi-fogged windows that the car needed to warm up a bit more.

It was then that I noticed someone in the side mirror, a young woman marching down the sidewalk carrying a bright orange beach chair. She wore a dark-colored parka with a hood ringed by fur, the face obscured. The woman stopped short beside the car, watching as we idled.

"What's she doing?" Izzie asked.

"I think she wants to reserve this spot," I said.

Izzie stared back at her through the window. "Reserve? With a *beach* chair?"

126

I nodded and stepped one leg out of the car, turning and calling to the person over the top.

"Do you need something?"

A flash of recognition passed over the woman's face, simultaneous with my own: Carmen Kangaroo.

"Oh. It's *you*," Carmen said.

"And it's you. You must live nearby."

Carmen dropped the chair to the ground, propping it against her leg.

"I found roommates there." She pointed diagonally across the street. "It's *way* nicer."

"Congratulations."

Carmen stooped down and peered through Izzie's window, lowered halfway; she looked inside the car, first at Izzie, and then into the backseat. At the sight of Lucy, Carmen's eyes widened.

"How do I know you?"

"Me?" Lucy said. "I don't know."

After a second Carmen tilted her head back and laughed.

"Oh, I know who you are." She looked back at me and shook her head, her laughter getting louder. "*That's* who you chose?"

An SUV approached now, slowed to a stop, and turned their hazard lights on.

Seeing this, Carmen swiveled on her heel, marched up to the car, and waved her chair.

"This spot is mine, asshole."

"You have a space saver," the other woman said through the window. "I have a *car*, ready to go. I take precedence."

"That's absurd!" Carmen shouted. "I've been waiting!"

I climbed back into the car and turned to face Lucy.

"You don't remember her from the tour?"

"Oh, right," Lucy murmured, still turned around, watching her.

127

I eased out of the spot. I imagined Carmen would plop into the spot in her beach chair, willing to get run over before giving it up.

Izzie piped in now. "Oh, was that the one with the animal name? Kangaroo? Oh, good God, no *wonder* you didn't want to live with her."

"Seriously," Lucy said, folding her arms in her lap and smiling, facing forward. "I'm sure you're thanking your lucky stars you chose me."

* * *

Lucy said nothing about Brad the whole ride, to my relief. I asked her not to mention him, citing some vague reason—that Izzie never liked Brad, and never approved. I also asked Lucy not to mention my parents. "Too sensitive," I had explained. "They're estranged from Izzie as well."

About thirty minutes in, Lucy pushed her phone up to Izzie and rested it on the center console. "Check this out. It's a dating app called SKIngle. Red dots equal single guys."

Izzie took the phone and swiped through. "Gosh. This is so... involved. I'm glad I didn't have to deal with this stuff when I was dating. It's a lot to keep up with, I imagine."

"It's exhausting," Lucy agreed. "I'm on three different apps. But it's not like I'm gonna meet someone through *friends* or anything."

"Have you gone on any dates?" Izzie asked her.

My eyes shot to the mirror. Lucy was smiling back at me, a wry smile. "Well, I went on one..."

I turned up the radio and picked at my hat, suddenly itchy, and unzipped my coat. I felt like I was suffocating.

* * *

When we arrived at the mountain, Izzie went with Lucy to help her rent some skis. I had my own so didn't join them. I was supposed to meet Corinne at the lodge for a check-in anyway. I hoped it wouldn't be required for the Events team to ski together, or even expected. But I at least needed to show my face.

First, though, I found a couple free cubbies along the wall for our belongings, and was filling them when I heard, "Margo!"

I turned, a pit forming in my stomach. "Astrid."

Astrid had on a full face of makeup and her hair was curled, flowing out of a red knit hat. Shanna stood smiling beside her, her face free of makeup and, in my opinion, much more attractive. Astrid had a naturally pinched face and a perma-sneer. Shanna had deep, kind brown eyes, and a genuine smile. At least, as far as I could tell, it was genuine. But look who she'd chosen for a friend.

Astrid looked around, exaggeratedly. "Flying solo today, huh? Guess you couldn't rally your friends or your *boyfriend* to come. You should give those tickets back to Corinne, yeah? Unless you were gonna be shady and sell them or something." Astrid winked.

To my immense relief, Izzie and Lucy came clomping over in their boots. When they neared, I said, "Astrid, Shanna, this is Izzie. And my roommate, Lucy." *I do have people to bring, you twat.* And it wasn't like Astrid came with a posse of non-work friends. All I saw was Shanna.

"Oh my God," Astrid said, staring at Lucy.

"What?" I said, growing irritated. Was she going to harass my roommate, too?

"Do you remember me?" Astrid asked, "From that speed-dating thing?"

Lucy's mouth opened into a surprised O. "Oh my God, *yes*."

"Speed-dating?" Izzie said, looking back and forth at them.

"It was this thing in the Seaport a couple of weeks ago," Astrid explained. "It was *hilarious*. The guys there were total mutants, and me and—Lucy, right? We just kept taking shots together to get through it. I kept meaning to text you back after—I'm *so* glad I had you there."

Izzie said, "Wow. Small world."

I stood there, frozen, thoughts swirling.

Lucy meets—and exchanges numbers—with someone named Astrid, and doesn't make the connection? How many Astrids are there in South Boston? And no way Astrid didn't mention where she worked—she was the biggest braggart in the universe, and our company was well known. Lucy *must* have known who Astrid was, I concluded.

I thought back to what I had told Lucy about Astrid that night, at Delaney's. Oh God, I'd complained about her—and I wasn't even certain what I'd said. And then, the late-night email, which we may have crafted together, or maybe...

Now, though, Astrid seemed genuinely surprised to learn that *Lucy* was my roommate.

Had Lucy kept this knowledge to herself? Or was this a ruse? Or maybe—I fiddled with my hat again—I was being supremely paranoid, and Lucy had never made a connection at all.

All I knew was it had been a bad idea to bring Lucy. A very bad idea.

Astrid linked her arm with Lucy's.

"I know it's, like, nine in the morning, but I still owe you a shot from the other night."

And then, without acknowledging Izzie, or of course me, and without a word to Shanna, who was left standing there with a look of bemusement on her face, Astrid led Lucy away.

"So," Izzie said, looking at me. "That's Astrid."

Margo

It was around noon and Izzie and I were hungry, deciding to eat lunch after this last run. I took slow, wide turns down the trail after Izzie and glided to the ski rack near the base, where she was already unclipping her boots. Izzie grunted as she wrenched the buckle open.

"By the way," she said, "you ever find that fourth ticket?"

I fished my hand into one pocket of my ski pants, and then the other, as I'd done all day, hoping it was stuck in some hidden recess.

"No. Must have left it at home."

We headed inside, and I kept watch in my periphery for members of the team—none of whom had contacted me to see where I was, all day. Except right as I was thinking this, my phone buzzed.

I looked at the text, then up at Izzie. "It's Lucy. She wants us to get drinks and food at the bar upstairs."

Izzie—who didn't get out much with Ray and Damon being so young and Steve working most weekends—squeezed my arm and squealed. "I think I hear a band..."

I shrugged and said sure, feigning indifference, while secretly I was furious, and apprehensive. Lucy hadn't answered my texts after, presumably, bumming around with Astrid all day. Not a good sign.

As soon as Izzie and I got upstairs we spotted them sitting at a round, high-top table: Astrid, Shanna, and Lucy. They were laughing about something but hushed once they saw me approach.

Astrid smiled into her pint glass. "We were just talking about you."

"You guys see Corinne?" I asked, forcing myself to ignore the comment.

"Clearly, you're not on the group text," Astrid said. "She couldn't make it. But she's letting me use this." She waved an AmEx, her corporate card.

"It's for everyone," Shanna said. "Corinne's treat. Margo, get whatever you want, on our tab."

"But she didn't say *junior* members." Astrid shrugged and smiled. "Sorry."

Izzie nudged me. "I'm paying anyway. We should find a table." Her eyes scanned the room. All tables were filled. "Hmm."

"There are seats right here," Lucy said. "Pull those two over." She smiled at me, but I found it to be forced, her eyes empty.

Izzie gave me a private, barely perceptible look—*Sorry to leave you with these beasts*—confirmed out loud that I wanted my usual, the lightest beer they had, and headed for the long line under the ORDER HERE sign at the bar.

I slid reluctantly onto the low-backed stool and returned a tight smile to Lucy. I was about to ask where she'd been all day—what trails she'd gone on, why she hadn't answered my texts—when Astrid leaned forward, wearing a crooked smile.

"Margo, I'm surprised you didn't bring your special someone." Now she addressed Lucy. "It's why she never goes to work outings. Too busy with her 'boyfriend,' " she said, making air quotes. "Have you ever met him?"

I shifted uncomfortably in my seat.

"They broke up," Lucy said. Then she gave me the world's least subtle wink.

"Ohhh," Astrid said in a smiling singsong. "My *apologies.*"

"Are *you* seeing someone?" I said, attempting to deflect. "Never heard you mention anyone."

Astrid tapped her phone. "Funny you should ask. Just got connected with a complete smoke show on SKIngle."

"Who?" Shanna asked.

Astrid pushed her phone toward the middle of the round table, for Shanna and Lucy to see. But I could see, too.

> Recent SKInnections: Brad Ellis.
> SKINFO***: Current Elevation: 900 feet.***
> Free Ticket to Triton = More $$$ for brews.

30

Lucy

Lucy watched Margo stare down at Astrid's phone, saw the wheels in her head spin.

Earlier, Lucy had left the extra ski pass at Will Call, the same pass she'd snagged from Margo's ski pants that morning, while Margo and her aunt had been packing the car.

The plan had been this: Margo would just *happen* upon Brad and Lucy, laughing and talking at the table, or cruising in from a run down the mountain. Then, Margo would be caught in her lies. She would be forced to admit in front of Brad—and her coworkers—that she'd made the whole relationship up. Instant mortification. Margo would flee the mountain in shame. The plan was *genius*.

But there was one problem. When Lucy had invited Brad to grab a drink at the bar—surely, he'd accept; she'd gotten him a free ticket out of the kindness of her heart!—he'd texted, "No, thanks. Doing my own thing."

She'd watched the red dot on the SKIngle app stop and reverse direction. He had been heading to the lodge, likely to the bar, but not now; he was spooked. The red dot later showed he'd gone back up Red Sister Trail, elevation 1,200 feet.

"Cool, cool," Lucy texted back, holding back what she really wanted to say: He was being ungrateful. He was detonating her plan. "Enjoy."

Now, instead of parading Brad around as Margo's fake boyfriend, all day Lucy had been forced to sit at this table, listening to drunk-ass Astrid go on and on about herself and her promotions and her Ivy League education and her expensive condo on West 3rd.

Lucy couldn't get a word in edgewise, but it wasn't a completely lost cause. She'd at least planted a few seeds. "Margo only has a GED, right?" Lucy said at one point. "It's so great your company accepts people like that in such professional roles!" And, "We have this rat issue, but we're trying to work through it. The plumbing, too; the toilet is constantly running...there are leaks in the roof...Margo tells me she's called a plumber. Hopefully she's telling the truth!"

Astrid and Shanna were aghast; they both agreed that Lucy was being taken advantage of, that she was living with a slumlord.

"You should really report her," Astrid had said.

Lucy had nodded gravely. "I feel so bad. I don't want to, but if it gets worse, I think I might."

* * *

Lucy wasn't exactly smart. This had been made clear to her over the years. Teachers. Specialists. Her parents. While there was some talk about specific learning disorders, there was a definite consensus that she had a slow cognitive speed; she had trouble mapping things out, thinking ahead, seeing the big picture. While she knew she was intelligent in other ways—cunning, inventive—she didn't always plan for every scenario.

In this case, she hadn't thought about what would happen if that horny hippopotamus Astrid ever laid her eyes on Brad on SKIngle. She hadn't thought about Margo discovering that Lucy had stolen the ticket. And now, there was no Brad there to make a big sweeping scene to overshadow this minor—in comparison—fact. "So you *never* dated!" Lucy had imagined herself exclaiming in faux horror. "I don't feel safe living with such a liar!" She'd imagined Shanna and Astrid with their mouths open (and where was this Corinne, she wondered, to whom the news of Margo's fudged résumé would be a fireable offense?).

And then, she hadn't anticipated Aunt Izzie to be so *nice* and level-headed and...normal. (According to Dan's notes, which sat wedged inside her Decomposition Notebook, serving as invaluable background information, Patty the Slut's sister, Izzie, was a "jealous pig woman." But even Lucy had to admit, Izzie was sweet as fucking pie.)

None of these imaginings had come to fruition. The plan had gone to shit. But she could recover. She could still make this work.

Lucy finally looked up and met Margo's glare, which was unceasing, fixed. Lucy tried to think. *What's the play, what's the play?*

Lucy decided. She was going for it.

She pointed at her phone. "That's Margo's ex, Astrid. I think he's off-limits. Right, Margo?"

Not the bombshell she'd wanted, without him there, but a picture on the app would work just as well. It would have almost the same effect. *Fake boyfriend.*

She heard Margo suck in her breath.

Astrid threw her head back and let out a cough-laugh. "Yeah, *right.*"

"He is. Tell her." Lucy nodded at Margo encouragingly.

When Margo said nothing, her face scarlet, Lucy shook her head and gave a rueful smile.

"He's still playing the field, I guess. Like I told you, Margs, you're *so* much better off without him. You're *better* than him."

Margo glowered at her. Silence at the table. Even Astrid didn't speak, but there was lots of kicking beneath the table. How they thought thirty pounds of ski boots knocking against each other would be inconspicuous, Lucy had no idea.

"What a coincidence," Margo finally said. "That he received a free ticket. The same day we were here." Then, she got up abruptly from the table and walked away.

Margo

"What do you *mean*, you pretended Dan's son was your boyfriend?"

I shook my head miserably and stared out the car window. We'd been on the road going south for a half-hour. Izzie was driving; I was too much of a mess. We'd left Lucy with Astrid, without a word, at the table, after I dragged my aunt by the arm out of the lodge.

I couldn't stop shaking. I'd known that it was no longer avoidable, that I had to tell Izzie about what was most mortifying, most disturbing, about this whole operation of mine, the fresh-start Margo Sharpe and the death of Maggie Nevins and what remained of it all.

Brad.

I supposed it was time to get it all out. Not mince any words. So, I began, right there in the car.

"I've always had a crush on him," I started.

"When did you even meet him?" Izzie asked. "I didn't even *know* Dan had a son until after he died—"

I squeezed my eyes shut and took a breath.

"I didn't. I've never met him. I stole a picture of him from Dan's house—him kicking a soccer ball—before Dan...did what he did. I know it sounds weird, Izzie, but I was, like, fifteen at the time, and I thought he was hot, and I was stupid. After that I always hoped he'd visit, but he never did.

"I asked Mom about Brad all the time, but she said Brad hated his dad, that his mom—Dan's ex—had 'turned him against Dan.' Anyway, for some reason, I kept up this fantasy after Mom and Dad died. I didn't feel I could date anyone real—that I could reveal who I was and not scare them away—so I just...pretended, that I dated Brad Ellis."

I shrugged, knowing how insane this—I—sounded. This next part, I couldn't even say without cringing.

"A couple years ago, I found out where he lived, and that's why... that's why I bought my place, honestly. Even after you and Steve told me not to, that it was a run-down piece of shit. It was all I could afford that was close to him."

"What do you *mean*?" Izzie, incredulous and shaking, was doing her best to keep her eyes on the road. "I don't understand any of this. What was your goal? Just to sit in your house your whole life and pretend this guy was your boyfriend? It defies logic. It's..."

She trailed off, tears streaming down her face.

I leaned my head miserably against the window, hands in fists at my lap. "You don't have to tell me how it doesn't make sense. It doesn't even make sense to me."

We sat in silence for a while. Scenes from earlier flashed before my eyes.

"Everything would have been fine if Lucy hadn't barged into my room and seen the pictures," I said to Izzie. "The one of Brad with the soccer ball, the picture I stole from Dan's...and there's one that

I...Photoshopped. A picture I found online. I made it look like he has his arm around me—"

"Jesus, Margo."

"I really am in love with him," I said, helplessly.

"You don't *know* him!"

"I know it *sounds* crazy. But that's the point. What's crazy is Brad's the only person on this planet who would understand how I feel. Because we have things in common."

"Like what?"

"Well, our parents were killed..." I trailed off, unable to meet Izzie's piercing side-eye.

"Don't pool them together," Izzie said coolly. "Ever."

"I'm not. Dan was rancid. Human filth. But—"

"But what?"

My quick temper, coupled with my nerves, caused me to finally say to my aunt what I'd been too afraid to say for over seven years: "*Mom* seemed to like him."

At this, Izzie jerked the car over to the right lane. A rest stop was coming up, fast, too fast; we wouldn't make it, we'd have to cut off two whole lanes of cars—

The tires squealed. My hand grabbed at the handle above my head, and the weight of my body pressed against the door as we swerved.

2013

Mom flitted by my bedroom in her thigh-length dress, then halted, doubled back, and poked her head in. "Time to make yourself scarce, Mags."

I nodded, waited for her to leave, then took a hit from a bowl I kept perma-packed in my bedside drawer, breathing out the crack of the open window.

Minutes later, my dad poked his head in.

"What are you still doing here? Listen to your mother. Time to head out!"

His eyes were a little glassy, his cheeks flushed.

"I'm *going*."

I gathered up my backpack and pillow and descended the stairs. There were people everywhere spread like spider legs up and down the hallways, tucked into nooks, leaning against walls. This many people here for a random summer party, no theme this time, was baffling to me. These people really have nothing better to do, I thought.

The garage's inner door was located on the opposite end of the house. En route, I made sure to avoid eye contact with the mothers of my classmates, the admins in the office at the high school, women who now looked alien, wearing sparkly tops and daintily clutching the stems of their wineglasses. In the kitchen were fathers of my field hockey teammates fumbling through conversations about work and fishing and irrigated grass.

Dan Ellis's bark-laugh sounded from the sunroom, followed by some advice about Rose of Sharon and how he'd be willing to cut a deal, half off if you made the switch to Ellis Landscaping...

Reaching for the garage door, my hip jostled the console table beside it, on which sat a bowl chock-full of car keys, and beside that a couple pairs of reading glasses, an empty beer can. Sam Cooke crooned through the speakers. No Mr. Big yet. Surely it would come on soon.

Once in the Volvo I tossed my bag and pillow across the console to the passenger seat. Mom and Dad had just gifted the car to me for my birthday, upgrading their own to a Lexus SUV, a model Dan had recommended. Dan *knew a guy* who could give them a *deal*. It still somehow turned into Dad spending too much. I'd already heard my parents fighting over it.

I got all the way to Jessie's street, two miles away, fighting summer traffic on 28—it was next to impossible to take a left from Memorial

Day to Labor Day—when I realized I'd forgotten my phone. It was like leaving my right leg behind.

I turned around and headed back.

The car started to rattle. Earlier I'd hit a curb outside Cumberland Farms—and then *again* when I reversed by accident—*two* curbs! Idiot, I thought to myself. You've had this thing for *one* day.

The rattling grew louder. I couldn't drive this down our pocked dirt road. No way.

Thankfully I'd reached Lamb Pond, so I parked at the Garritys' private pull-off, fronted by the private dock they let us use, and started to walk down Punkhorn Lane. I dreaded getting back to the house and catching Dad in some cringe-worthy, flirtatious banter with one of Mom's fake friends, but at least I could interrupt him long enough to mention the rattle. He could call his mechanic first thing in the morning. Then, hopefully there would be someone sober enough to drive me back to Jessie's.

I walked, unhurried, taking in the crisp, starry night. I was still a little high and felt calm, serene. The road was dark and quiet at first, the slap of my flip-flops and the chorus of peepers the only sounds of the night. But soon enough, there came the music and the lights and laughter.

As I passed Dan's house, I heard a woman's voice, followed by a man's. Hushed tones, giggling. Then, two figures stole across to Dan's adjacent yard. Something stopped me from calling out. Instead, I stepped to the right, into the Punkhorn's woods, and hid behind a thick oak.

"Did you turn the motion sensor off?" It was Mom. I knew it for sure now.

"Yeah," Dan said. He held his hand on Mom's lower back, and I could see their heads swiveling to look back at the house where the party was still very much going strong.

The side door opened. Dan and Mom stole inside. It shut. The light in his kitchen went on. A flimsy shade was drawn over the screened door, but from my angle I could see their dark figures through it. And then, one figure pressed against the door, followed by the sound of the shade banging. The outline of Mom's long hair, and a second figure, a bald head, descending upon it. Another bump against the door, a sharp gasp.

I turned, bowing over a tree stump, and retched.

32

Lucy

"Brad!" Lucy called out. "There you are."

He'd been standing outside by the fire pit, alone, beer in hand, looking off at the mountain. At the sound of Lucy's voice, he waited for a beat as if bracing himself and turned.

Lucy strode toward him and jutted a thumb at Astrid. "*So* funny that you connected with my friend on SKIngle. Small world."

Astrid hung back a little, uncharacteristically shy, and said in a small voice, "Hey."

"Astrid works with *Margo*," Lucy said. "Isn't that funny?"

Astrid giggled. "Lucy told me all about your so-called *girlfriend*." She paused, then flashed a smile. "Though, seeing you in person, I guess I don't blame her for stalking you."

Lucy smiled too; she wasn't in the least bit jealous of Astrid vying for Brad's attention. Two words in and Brad would want to boot

Astrid off the side of the mountain himself. In fact, Lucy actually wished Astrid were more attractive, or had some fashion sense. It would boost Lucy's own social capital; then maybe Brad might answer her fucking texts for once.

Lucy glared at Astrid now, wishing she could lick her finger and wipe it over the clown makeup on Astrid's face, and then throw that awful plum-colored coat into the fire.

Brad took a long swig of his beer and looked at Lucy. "Can I talk to you a sec?"

Once they were out of Astrid's earshot, he said, "It's official. As far as I'm concerned I've got *two* fucking stalkers."

"No, it's not like that," Lucy said, pulling out her phone and fumbling with it, knowing her time was limited. She held it up. "See, this is what—"

But he wouldn't let her speak. "I told you I wasn't interested in whatever information you're *claiming* to have about my dad." He waved his hand back at Astrid. "Baiting me here with a ski ticket? I mean, come on. I wouldn't have taken it if I knew you were here. You said, 'I have a ticket I can't use'; like, how would *you* interpret that?"

Lucy wished he'd speak more quietly; she sensed Astrid swanning her neck and inching closer. She widened her eyes and changed tack.

"I'm *so* sorry, Brad, I truly wanted to give you space until you were ready. But just so you don't think I'm some *random stalker*," she chuckled at this, shaking her head, "I wanted to show you one thing as proof that I *do* have important information that will change your life. I'm not being hyperbolic." She'd heard Margo say this word to her aunt earlier in the car, after Izzie told Margo she'd "been single for a million years," and to please consider dating some dumb lawyer at her husband's firm. It had taken everything for Lucy not to spill the story about Brad right then and there, but she'd exercised patience. She was *learning*. Thanks, Dr. Reynolds, you dickwad.

146

Now, someone called Brad's name, a guy in a blue ski parka holding two draft beers.

"One sec," Brad called back.

Lucy shoved the phone in his face. "Please. Look."

"What am I even looking at?" he said. "Oh. This is that trunk you were telling me about."

"Yes. This was *Dan's* trunk," Lucy said. "He sent it to me. He'd arranged it before he died. He wanted me to know what Margo did so that I could get him, and *you*, justice—"

"How the fuck do *you* have something of my dad's?" Red striations had formed on the whites of his eyes, which were watery from the cold, and as he spoke, puffs of air escaped his perfectly formed lips. His gaze hadn't strayed from the picture. He was squinting at it, brows furrowed.

Got you, she thought.

Now, it was Lucy's turn to play coy. She snatched the phone back, put it in her pocket, and then coquettishly shrugged her shoulders as she walked over to Astrid.

"Sorry, girl," she said loudly, linking Astrid's arm and leading her away, "turns out he's not interested."

* * *

Lucy didn't mind when Astrid dragged her right back to the bar, where she downed shot after shot, mooning over Brad's rejection—whining and perseverating over why he'd even *SKInnected* with her in the first place. "Why'd he swipe, then, if he was just gonna be an asshole?"

Shanna joined them but didn't last long, eventually shaking her head in disgust at Astrid's too-loud honk of a voice, her rudeness to the bartenders. In order to secure her only option for a ride home,

Lucy was as nice to Astrid as she could muster. She told her that maybe Brad thought she was someone else, that it was an honest mistake. Don't take it personally.

She didn't tell Astrid the truth: *Your picture is from a decade ago and filtered to shit.*

They stayed three more excruciating hours until it bled into the loud shoulder-brushing of après-ski. Lucy took one out of the ten shots offered to her, tossing the others behind her shoulder into someone's ski bag.

Finally, Lucy commandeered Astrid's keys, took her arm to steady her, and led her out of the bar.

She'd accomplished a *lot* today. Brad had agreed to meet tomorrow. He was officially *hooked*.

Margo

"They weren't having an affair," Izzie said. She sat across from me in the rest-stop food court.

I looked up from my fountain Coke. "I don't know how you define an affair, Izzie, but *come on.*"

"Honey, do you know what all those parties were for?"

I looked at her blankly. "No."

Izzie waved her hand exasperatedly as if she was explaining how to go number two to a toddler. "You had to have heard the rumors?"

I squirmed in my seat. "You mean, like, what all those Botox beasts in the Marshside Moms Facebook group would say about Mom—about her being a tease, and that she drank too much, and that it was *her* fault she'd led him on?" I felt my face grow hot, my heart rate quicken.

Izzie shook her head at this, and I knew I wasn't going to like what she said next.

Izzie took a labored breath. "Mag—Margo. Your parents were *swingers*. Those were swingers' parties."

I sat very still.

Izzie twisted her wedding ring.

"You remember that key bowl. By the door. It was for this game..." She began to ramble, her speech hurried. "Anyway, I never liked going to the parties myself, hence why I rarely showed up for more than ten minutes, just to show my sister I wasn't a total wet blanket. Steve, on the other hand, refused. He used to say, 'Never mind the swinger thing; the fact that it's your *sister* makes this so much weirder.'"

"Oh my fucking *God*!" I finally burst out, startling a mother beside us who was tending to her kids.

"Sorry," I said, then lowered my voice and turned back to Izzie. "Are you telling me what I saw that night, between Mom and Dan... that was, like, *sanctioned* by Dad?"

Izzie winced. "Sort of. It was...complicated. I remember that exact night. Patty called me afterward. She'd had too much to drink, and once she got to Dan's, she had second thoughts, but he wasn't taking no for an answer."

She stopped, looking as if she was about to say something, and then thought better of it.

"Anyway, it made her reevaluate their...arrangement. Your dad knew it was no competition whatsoever, trust me. Anyway, when your mom rejected him, Dan was not pleased. To say the least."

I was trying to listen, to turn over every word, but I was lost in my own thoughts, feeling as if all my memories had been slashed by a teacher's red pen: "Revise!"

"I thought you at least had an inkling," Izzie said, breaking the silence.

"No, I didn't. But how is that fair?"

150

"Fair?" Izzie said, frowning.

"Don't swingers *swap*? Who did Dad get? Dirty fucking Dan didn't bring anything to the table! She goes for this...this pathetic *turd*? What did she see in him? He was bald and pudgy and such a douche—"

Izzie rubbed her eyes. "He worked on her for a long, long time. You remember him coming by all the time, offering her flowers and free landscaping, any excuse to go over there. And your mom, at first, was flattered by all the attention. She felt bad for him. He'd portray himself as this sweet, *lonely* guy." Izzie shuddered.

"So, he was a pity lay."

Izzie scowled. "Margo."

"There's no use beating around the bush." I paused, then said, "Ew. Bush. Oh, God."

I covered my face with my hands as my thoughts flew, puzzle pieces suspended in the air, interlocking. I couldn't think straight.

So. Mom wasn't the awful cheater I thought she was; Dad *knew*. I wondered if that made what I had done worse (*yes*); I wondered if I could have just gone to Dad, asked him for help (*yes*), before taking things into my own hands. And doing what I did—I could have warned them.

Oh, God.

Izzie sighed and stood. "We should go."

Walking out of the food court, I had to steady myself on nearby tables. I felt untethered to the earth, wobbly.

"Are you all right?" Izzie asked.

"I'm fine. But can you drive still?"

"Of course."

Before we got into the car, Izzie said, "There was something going on with Dan." She tapped at her own temple. "I mean, *before* he lost it. You remember him calling her that summer, at all hours of the night?"

I did.

"He was positively convinced she was leaving Andrew. He made all these wild accusations. Then, as we all know, he just *snapped*. It was baffling how quickly it all changed. You just never know with people, I guess."

I tried my best to keep my expression neutral, but my heart was in my throat.

I got into the car so I could avoid Izzie's tear-filled gaze.

Izzie got in, dabbing at her eyes, then started the car. "I wish I'd listened to my gut, even when your mother and father said how *harmless* he was, that he just couldn't handle the emotional toll of their 'lifestyle'—that they'd all make up, like they always did. I wish I'd done something. I feel like it's my fault."

"It's not your fault," I said quietly.

But it is, at least partially, mine.

* * *

The house was dark and quiet when we got inside.

Izzie slipped into the bathroom and I took that opportunity to case the apartment, making certain Lucy wasn't sitting in a dark room, listening.

"Hello?" I called out.

We'd spent a long time in that food court, talking. Lucy could have driven home in that time. She could be lurking.

"Think I can ask Steve for eviction advice?" I asked after Izzie came out, wiping her hands on her pants.

Izzie squared her shoulders, took a breath, and faced me head on in the hallway.

"I've gotta be honest. I'm worried about you. This whole Brad thing...it's unhealthy."

"But she—"

"Yes, it seems like Lucy is up to something"—Izzie held up her hand before I could say anything more—"and I mean, sure, does Lucy *likely* have a thing for Brad? Yes. But that's none of your business, is it? You don't *know* him."

"We have a connection," I said, quietly.

"Frankly, Margo, do you really think Brad Ellis wants to sit down and talk about what his father did? With you? Do you think you guys will run off into the sunset, all because your parents were tied up in some sick game?"

"Maybe he's hurting, too. Maybe we would find common ground."

"What if *he* blames your mother, just like everyone else? Because you know what the note said..."

This statement hovered in the air between us, too flagrant, too painful to face.

"You're right," I said, finally. "The Brad stuff is all in my head. I need to just...let him go."

I was happy to see Izzie's shoulders relax as she breathed out. Izzie didn't know that this was merely propitiation. A fend-off. I would *never* be done with Brad.

Seeing Izzie's hand reaching for the doorknob, I whimpered, "Sure you can't sleep over?" I imagined Lucy striding inside any minute now with Astrid in tow, snide remarks about Brad spewing from each of their vile lips.

"I'm sorry, honey, but I have to get home. Steve's about ready to off himself after being alone with the boys all day," Izzie said, rolling her eyes. "Yes. For *one* day."

She planted a kiss on my forehead, then looked at her phone and gathered her keys from her purse. It seemed her mind had already gone to bedtime stories and grocery lists.

Right before the door shut, Izzie said, "Wait. Here." She pressed into my hand a folded piece of paper.

I didn't look at it, instead watching Izzie get into her car through the bay window.

When she was gone I opened my palm and unfolded the paper. On it was a list of phone numbers for multiple area therapists. The paper was thinned, the writing faded. It had been written, it seemed, a long time ago.

* * *

I stand at the foot of my parents' bed. They're in the bed, sleeping. A heart-leap of happiness—the last seven years never happened. Any of it.

Except, as I turn my attention back to what's before me, it dawns on me, slowly, a sickening recalibration. They're not sleeping. No. They're not sleeping.

"Your body is a temple" was one of Mom's favorite sayings, so she'd have been glad that hers was left on display—nude, and mostly untouched from the neck down. Her arms are bronzed from employing her lethal backhand at the club's outdoor courts for hours on end. Her breasts, Dad's fortieth-birthday gift, defy gravity, perked and taut. My eyes travel lower, to her emergency C-section scar, my begrudged entrance to this world, the result of a bunk pack of birth control pills. (Mom and Dad never wanted to be parents.) Finally, her tattoos: On her inner arm, in small, tasteful, lowercase script: *As you wish*. On top of her left foot, Dad's initials, TAN, for Tobias Andrew Nevins. This, however, was not untouched. The "T" had been scraped with something sharp, something bloodletting, into a "D." DAN.

My eyes travel to the right, to Dad. His chest is waxed—it's summertime, and in his muscles, even as he lay inert, I can see all those hours playing racquetball, kayaking with Mom, lifting at the gym. There are no tattoos, but he wears a gold locket around his neck with

Mom's picture on one side, and on the other, his dead mother. When anyone teased him about his dainty little locket he'd shrug and say, "The only problem with this locket is that it doesn't fit a picture of my number one," and then he'd wink at me.

Now, *above* their necks is another story. Two sets of professionally whitened teeth glow as if lit by black light, surrounded by tendons and flesh that is ripped and cleaved, sliced and sluiced. Their hair is matted—Mom's blonde now in colorless, dreadlocked snarls, Dad's flecked gray-brown, caked in blood.

Then, a sound. Behind me. I ignore it.

Abruptly, Mom—or rather, her corpse—sits up. Yellow petals fall from her eyes, leaving two gaping black holes. She picks at the drenched crimson sheet.

"Mags." As she speaks, rags of chin-skin flap left, right. "Do you think..."

"Mom," I say, as his soft laughter erupts behind me. "I'm so sorry—"

"I said, do you *think*," Patty repeats, raising the sheet higher, "that the cleaner can get this out? She's coming tomorrow to tidy up after the party."

Heavy breathing warms my neck. He's standing behind me. The smell of dirt materializes, a sprinkler on a hot summer day. Then the rot of his breath.

A light scrape on my shoulder deepens. I open my mouth to scream.

* * *

"Margo?"

At the sight of Lucy, standing there at the end of the bed, so still, but almost...*swaying*, I jumped back. The back of my skull banged against the headboard.

Lucy's words came out in a low purr.

155

"You were crying out in your sleep. Are you all right?"

"I'm fine." I wiped the hair back from my face, moist with sweat.

"Bad dream?"

"Something like that."

"What do you need—water? Anything?"

"No," I said, but Lucy rushed out anyway and returned with a glass. I took it and sipped a couple of drops only. I didn't trust anything Lucy did or said. Not anymore.

The light from the moon streamed in from the window, giving Lucy a ghostly hue.

I reached for the covers that were tangled at my feet and smoothed them, pulling them up to my chin.

Lucy turned.

"Is Astrid here?" I asked.

"No," she said, looking at me. "She dropped me off. Why?"

"No reason. But, umm, after work tomorrow, I hope you'll be home. I need to discuss some things with you."

"I'll be here. *Really* looking forward to it," Lucy said. She gave me an odd grin, her face in the near-dark still imbued with that white hue from the moon. "You do this all the time, you know, Margo. You talk in your sleep—well, *scream*—quite a bit."

Lucy

ASS TURD: "GIRL!!! Thx for driving my ass home. I got so fuckin drunk."

ASS TURD: "Can't find my pants."

ASS TURD: "CAN'T SLEEP!! U?"

It was four in the morning. Lucy lay in bed, her ski bag tossed to the floor, her phone clutched in her hand. These late-night texts had been streaming in for hours.

She couldn't sleep. Ever since she'd walked home from Astrid's, spent a little time eavesdropping on Margo and her aunt from the hall closet, and then tended to Murder Margo's night terrors, she'd climbed back into bed, where all she could think about was all the work she had to do before Christmas, in just six days. She'd have to take a hiatus and head home to spend the holiday with her family, in Pennsylvania.

This, she dreaded.

Lucy's mother had left several voicemails over the past couple of weeks, each growing in urgency and exasperation. The final message, left while Lucy was on the mountain, said, "Unless you want your father and me to show up in South Boston so we can all open presents together, AS A FAMILY, you will come *home.*" Her mother had screamed this into the phone, and her mother *never* yelled.

Lucy was spooked enough to text her sister. "Savannah. Tell Mom *fine.* I'll come home in a couple of days. But until then, tell her to stop fucking calling me."

Savvy responded immediately. "What is UP with you lately?? They r so worried."

Lucy thumbs-downed the message.

Now, staring at the ceiling, Lucy shifted her thoughts to Brad.

Today was the *big reveal.* She was giddy, but also apprehensive, scared. She had to play it right; she couldn't afford to mess this up with him. Any rash reaction would screw up Lucy's long game. She couldn't cause Margo's radar to go off, either, not after all that eviction talk with that aunt of hers while Lucy was folded in the closet behind a giant coat, the one place that Margo hadn't checked.

Lucy giggled, thinking back to Margo's aunt essentially telling her she was absolutely out of her mind for this one-sided obsession with Brad.

Time somehow crawled to 4:45 in the morning. Lucy stretched into a starfish and yawned, then rose from bed. It was time to make like she was going to work, as she did every weekday morning. Quick shower. Put the coffee on, right at five. Set the knapsack with the big buckles by the door, top flipped open, packed with notebooks and a clear pencil case filled with unused red pens.

She listened for Margo's phone alarm at six, and next, for the shower to turn on. It was a baffling phenomenon, how Margo managed to wash her hair every day, but still, it looked like she'd slept in a vat of bacon grease.

After Margo got out of the shower, Lucy slung her knapsack over her shoulder and made sure to announce her exit by slamming the door, loud.

She walked to her car, slipped her "work bag" into the trunk, and drove to a private garage, basement level. She locked her things inside, and then headed back out on foot.

Her destination: M Street, to Brad's. Her plan: Begin Stage Three.

* * *

When Brad opened his door, it looked like he hadn't slept in days. He was still handsome, though.

"It's early," he said, his breath rank. "Tell me again why I couldn't just meet you at your apartment? Isn't she at work?"

"We'll walk over there together," Lucy said sweetly. "So you don't get lost. And plus, I wanted to show you something before we left. Something we can only see from here."

She ignored Brad's frustrated back-of-the-throat sigh and waltzed past him, inside, trying not to sniff the putrid, hungover-man smell that permeated the whole apartment. She caught sight of herself as she passed a large, full-length mirror (when she finally told Brad everything, and after they inevitably grew closer, she would help him redecorate his apartment; full-length mirrors go in the *bedroom*). Her hair was growing so damn slowly. She'd done it to herself, as much as she regretted it, and even if in the end, it wasn't her fault. It was her mother's, technically.

Jackass Judy had just told Lucy she'd been lying to her own daughter for thirty years.

Lucy took the news calmly at first. Judy waited for her reaction, and Lucy simply said she needed a minute, and went to the bathroom to collect herself.

She'd felt strange, out of body—like parts of her didn't belong anymore. Not her eyes or her nose or her hair. It was the oddest sensation, wanting to divest herself of...herself.

After a while she strode back to the living room where her mother was waiting in the easy chair and swiped a pair of scissors that were next to her on the table. Lucy began cutting, chopping at her shoulder-length locks like she was Edward Scissorhands, nicking her cheeks while her mother screamed, until her sister flew into the room and wrenched the scissors out of her hand.

But not before a Saturn ring of hair had gathered on the floor around her feet.

Cue the whole debacle with Dr. Reynolds and the new "protocol."

Brad now stood with his arms crossed, watching Lucy as she stood awkwardly in the center of the room, taking everything in. She let him watch her, wondering if he saw her any differently yet. She'd played up the dark makeup around her eyes this morning. Her best feature, if she did say so herself.

Finally she looked into his eyes. His expression was one of disgust. This stung. She gave him a hurt look, a little pout of the lips. He looked away.

She sighed and checked her phone for the time, listening for sounds outside.

"So—" Brad started to say.

"Wait." She ran to the front window and lifted his blind. "Here it comes."

"What?" He dipped his head down to look.

She pointed.

Sure enough, the bus had squealed to a halt a few feet before Brad's front steps. And to Lucy's satisfied glee, peering forlornly out the bus window was a black-haired ghoul staring straight into the lifted blind at Brad and Lucy, a look of shock slowly crossing her face as the sight sunk in.

Margo

I knocked on the glass door. Corinne looked up over her glasses. Her eyes looked red, as if she'd been crying.

"You ready for me?" I asked.

"Ready for what?"

"Our check-in."

"Astrid didn't tell you?" Corinne said, tiredly. "I've given her a promotion. You'll be reporting to her now."

"No," I said, lingering at the door. "She didn't tell me."

My stomach roiled at this new disgusting fact. How could Corinne be such a terrible judge of character?

"Need something else?" Corinne said, looking up.

Watching her for a moment, I sensed distress, pain. I wanted to ask if Corinne was okay, in my own roundabout way.

"Missed you at the ski trip."

"I had a family thing," she said.

I looked to the right side of Corinne's desk, at her funky red credenza that didn't fit the soulless air of the rest of the office, and noticed the photo of Debbie was no longer on top of it.

"I heard *you* had a good time," Corinne said, arching a brow.

I looked back at her, startled.

"But how about we be mindful that these are work-sponsored events, yeah? Next time, watch the booze intake."

"What? I didn't—"

The phone rang. Corinne nodded at the door for me to leave. As I did, I heard Corinne say, low and urgent, "I told you, stop calling my work."

When I returned to my desk I noticed a meeting invite had popped up, one that was ten minutes overdue, with Astrid. I could have sworn it hadn't been on my calendar earlier.

I rushed to the small meeting room. Astrid was sitting at a circular table, facing me. Her laptop was open, and she had a notepad filled with handwritten notes.

"Not a good look, late to your first meeting with your new manager," Astrid said, smirking.

"I didn't *know* you were my manager," I said, curtly. "Corinne just told me."

"I told you on Saturday. At the mountain. Were you too drunk?"

"No," I said, sitting up straight. "I was barely drinking. You—"

"What about me?" Astrid said, smiling wickedly.

I pursed my lips. Don't freak out, Margo. *Don't.*

"Your roommate and I had a great time. I learned so many things about you."

"Like?"

"Like, about your personal life."

"My personal life has no bearing here," I said, jaw clenched.

Astrid wasn't listening, it seemed.

"We met up with Brad," she said, inspecting her fingernails. "He's gorgeous. I'm so sorry you guys broke up."

"Can we talk about more appropriate things, like work? Isn't that why I'm here—?"

"Oh, yes. Of course. Just trying to get to know my employees a little bit."

Astrid launched into the coming week's tasks—client-facing tasks, none of which were part of my job description. I could hardly concentrate on anything she was saying. All I could see was Lucy's face through the window this morning, and Brad ducking down to look beside her, catching me watching from the bus as it passed Brad's house.

Lucy's look of jubilation.

When Astrid was finished drowning me in senseless tasks, she said, "Your roommate also mentioned something interesting about your parents, which I found so funny."

I leveled my gaze. "What's *funny* about my parents?"

"Well, I remember Corinne saying that you'd told her this awful story about them. How they died in some tragic accident? Which of course I always found to be so *sad*. I've always felt so *bad* for you."

Tears bloomed around my eyes.

Astrid went on. "But you told your roommate that you're 'estranged' from your parents." She made giant air quotes with her witch-fingers. "So, they're alive? You lied?"

I set my jaw. "Trust me. They're *dead*."

Astrid smirked. "Okay. Sure. And *where* did you go to college again?"

I got up, unbridled rage coursing through me.

"I need to be excused. Actually, I need to go home."

Astrid called after me. "We get one mental health day per year, Miss Sharpe. I assume you'll be using yours today?"

163

36

Lucy

"The place is such a dump, right?" Lucy said as she led Brad down the hallway.

He nodded slightly. "Looks that way."

"And look at what a slob she is. Disgusting." She pointed to the sugar trails by the coffeemaker, the stacks of dishes in the sink. "Everything leaks, and it's like she spends her days taking fifty-pound dumps, that's how often the toilet gets clogged."

Brad stood by the glass sliding door and looked out, hand on his hips.

"This place isn't so bad. Least she's got a nice deck. Better than my apartment. For what you said you pay in rent? I'd kill for this spot. Instead I've got that piece-of-shit place with my roommate, who's always hassling me about bills and shit while I'm, like, Chill, dude—I'm fuckin' broke, just like you. You don't even pay utilities, you said. Consider yourself lucky."

Lucy—while pleased that Brad was stringing together more sentences than he ever had before, actually having a conversation with her—snorted. "*Please.*"

Upstairs, she tried Margo's door. Locked.

"Dammit," she said. "I wanted to show you the creepy pictures of you she used to have on her dresser. When I found out she was making up your relationship, she put them away, in her nightstand. To go along with her vibrator." She coughed out a laugh and shook her head. "But it's okay. I took pictures of them for proof, on my phone. Look."

He pinched at the screen with his fingers, expanding the photo.

"How does she have this picture of me? That's...*Dan's* yard. Literally one of the three days in my whole life when I visited him. I think in this one I'm, like, fifteen. He hated when I kicked the ball against the house. He was such a *dick*—"

"I'm sure your dad just wasn't used to having a kid around," Lucy said, dismissively. "I'm sure he loved having you there. Okay, now look at the next one," Lucy said, tongue poking her cheek to keep from laughing.

He swiped to the following picture. "Uh, don't think this is it."

He showed her and she took the phone.

It was a picture she'd saved from the company "Dr. Ratz!" that sold large-sized rodents online. Staring out at them was a picture of Remy, the male. He'd squealed the loudest.

"Oh, right. You need to swipe this way." She handed back the phone.

His eyes widened.

"How the fuck did she get a picture of me with my arm around her? Is this at Delaney's? How did she do this?"

"Told you she's a complete weirdo." She wagged her head toward her room. "Now, on to the main event."

In anticipation of Brad's visit, Lucy had made her bed and washed her sheets and hung her clothes in the minuscule closet. She'd dragged the trunk to the center of the room, a feat that had taken all of her and Astrid's strength. It also took strength to refrain from clocking Astrid every time she asked to see what was inside.

"Told you it was big," Lucy said now. Her breaths were short and she was sweating.

"You gonna open it?" Brad said. "I'm missing work for this."

She stepped forward and brandished the key.

"Promise me you'll take this information seriously. That you won't try to act too impulsively. I have been planning this for a long time, ever since this information came to my attention." She shut her eyes, relishing the drama. "It's a matter of life and death that we stay the course and keep our cool."

She opened her eyes. He looked unconvinced. Bored. She would have to drum up enough enthusiasm for both of them. She didn't understand how he could be so unimpressed by all this. It was an adventure, a mystery. True crime in live time.

She kneeled in front of the trunk and began to turn the key slowly, dramatically. Her heart pounded in her chest. This was it. This was the moment...

Right then Brad's phone vibrated.

He checked it. "Fuck. I gotta go."

"What do you mean?" she said. "You can't go now."

"I'm supposed to be on-site at Fidelity. I thought the meeting was tomorrow but it's today. I'm already on thin ice with my boss, and if I get laid off again..."

He turned toward the door, muttering to himself, head in his phone.

"I really need this deal to go through. Fuck, fuck, fuck."

"But we were just about to—"

"I'll come back later. After work. It's fine."

She tried to keep the frenzy out of her voice.

"I can't guarantee she won't be here then. I only have so much time before she tries to evict me. I heard her talking to her aunt about it last night. And I wouldn't be surprised if she was planning something even more extreme. Something way worse than eviction. This is a matter of life or death, Brad. We gotta get this plan in motion. Are you even *listening* to me?"

"Jesus," he said, jerking his head up from his phone. He was still standing in the doorframe. "You don't need to yell. What plan?"

Suddenly she heard the squeal of bus brakes outside the window. She glanced down at her phone. She flew to the window and looked out. The bus went by without stopping. No Margo.

Lucy let out her breath and turned back to Brad.

"I thought that was her. Astrid's supposed to tell me when she leaves work today, and every day, but she's no use half the time. Head up her ass." She rolled her eyes, then pointed at the trunk. "Can we at least get this out of here, keep it at your place? It's a miracle she hasn't tried to break into it already."

A miracle that she was such a moron. If it were Lucy, that would have been the first thing she'd have done.

"Where the hell will I *put* it?"

"Life or death, Brad. Seriously."

She tried to breathe evenly.

"Jesus," Brad said. "Fine. I'll come back and get it. There better be gold nuggets in there or something. Something that'll make this worth my time."

"There is," she said, calling at his back as he made for the stairs. "I promise."

37

Margo

The bus trundled down M Street. I stared straight ahead as it passed Brad's building, willing myself to listen to Izzie, to *stop obsessing over someone you don't know,* and to stop thinking about what I saw this morning: Lucy's face in Brad's window.

The bus neared the stop by my house. I did not pull the stop string. The thought of returning home, facing Lucy and reckoning with whatever shit she seemed to be pulling to ruin my life, made me sick. Instead, I stayed on a few more stops and got off at The Sham.

Inside was the weekday crowd. Owen wasn't there, or anyone else I knew. I wasn't sure why I thought he'd be there. It was only three in the afternoon. And what would I appeal to him for, anyway? Advice on how to reconcile all my *lies*?

I ate quietly alone in a corner, staring at a replay of a Celtics game playing with the sound off on a local sports station. The numbness of solitude and blur of green uniforms eventually calmed me, as did Uncle Steve's email response to my inquiries about eviction, which had miraculously come through despite the spotty service, complete with the necessary downloadable forms. I read through each of them at least five times.

Eventually I dragged myself up from the table and slipped cash under the ketchup bottle.

Outside, I pulled my scarf away from my neck, feeling itchy and hot. It was unseasonably warm for late December. I looked at my phone to check the time, only to see an alert stripe across the screen: *Balance below $0.*

That can't be, I thought, blinking. There'd been almost seven grand in there, between Lucy's rent money, dog-walking savings—Owen had begun to pay me more; he'd insisted—and a small loan from Izzie to help pay the contractor for the Punkhorn house.

My fingers rapidly tapped the screen as I logged into my banking app. The most recent transaction was ATM MERCHANT SHAM-ROCK, $22.00. No surprise there; they didn't take cards, and I'd withdrawn cash. I'd declined to see my balance, and now I regretted it.

My eyes flipped to the transaction below, to the Zenpay deduction in the amount of $7,000, posted to my bank today. At confirmation of this, I gasped.

I began speed-walking in the direction of my house as I logged into the Zenpay app, looking up every few seconds to be sure I wouldn't walk into a pole or a person. I navigated to the Zen Payments screen, where it showed two days ago that I had evidently "paid" a user with the moniker "6f1ng€rdM@n." The picture attached to the profile was an illustration of a rat. And sure enough, the amount sent from my account: seven thousand dollars.

I went to the Zen Friend screen, to my only two connections, the only two people who knew I even *had* the app, who had any sort of proximal access to my phone.

These two Zen Friends were none other than LSomers13 and ASTaRIDborn.

* * *

"Lucy?" I bellowed, stomping down the hall toward the lighted kitchen.

When I got to the kitchen entryway, Lucy was at the table, and beside her sat Astrid. They were here. In *my* house. Waiting.

I forced my mouth to stay shut, my fists to relax by my side. Astrid was my boss. I had to keep it together, as best I could.

Lucy cocked her head. "What's up? You seem...*perturbed.*"

Through gritted teeth, I said, "I need to talk to you, Lucy."

Astrid sniggered at this.

"In *private*," I snapped, then stalked to the living room through the connected half wall. I wished I'd have more privacy for what I was about to say, wished there was a door to close.

Whispers in the kitchen. Giggles. A moment later Lucy trudged into the living room and plopped onto the couch.

I remained standing and looked down at her. "I'm missing a lot of money. Seven *grand.*"

Lucy's expression betrayed nothing. It was blank.

I stepped closer and leaned forward. "Did you hack my phone?"

"Ex*cuse* me?"

"You're the only person who has my Zenpay. You and"—I nodded at the kitchen, where I could see Astrid leaning in her chair, trying to get a view into the room—"her."

A few weeks ago, for someone's baby shower, Astrid had bullied me into to giving her my Zenpay name, falling just short of calling me cheap after I'd tried to resist. We were in the conference room, and the whole team was watching. I caved. Meanwhile, even Owen didn't have my Zenpay; he paid me in cash, and Izzie was terrible with technology. She still wrote me checks.

"Okay, so how exactly would I 'hack' you?" Officially gone was Lucy's sickly sweet tone. This was almost a growl.

"I don't know," I said. "But you found a way—just like when you sent that bullshit email to Corinne."

Lucy shook her head, slowly. "No idea what you're talking about."

I ignored this and glared at her. "Not only are you *stealing* from me, but it's also clear you've been busy trying to get me fired. Befriending my coworkers at dating events? What a *coincidence*."

"Umm, don't flatter yourself," Lucy said. "Yes, by chance, I ran into Astrid and then we hung out on the ski trip. We have a lot in common. Fast friends."

Lucy sat back. She appeared oddly calm, which infuriated me even more.

"Right. The ski trip. The one where you stole a ticket for Brad. Don't think for two seconds I don't know you've been after him this *whole time*."

At this, Lucy burst into a laugh and draped her arm across the back of the couch.

"You know what? Cat's out of the bag. You and Brad are *certainly* not dating and never have. Stop fucking lying. He doesn't *know* you. And how might I know this for sure, you may ask?"

Lucy smirked, tapped her phone, and flashed a picture in front of my face. In it Brad was in a ski coat, standing with a beer in his hand. The ski lodge loomed in the background, and the photo was dated the day of our trip.

Next, Lucy swiped to another photo. This one was Brad again, in my living room. It appeared as if he was headed toward the front door, but had turned his head back quickly, as if the picture was unexpected. He almost looked like he was frowning. The date above the picture said, "Today, 11:00 a.m."

"He was *here*, in my house?"

The door was locked to my room. A small mercy. But equally sickening were the images arising now of Lucy and Brad canoodling on the mountain after Izzie and I left. And then?

With horror, I allowed myself to consider the nauseating possibility I'd so cavalierly taken for granted could *never* be true: Brad didn't like Lucy, did he? He liked blondes, yes, but Lucy was positively weird-looking. Like an electrocuted rodent.

However, I quickly calculated how many times (*that I knew of*) that Lucy and Brad had hung out. First: their sham of a date at the pizza place. Then: the mountain. And today. In my own house. Three times. So, maybe it wasn't a one-time hookup or some drunken mistake, a lapse in judgment. There was a strict one-night maximum with Brad Ellis. I would know; I'd tracked each one for *years*.

Now, I couldn't help it; tears began to form in my eyes.

Lucy began to rise from the couch, carefully, as if I was some wild animal, afraid I might make a sudden move. She crept slowly around the coffee table, giving as wide a berth as she could manage in the small room.

"The rats!" I spat out suddenly, desperate for something, *anything*, to prevent Lucy from gaining an edge, from painting me as the villain. "You planted them under the floorboards. By the fridge. I know that was you. You lied about needing the exterminator—"

Lucy whirled around to face me. "Jesus Christ, you're such a slum-lord! By the way, over by the fridge? There's a bunch of mold there. I wouldn't be surprised if there were nests of vermin everywhere. Look at the way you trash this place, all the leaks, and your nasty dishes—"

"Those are *your* dishes!" I screamed.

Lucy shook her head and looked meaningfully at Astrid, who had become an official spectator, now leaning against the half wall.

"And me getting sick," I went on, aware of the screech in my voice but unable to control it, "I *know* you did something to my food—and then ridding the house of every roll of toilet paper—do you think I'm *stupid*?" Out of the corner of my eye, I could see the gleeful expression on Astrid's pig face as she shoveled popcorn into her mouth from a bag of Smartfood. Her eyes darted from me to Lucy.

"Who can believe *anything* you say?" Lucy said, positioning herself beside Astrid. "Everything is a lie. Who even *are* you?"

Who am I? I thought suddenly, a jolt to my chest. Who *am* I?

The question disoriented me, so much so that I didn't hear what else Lucy was saying, nor did I care. Something about being a stalker with mental problems.

"You know what?" I said, after a minute.

Lucy, miraculously, stopped talking.

"Here's the truth," I said evenly. "I'm not estranged from my parents. They *did* die. They were murdered seven years ago, when I was sixteen years old."

Lucy froze for a moment, mouth half-open, but then recovered. She rolled her eyes.

"Oh my God, which is it? Margo here thinks we're gullible. Too bad we know she's full of shit. Let's go." She tugged at Astrid's forearm.

"No," Astrid said, pulling her arm back. "I want to hear."

Standing in the middle of the living room, I took a deep breath in. What was the use? Everything was wrecked. This paper-thin identity of mine had been compromised. I'd been a fool to think it wouldn't be.

* * *

I told them everything.

About my parents in bed and the blood-soaked sheets and Dan's bloated, shiny-headed body that hung on the exposed beam, the body I didn't see until all my screams had been expended from my lungs.

174

I told them about the garden shears Dan had used on my parents' faces and the suicide note in which he'd claimed to have been *conned*. Patty had *led him on* and emotionally abused him so badly that he'd had "no other choice." There were also "voices" who told him to do it, demons who'd taken on the form of government officials. They told him he could make the world a better place if he eliminated my parents from this earth.

"He was sick and demented. He killed my parents, and then himself. You can look it up. Nevins murders, Cape Cod, 2013."

As I spoke, I noticed Astrid's face, her expression half-believing, half-pitying.

But Lucy did not appear pitying. In fact, she seemed bored. Disgusted.

I barreled on.

"My birth name is Maggie Eleanor Nevins. I have my GED. I couldn't afford college, and I was still too much of a wreck to attend anyway. I lied to Corinne to get a better job than that janitorial shit I was doing, cleaning up the messes of all you rich college girls who have no worries and no problems. All you care about is happy hour, and you never remember to recycle your Starbucks cups, like a bunch of savages. So, whatever. Go ahead and tell Corinne," I said, wiping my cheeks with my sleeve. "I don't care. I don't care about anything anymore."

Silence hung in the air. No one moved.

Not until I wiped my face once more and said, "Now I would appreciate it if you both got the fuck out of my house."

Lucy

Astrid sat crouched over her phone, swiping, tapping, squinting. "Honestly? I, like, feel *bad*."

They were sitting at a high-top at Delaney's.

Lucy took a sip of her tequila soda, then said, "Don't. She's *lying*."

"No, she's not," Astrid said, eyes bugged. "It's *true*." She held out her phone, showing search results for "cape cod double murder suicide 2013."

Lucy scowled, not bothering to read it. What a *performance*. Margo was supposed to remain the pathetic lying hermit she'd made herself into—at least, for a little while longer—so that Lucy and Brad could dismantle her, bit by bit...

"Oh my God, someone posted the last *love* letter between Margo's mom and dad. That is so sad. They were high school sweethearts. By the way, the dad? A fucking DILF. Andrew Nevins. Holy shit. The mom was hot, too, though her fake boobs are re-diculous. No idea why the mom would cheat on him with Brad's ugly-ass dad, though. Look at this guy. Gross. Brad must take after his mom..."

Lucy bit her tongue—Dan wasn't *that* ugly—and let Astrid natter on.

She supposed it wasn't the worst thing, that Margo had outed herself before Lucy had had the chance to. It was all the same anyway: Astrid would go back to Corinne and get Margo fired for lying about her education, as was the plan, and Margo would be back on her heels, miserable and poor. Yes, she thought to herself, it wasn't the end of the world after all. If anything, it would speed things up.

Because there was so much more to come.

At this, she smiled, not even minding that Ass Turd had ordered another round on her tab. Thankfully she had plenty of money. Dan had made sure of that.

39

Margo

Zenpay customer service was a joke. I had a chat window open, but there was no real person on the other end, just automated responses and links to their "Help Center." When I did speak to a person, they put me on hold for hours. All I learned in the end was that since it appeared I had authorized the payment from my own device, there was not much else they could do.

Owen was working, but over text had insisted I file a police report.

I put in a call, and a young officer with a shaved head arrived shortly after.

"You found her on Craigslist?" he asked, peering around.

"Yes." I chewed my lip.

"You know they got more secure modes of finding roommates nowadays."

"I'm aware." Then I said, hoping I sounded confident, assured, "I've got eviction stuff ready. I just have to serve her the Notice to Quit."

The officer jotted something down. He said I likely wouldn't recover the funds; he'd unfortunately seen this happen many times before. And that was it. He left.

Owen and Tommy stopped by soon after with Bearie. I nuzzled with the dog on the couch as father and son went to work installing cameras.

"I feel bad I can't pay you," I kept insisting, but they waved me off.

When they were finished, they showed me how to work the app on my phone, how it was connected to Wi-Fi. They showed me how I could see the front stoop and the back deck and all other common spaces.

"Illegal if you do her bedroom, or the bathrooms," Owen warned me. "So obviously, we left those out."

"Obviously," I said, but I was disappointed. I wondered if I could sneak one in anyway. A nanny cam of some sort. But how would I pay for that?

When they were finished, Tommy walked to the couch where I was sitting and sat down on the opposite end. Bearie positioned his body so his head was in my lap but his hindquarters were draped over Tommy.

"Sounds like this roommate of yours has been up to something from the moment she moved in," he said. "Any idea why?"

"I don't know, exactly. I just know it seems to involve...a guy."

Tommy nodded knowingly, and my cheeks flushed. A *guy* that was never mine in the first place. A *guy* I didn't really know.

Lucy was right. I was pathetic.

Then I heard myself say, "Not a guy I'm seeing anymore, though."

Tommy betrayed a small smile, which he seemed to be fighting, and nodded. Then he got up to leave. Owen followed, and at the door bent down and scratched Bearie's ears and told him to be a good boy, and that he'd miss him. Bearie was staying the night, as the father-son duo was headed to Foxwoods to watch a UFC fight.

"Thank you for being so nice to me," I said weakly to Tommy and Owen's backs.

"You got anywhere to go for Christmas?" Owen asked.

"Just hanging around here," I said. "Small family."

It was true. Izzie was in California with Steve's side of the family. It was nothing new, being alone over the holidays, but each year the absence of my parents felt like a deeper abyss of grief. I almost wished their deaths were fresher, sometimes. Not the gore, the macabre shock. But the nearness of it. At least back then I thought about them more. Kept them alive in my mind. Now, it was like they were drifting further and further away.

Owen placed his large hand on my shoulder. "Tawna's making Christmas dinner. You're welcome to come by. In the meantime, cameras are your first step. But you gotta get that roommate the fuck out of here, yeah?"

I promised I would.

Owen descended the front steps, where Tommy was waiting.

Tommy called up to me, his eyes azure, like the sky over his head. "You need anything, day or night, I live a block away. I'm serious."

I nodded and shut the door before they could see my tears.

* * *

"I wanted to leave this for Lucy."

It was a couple of days before Christmas. Astrid stood on my front steps, holding up a small green gift bag.

"Can I come in for a sec to leave it under the tree?"

"Sure," I said. I opened the door wider and let her in. "I have something to give her, too. Do you know where she is, or when she'll be back?"

"She could be at Brad's," Astrid said, marching into the living room and placing the gift under Lucy's small, knee-high tree, the needles of which littered the floor. She looked at me. "I know what you're thinking. I was the one who SKInnected with him on the mountain and all that. But Lucy and I don't let guys come between us. So, it's, like, cool that she's seeing him. I don't mind. Even though I think I'm better-looking. But whatever."

Oh, how I wanted to scream.

"Or," Astrid said, as she made her way to the door, "she might have already left for Pennsylvania, for her parents' house. She told me you had a dog here, so she was thinking of leaving town early. Kinda shitty for you to let a dog stay here and endanger her health, by the way. You know she's deathly allergic to a whole bunch of stuff, including dogs."

A shiver ran down my spine. "The dog's only been here since this morning. Lucy hasn't been home in days. How does she know there's a dog here?"

Astrid shrugged.

As if on cue, Bearie bounded out of the kitchen and jumped at Astrid. She let out a yelp and backed against the wall. But Bearie kept at it, nuzzling his huge snout in her hand. Eventually her look of disgust softened and she patted him lightly on the head with a flat hand.

"I guess you're not so bad. Lucy said you were disgusting."

As if offended, Bearie retreated to the kitchen.

How would Lucy know? I'd never had Bearie here while she was home. Even the walks I took him on, I took when she was holed up in her room.

She's been watching me this whole time, I thought. Constantly.

Astrid wiped her drool-wet hand on her pants and gave me a small smile.

182

"Thanks for letting me leave the gift. That was nice of you."

I crossed my arms and eyed her warily.

"You're being awfully civil. I'm surprised you're not insulting me."

"Well, I know you lied and stuff? But I dunno." Her eyes fell to the floor. "I feel bad for you. I thought you were, like, just a freak weirdo cleaning lady who tricked her way into a job. I always thought Corinne liked you the best because you were the pity case. I couldn't compete with that. It was like kicking a puppy. Also, I guess I was embarrassed. About the—well, you know."

"Nail jar," I said.

Astrid's eyes—on which the lashes seemed spare; I'd never noticed this before—flicked back to mine. "It's a *condition*."

"I wouldn't have said anything," I said.

"That's not what she—" Astrid stopped, her eyes on the camera above my head. "I gotta go. Merry Christmas, Margo."

"What did she tell you?" I called after her.

But Astrid had already let herself out.

Lucy

Savannah brought her new boyfriend home for Christmas. This, Lucy viewed as advantageous. Her parents wouldn't want to air dirty laundry in front of such an esteemed guest.

The disadvantage, however, was that the boyfriend was an insufferable fucking loser.

"Lucy, you went to community college down the road, your sis tells me?" he asked, after *mmm*ing too loudly over her mother's dry ham. Her mother had gone all out, the complete array of cracked china splayed across the table.

"Yeah," Lucy said, stabbing at her roasted potatoes. "I'm the brains of the family."

He grinned. His ears were too flat against his head. His mouth was too big. And so was Savannah's stupid smile when she looked at him.

"I can relate," he said. "My brother went to Yale. Makes UVM seem like, umm—"

"A shitty community college down the road?" Lucy asked sweetly, popping the potato into her mouth.

"Lucy, don't be rude," her mother scolded.

Savannah let out her resigned "It's hard being the good one" sigh that Lucy despised, and changed the subject.

"Luce, your hair is looking a lot better. You look great. I hear you got a new job. And you're seeing someone, Mom said?"

Lucy thought she could feel the table wobble a little, and caught a surreptitious glance between her parents at the other end of the table.

"I'm seeing someone, yes," Lucy said, smoothing her napkin on her lap. "He's very special to me. It took me a long time to find him."

Savannah raised her brows. "That's great, Luce. You have a pic?"

Lucy handed her the phone. "I met him on a dating app. My roommate had been stalking him. It's a hilarious story." She popped another potato in her mouth.

Savannah took the phone, peered down, and then looked up from the photo. Her boyfriend craned his neck to see and smiled, biting his lip, it seemed, to keep from laughing.

"He looks like a model," he said. "Good for you."

"He does," Savannah agreed, handing the phone back and tossing a furtive glance at her parents. "I'm really happy for you."

They didn't believe her, Lucy knew. A mismatch. Just like she'd deemed Brad and Margo—*Maggie*—back in the early days when she believed Margo (how hilarious) about their sham of a relationship.

"I know what you're all thinking," she said now. "But we have a lot in common. We're actually working on this genealogy project together." She took a sip of her wine and glared at her mother.

"What do you mean, genealogy?"

"Just looking into our families."

186

"Isn't that how all this madness started in the first place?" her mother said.

"Honey, don't say *madness*," Lucy's father whispered, widening his eyes.

"Yes, Mother, it's how I found out you're the world's biggest liar."

"Lucy!" said all three of her family members in unison, and in the same admonishing tone.

Lucy chewed the desert-dry piece of ham and washed it down with a big gulp of water. Then she got up and said to Savannah, "Happy for you, too." She nodded at the boyfriend. "He's a real *prize*."

* * *

Lucy stopped at a red light, signs for the highway visible just up the road, and opened her burner phone, now officially her primary phone. The other, accessible to all the undesirable people in her life—her parents, Margo, Savannah—was somewhere in the Susquehanna River. All the voicemails and texts went with it. ("Come back here, Lucy—we have to talk. After that display, we've contacted Dr. Reynolds!")

It was all so preposterous. She was almost thirty years old. They could do *nothing*. Never again would she agree to be sent away to that godforsaken facility, Serenity Meadows—*vomit*—with the stupid bonsai trees everywhere and those awful soft shoes they made you wear. If she ever had to see that place again, she'd set fire to it.

She was sick of everyone's condescending attitudes, sick of everyone just expecting her to fall in line with the bombshell news she'd received from her mother, acting like it didn't change everything. She had a purpose for once: to make things right for a poor, vulnerable man named Daniel Ellis.

The light turned green.

Glancing up from the photos that had just come through—captioned "bed rodents"—she laughed and laughed and drove and drove, thrilled to be heading back to Boston so that she and Brad could get back to work.

Margo

I stood in the bathroom mirror. Enormous black circles had appeared under my eyes. Skin, oily and pale. Blonde roots lined my middle part. Roots that now I wasn't sure were worth hiding anymore.

I remembered buying that first box of hair dye. I would never forget the feeling of the plastic gloves, of squeezing the black ooze from the tube onto the strands, and my pale forehead, stained like smudged ink.

I flipped the light off. I couldn't stand the sight of myself any longer.

As I left the bathroom and entered the hallway I noticed a rank odor that was getting stronger the closer I got to my bedroom.

The door was ajar. I was sure I'd locked it.

I burst inside. It was dark, but the hallway light illuminated just enough to see what was on the bed: red streaks across white, unmade sheets; the matted fur, the coiled tails, the snouts—two, side by side—this time not underneath a floorboard, but atop the pillow. Two gargantuan, freakishly large rats.

I let out a wild shriek and ran from the room, shutting myself in the bathroom, whole body trembling.

Cameras.

Fumbling with the phone in my pocket, I checked it for activity. Unfortunately, I had the non-paid version of the app and could only get still-shots for history. Owen had suggested I upgrade, but that had proved too expensive. And having the cameras for less than two days, resting on the assurance that Lucy was in Pennsylvania for the week, I hadn't yet set up phone alerts. For what felt like the millionth time, I scolded myself. *Fool.*

Now, I checked the motion alert history. I navigated back to the very first still-shot on the stoop and saw that only an hour ago, while on my walk, someone dressed in dark clothing and a ski mask (the images were in black and white) had been hunched over the front door lock, turning a key. The next capture was the upstairs hallway. The person's face was tilted to the floor. She, or he, carried a garbage bag that appeared half full. And the last image: the person opening my locked room—with another key.

My own bedroom camera afforded only one still-shot, of the person walking toward the bed. I zoomed in as best I could but still couldn't make anything out that would identify whoever it was. All I could tell was that the person seemed short, very short, and thin. Lucy and Astrid were far taller than this person, by at least six inches. And no way were those Astrid's shoulders—too slim.

Terror coursed through me. And déjà vu. The rats, and the way they were positioned, side by side and bloodied in the bed, were staged, just like the scene I'd recounted to Lucy and Astrid just days before. The scene I'd come upon in my parents' bedroom.

I reopened the door, slowly approaching the bed, and scrutinized the bludgeoned rats—how bloody they were, how mutilated. How *large.*

"*Princess Bride,*" I suddenly remembered Lucy saying, in response to the sign in the living room. "*Love* that movie."

These rats were, I saw now, ROUS.

Rodents of Unusual Size.

The last time I'd been this angry and threatened and cornered, I'd dealt with it—poorly. The sick thoughts that swam through my mind now, the avenues for revenge and retribution, were all too familiar. I'd been down this road before, and it had not gone well.

2013

"What's up *your* butt?" Mom slipped the straw back in her mouth, her eyes narrowed at me.

We were sitting around a table on the deck: me, Dad, Mom, and Dan. A pitcher of margaritas sat at the center of the table. Earlier, Mom, as an olive branch, had offered me a small glass, *just this one time.*

I glowered at my mother and swallowed the rest of my margarita in two large gulps. Every time I looked at her I replayed what happened that night, what I saw from behind that tree. She sickened me.

"Why aren't you at the Lobster Shack?" Dad asked. But he wasn't looking at me, or anyone; his head was down in his phone. He was in the hole from renting a space he couldn't afford down in the Port, and was courting another client. Another one of Dan's business suggestions. Dan does so well for himself, Dad had argued. It was *smart* to listen to him.

"I got cut," I said, picking at the side of the table. "Too many servers on, and none of us would make any money. Tracey said I could take her double on Saturday to make up for it—"

Dad got up, abruptly, interrupting me.

"Sorry hon," he said to me, and then to Patty, "They want a meeting. Right now. The CEO is vacationing right in Chatham, so he said he'd give me a few minutes. This could be *huge* for us." He slid his chair with the back of his legs and pressed a kiss onto Patty's forehead and then on mine. "Love you. Be back for dinner."

As he skirted the table he rested his hand, lightly, on Dan's back. "See ya, buddy. I'll tell you how it goes."

"Good luck, bud," Dan said.

Once Dad was out of sight, out of the corner of my eye I saw Dan's lip curl. He caught me looking.

"Mags, you must have plans with friends on this glorious day off?"

"Nope, staying right here. At my house. Where I live. Do *you* have plans?"

He shrugged sheepishly, a fake, oafish shrug that wasn't fooling me. "I'm just hanging alone."

Patty swirled her straw in her drink. "Maybe you and I could do something."

"I'd love to," Dan said.

"I was talking to Maggie," she said, and I thought she said it a little sharper than usual.

"Want to?" Mom said.

"I'd love to," I said, smiling at Dan.

"I thought you wanted me to go with you to find some perennials," Dan said. "Remember, it's my expertise, and you're getting me all for free."

"I changed my mind," Mom said.

Dan stared at her, and then looked at me.

I grinned at him.

He got up from the table. "Fine."

Mom didn't look at him. She reached for a chip at the center of the table and was about to dip it into the salsa bowl when he said,

"Dress looks a little tight, Patty. Remember that diet you said you wanted to start..."

He made his way to the little white gate separating our yard from his, whistling as he walked.

Patty's arm hovered in the air, and she dropped the chip.

"You're a fucking creep," I called after him.

Dan turned, the sun gleaming off his bald head. "Excuse me?"

"You heard me," I said. "Run along now." I twiddled my fingers in a running motion.

Surprisingly, Mom did not scold me, did not tell me I was being rude. Instead she said, "Yes, run along now, Dan."

Mom and I spent the rest of that afternoon shopping. She bought pounds of makeup and face creams and diet pills, and treated me to a nice dinner at Wequassett, overlooking Pleasant Bay. She'd had to pull out her "emergency credit card," saying, "Just our secret, Mags. Okay? Just this one time." We had a wonderful day together, one of our best. And last. We didn't mention Dan's name once.

That afternoon, the silent agreement with my mom—if it even was an agreement—incited something in me. I likened it to an instinct, a deep need to protect.

This man was not right. I'd always known it. For the remainder of that summer, when Mom stopped asking him to come by, and he'd show up on his own anyway, and my mom began locking the door, pulling the shades, biting her lip, and avoiding him—and his visits only increased—my resolve grew even stronger to keep that vile man far, far away from my family. I would do whatever it took.

42

Margo

To be alone on Christmas Eve was depressing on its own, but even worse was picking out paint colors for the house in which my parents had been slaughtered. It was like a bad Christmas-turned-horror movie, with orphan Margo voluntarily revisiting the roots of her pain and dysfunction. But really, there wasn't anything else for me to do, let alone anyone to see. It was as good a time as any, I figured, to sign off on improvements with the contractor.

When I got to the Punkhorn house, Jessie was already there. She was standing out in the cold, her blue binder and clipboard pressed to her chest. The contractor was late.

"How are things?" Jessie asked.

"Could be better," I said. Then, noticing Jessie's drawn face, and her own under-eye circles, I added, "Hey. A while back—the day you were supposed to come skiing, and had to cancel—Izzie mentioned something about your mom. Is everything okay?"

Jessie swallowed, her eyes on the empty road. It was so quiet the occasional rustling of trees sounded loud, pronounced.

"Mom's been terminal a few years now, and they've been juicing her with every cocktail under the sun, but...they've run out of combinations. It's why I'm here. I had to leave my job and apartment in New York to come back here and help out. I had no idea how long it would take. Still don't. They just keep saying, 'Days or weeks, it's hard to say.' And now it's been months." She shrugged. "Izzie was the one, actually, who hooked me up down here. I ran into her at the grocery store and told her everything, and she got me in touch with the realty company. She's been a lifesaver. She also found us the best nurses..." Jessie paused; she looked near tears. "Anyway...that's why I'm here."

"God, Jessie, I'm so sorry. I wish I knew. I feel so terrible."

Jessie shook her head. "I feel weird even talking to you about it. Your situation was *so* much worse. And more sudden."

"Don't think that way," I said. "Quick and sudden is shitty, but slow and prolonged? None of it can be easy."

Jessie looked down at her watch. "Sorry to rush things, but I have to get back to my mom's in a bit. Even if she's not really...with it enough to realize, it *is* almost Christmas. On we go."

I followed her inside.

We talked about repainting the yellow door—black this time—and the plantings outside, mostly hydrangeas. It felt wrong to talk about such things. She needed to be with her mom. But I also sensed she was relieved to have a break, to be out of that house. She was an only child, just like me, with a father who wasn't in the picture. The entire burden fell on her.

"What are you thinking for shrubs and flowers and stuff?" she asked.

"Anything's fine, as long as there are no daffodils," I said, surprising myself. I hadn't meant to bring it up. But a memory—quick,

196

fleeting—flared of Dan. In it I could see his sweaty face and neck, soaked gray T-shirt, dirt under his fingernails and trailing him as he dragged the yellow flowers into the kitchen. I could see my mother reaching for a vase—*Oh, Dan, you shouldn't have. And daffodils. You know yellow's my favorite...*

"Noted. No daffodils." Jessie scrawled on her pad. Then she looked up. "So, anyway. How's it going with your, umm, roommate?" Jessie gave me a strange look. "And your dating life?"

"I take it Izzie told you about the whole thing with Brad."

Jessie breathed out. "She's worried. She asked me to talk to you about it. She's, like, our friendship counselor." Jessie smiled.

This was a perfect opportunity for deflection.

"Look, about what happened between you and me," I said. "I wanted to say I'm so, so sorry I ignored all your calls and letters, and that I made Izzie swear to secrecy about my new name. I know it all sounds really dramatic and stupid."

"You wanted a fresh start," Jessie said. "I get it." Jessie stood up straight. "I was really hurt, though. I can't lie."

Right then, the contractor walked through the front door and cleared his throat, a middle-aged guy with his own clipboard. We had to put this conversation on hold. Or maybe Jessie would forget about it.

Jessie looked down at her phone. "Shoot. Sorry to have to jet so soon, but duty calls."

"I'll be back in a sec," I said to the contractor, and followed Jessie to her car.

"Maybe..." I trailed off, trying to keep the hope, the excitement, from my voice. "Maybe we could go skiing together. I know you couldn't go last time with me and Izzie, but...I'd love it if we could go, just you and me? Like old times."

"I'd love that," Jessie said. She reached for the car door handle, but first paused and looked deep into my eyes. "And then you can tell me the whole story. About what sent you running from Marshside. Like, not just what happened with your parents, but, like...what *really* happened that summer. Why you got so distant...so weird. And no bullshit this time. How does that sound?"

My face fell.

"Right," I mumbled, slowly backing away from the car. "Sounds like a plan."

* * *

The streets of Southie were nearly deserted the night of Christmas Eve.

I walked along with Bearie, fraught with worry: how to pay the contractor for all his work; how to keep my job in the likely case Astrid told Corinne I'd lied on my résumé; how to tell Jessie—and by default, Izzie—the truth after all these years, about what I did.

Because I would have to. I couldn't live with it any longer. I couldn't let it sit inside me, rotting me from the inside out.

Lastly, there was Lucy: What did she have planned next?

I was nearing the end of the walk when a voice rang out behind me.

"Hey, how's that roommate working out for you?"

I swiveled. I'd walked right past Carmen Kangaroo, who was sitting on her front step with her phone on her lap. I walked back to her, tugging Bearie lightly on his leash to follow. From the squiggly lines on Carmen's phone screen, I could see she was waiting for a Lyft.

When we got close, Bearie sniffed Carmen's face and she smiled, nuzzling her face into his cheek. "You look like a big bear!" she said.

I cleared my throat. "She's, uh, not working out well. My roommate. Big mistake."

Carmen made a circle around her ear with her finger. "Not surprised. She's a cuckoo bird."

I stepped on Bearie's leash and tied the end of the poop bag; he'd just dropped one in the middle of the sidewalk.

"Why do you say that?" I'd really wanted to say, *How* do you know that?

Carmen looked down and tapped her phone. "He *canceled*? What an asshole." More tapping, and then she looked up again. "What'd you ask me? Oh. Why is that Lucy girl a cuckoo bird. And trust me, I don't use that term lightly. I've got anxiety and ADHD, and I'm heavily medicated. Proud of it, too. But this Lucy girl...Jesus. Well, for starters, she's *everywhere*. At the bars, at the coffee shops, out at night with that pig-faced girl, everywhere. She must hate being home."

She watched for my reaction. I nodded for her to keep on going.

"Anyway, after *you* rejected me, I answered Steph's ad on SouthieCares for this place." She wagged her head to the building behind her, an expensive Pottery Barn wreath hanging on the front door. "I guess Lucy interviewed here first, and then I came after. Steph said I was a breath of fresh air, compared to *her*."

The door opened and Carmen turned. A striking blonde emerged. She was wearing an expensive-looking coat and Mary Jane combat boots.

"Lyft guy canceled," Carmen told her. "Got an Uber. It's coming in two minutes."

The blonde nodded and then leveled her gaze at Bearie.

"Oh my God, that *dog*. He's huge."

I waved a hand, the one with the poop bag. "Hi."

She nodded at me politely.

"Steph," Carmen said. "Tell Margo here about that Lucy girl. The one who interviewed before me. The one with the weird hair."

Stephanie rolled her eyes. "Oh, that girl. It was like she was playing Twenty Questions, but like, didn't stop at twenty. She asked when I would be home every day, if I had a boyfriend, if I knew anyone else in the neighborhood...and then she dropped some names, and I didn't know any of them. You said your name was Margo? I think she asked if I knew you. She was obsessed with some guy named *Chad* or something? Asking if any of us had been on a date with him, or seen him around. I was like, 'Why, who's that,' because she seemed to be getting all worked up, like pulling on her hair and sweating? It was so nasty.

"Anyway, she said she'd moved here because of him. When I asked if they'd dated, she laughed—and I don't mean, like, a normal laugh; she cackled like a *witch*. She said he already had a girlfriend. But she kept laughing at these random times, like a serial killer or something. Oh, and she kept looking out the window of the bedroom and the living room, like, staring out, and then asked if it would be okay if she repositioned my couch so that she could see out the window from it. I don't know. The thing is, she wasn't that bad at first. Her emails were normal, and we'd even talked on the phone. But once she got here, it was bad vibes all around."

"She didn't act like that at *all*, at my place," I said. I looked at Carmen. "Right?"

"True," Carmen said. "She was all quiet. Put on an act. She was a kiss-ass." She rolled her eyes.

"Well, I'm glad I saw what she was really like," Steph said. "I remember I couldn't wait to get her out of here. Then Carmen came—and I'll admit, you're a *lot*," she smiled, and Carmen smiled, and even I smiled, "but deep down you're a good person. Even if you're a complete neat freak."

"You're making me blush," Carmen said. Then she looked across the street and pointed to an approaching sedan. "I think that's him." She waved.

The car pulled up to the curb.

"I'm evicting her," I said, as they climbed into the Uber. I wasn't sure why I was even telling them. But even if neither of them were the ideal recipients of my thoughts, it felt good to say it out loud.

Stephanie, who'd climbed in first, called behind her shoulder, "Good idea. I'd sleep better if she was off our street."

Carmen settled into the seat beside her and lowered her window. "Wait. Margo, it's Christmas Eve. Are you in the city alone?"

I nodded.

"Are you heading somewhere tomorrow, like, your parents' or whatever?"

I hesitated a moment. Then I said, "No. My parents are dead."

"Both? Really? Mine, too," Carmen said. "Cancer and a heart attack. Like a fucking *month* apart." Carmen widened her eyes. "I've never met anyone our age with both parents dead."

"Me neither."

"Wanna come with us?" Carmen asked. "We're going to drink our sorrows away at Delaney's. Steph's parents are alive—"

"Technically," Steph cut in, leaning over Carmen's lap.

"But she doesn't talk to her mom," Carmen said, "and her dad's a deadbeat douche, and her brother ran far, far away from it all—"

"Okay, could you not tell my whole life story to a stranger?" Steph said.

"Thanks, but I'm okay," I said. I could tell the Uber driver wanted to get going; he kept casting annoyed glances at me. "You guys go ahead. Have fun."

I didn't deserve all this kindness. From Owen, Tommy, or even Carmen Kangaroo, whom I'd written off without even getting to know her.

Carmen shrugged. "Maybe another time? And good luck with what's-her-face."

Margo

It was three in the afternoon, Christmas Day. I lay in bed, the covers pulled up to my chin, shivering.

Earlier, Izzie had called from her in-laws' in California, twice, to wish me a Merry Christmas, but I'd let the calls go to voicemail. I had no plan to mar Izzie's holiday with my problems, nor Jessie's, who'd also called. Even Owen was trying to fold me in. "A reminder that you're welcome to come by the house," he'd texted this morning. "Tawna made a roast. And Tommy will be there." He added a smiley-face emoji to that last comment.

"Got my own thing going," I texted back. "But thanks, and Merry Christmas. Give Bearie a squeeze for me."

My "own thing" was me spending all day agonizing over why— *why?*—Lucy seemed so intent on destroying my life. It was obvious Lucy's obsession with Brad was the driving force. But why

203

the rats—why the friendship with Astrid, making life hell in my own house?

Oh, *shit*, I thought, suddenly, shooting up from bed.

A flash of memory, a snippet of something I'd seen on Lucy's phone a couple weeks back. What did it say? I fought to grab at the memory before it flitted off, out of my consciousness. *What was it?*

And then, a bit of it came back.

It was a day I'd come home early from work, unexpectedly. Corinne had dismissed everyone around lunchtime; she was feeling generous, she said, telling us all to enjoy the afternoon.

I'd arrived home very early, surprised to see Lucy's car parked out front. Later, Lucy would claim she'd taken a personal day, for a few appointments. But at this juncture, I wasn't sure why she'd be home, or if she even was, physically, in the house.

When I walked past the bathroom, I could hear rustling inside, and then the creak of the toilet seat. Then in the kitchen I saw Lucy had left her phone on the table, the screen still lit. A podcast of some sort, called *Dirty Vines*, appeared to be playing. No sound was emitting from the phone. She must have been listening with her earbuds.

The toilet flushed.

I clicked off Lucy's screen and scurried to the fridge, opening the door leisurely right as Lucy appeared in the entryway.

"Didn't hear you come in," Lucy said tersely, extracting an earbud. She snatched up her phone and went up to her room.

I didn't think much of it at the time, other than Lucy hadn't even said hello, and how strange it was that she'd taken a random day off, when I could have sworn I'd heard her leave that morning. I'd been thinking more about how her personality had completely changed from the first day I'd met her, when she'd toured the place, sweet and shy and amenable, oohing and ahhing, and, as Carmen had put it so delicately, kissing my ass.

Fake.

Now, I leaned over, pulled my laptop from beneath the bed, and googled *Dirty Vines*.

The first result yielded a landscaping company out of Colorado. I scrolled down, and then saw it, recognizing the image result. *Dirty Vines: A True Crime Podcast.* A black-and-white blurred photo of a young girl in the woods loaded on the homepage. The title of season one was "Marshside Murders."

My breath caught at the mention of my hometown: *Marshside.*

I ripped through the episode notes. The first season featured a mystery about a young girl from Marshside named Maxine Lang, the victim of an assault. It had happened decades ago. Her name was vaguely familiar, but the perpetrator was long dead, and the case had been solved. Subsequent seasons featured different, far-flung crimes in locales other than Cape Cod.

Was it a coincidence? Despite the Cape being a widely recognized vacation destination, my hometown was small, a fishing village and a conservation haven and a tourist trap, depending on what part you lived in, or who you were.

Still, I feverishly searched every single episode note, every listener comment, and even listened to snatches of audio, for any mention of the Nevins murders. There were none.

Hosts Sly and Skye Stevens had covered a missing mom in Arkansas (season two), then a human trafficking ring out of New Mexico (season three), and the fourth, current season seemed to be a mashup of "favorite listener episodes with bonus extras."

I slipped my laptop beneath the bed and lay on my back, picking nervously at the sheet, part of an old set belonging to my parents. I heard my quick, shallow breaths—the self-conscious kind, where you're fully aware that your breathing is off, and you try to correct it and find yourself practically hyperventilating.

To calm myself I tried to reason that many people listened to true crime podcasts and murder documentaries; it didn't mean they had any proclivities for what was contained within them. It was perfectly normal. And the first season just so happened to feature Marshside. Probably a coincidence.

Or.

What if Lucy was embarking on some undercover investigation? What if she was some true-crime addict loser who got off on cold cases, some wannabe detective? What if Lucy's whole ruse to live here was to expose my past, to concoct some fucking *exposé*?

Because if that was the case, there was the potential for me to be in deep, deep shit.

I continued to lie there, blinking back tears, staring at that ceiling like it contained an answer.

But not if I get to her first, I thought suddenly.

The thought was thrilling, revolting, frightening. I felt my heart beat faster.

Not if I get to her first, I thought again.

And silence her.

* * *

The next day I got out of bed, showered, and made a real meal (canned soup). And when I was done with all that, I organized my materials.

Leaning on the kitchen counter with my hip, I neatened the stack of eviction papers and folded them in thirds, then slipped them into an envelope. I was so sick of startling at every noise outside the house, every voice on the street. Last week, Uncle Steve had warned me that Lucy might take me to court, and that the ensuing procedures would be lengthy and expensive, but still, I had no reservations.

Then I called a locksmith. He came within an hour to change the front-door lock. This was illegal; Lucy was due ingress as a paying tenant. But I couldn't afford to be blindsided. I wanted Lucy to have to beg to come in, to be forced to face me head-on. The lock was another $300 I couldn't afford, charged to my credit card, but it was worth every penny.

I just didn't know when Lucy would come home. Or if.

* * *

Then, the day came. A knock at the door, New Year's Eve. It was her. I knew it.

I rose from the kitchen table, slowly. Choice words (*stalker, animal abuser*) raced through my mind as I clutched the envelope and strode toward the door.

But when I looked through the peephole, there were not one, but two figures on the stoop, a blond male around my age, wearing a hoodie and jeans. And beside him? The one and only Bradford Daniel Ellis.

They knocked again.

When I still didn't answer, didn't move, Brad spoke.

"Margo. I can hear you. I know you're home. Let's cut the shit, okay? You know who I am. And I know who you are." He glanced at his friend, then added, "I need to...have a word with you."

Brad's little speech sounded foreign and incongruous coming from his mouth. Sure, I'd overheard snippets of him talking now and again at Delaney's, sitting on a stool nearby, hiding in plain sight, an unattractive, greasy-haired warm body and nothing else. Brad, oblivious, would be busy citing his fantasy picks or the winners of his work March Madness pool or whatever girl he'd "bagged" the night prior. I chose to ignore this talk, preferring when he shared his schedule for Meals on Wheels, or his latest "basketball date" with Corey, his volunteer Little Brother. Even our fake text conversations featured Brad as the ideal supportive boyfriend: kind, understanding, optimistic. I'd text from my own phone number, having saved it under "Brad<3."

No one was supposed to know any of this, *ever*; it was an interior world that only I was privy to. And, in my defense, I'd told myself that one day I'd have these conversations with him in real life. I'd told myself they were "therapeutic manifestations"—some crap I read in an article once that made me feel better for texting myself things like "Bye, hon," and "You looked so cute today. Did you get my flowers?" I cringed now just thinking about it all. It's wild what you'll excuse about yourself when no one is watching.

Now, in real life, the real Brad was on the opposite side of that door, and he didn't sound supportive or kind. In fact, he sounded like an asshole principal. *I need to have a word with you.*

I kept my eye glued to the peephole and calculated my odds. Two six-foot-plus monsters and *me*. This couldn't end well, especially if there was some sinister plot, something his putrid little girlfriend Lucy had put him up to.

I took out my phone. I bypassed 911—too dramatic—and texted Owen: "SOS, Can you come by?" No answer.

These seconds mattered.

I tried Tommy, who answered immediately: "Be right there."

Brad lifted his fist to pound again. I called through the door, keeping my voice level: "Please wait until my friend comes. Then I'll open the door. I don't feel safe."

I watched as Brad glanced incredulously at his friend and then back at the door. "We're not gonna, like, *attack* you, Margo."

The envelope crinkled in my hand, damp with sweat. "I don't believe you."

Right then I saw Tommy coming from across the street, hands in his pockets, his beard fuller and longer than when I'd last seen him. He wore Carhartt jeans and a heavy coat. When he got closer it was clear he was shorter than the other two men, but he had that defiant

South Boston grit straight out of a Ben Affleck movie. I was certain he'd seen his fair share of Brads.

"Do we have a problem here?" Tommy said.

Brad held his hands up. "Hey, guy, I'm not here to start anything—"

"Don't call me 'guy,' " Tommy said.

"Okay, *sir*, we're here to grab something heavy. A trunk, in Lucy's room. Then we're out of here."

I opened the door.

Brad whipped around, as did the friend. I looked past Brad at Tommy. "Thanks for coming. Now everyone can come in."

Tommy stood beside me in the hallway. In effect, we blocked any access to either the living room or down the hall. The only place to go was upstairs.

Tommy crossed his arms. "You know these guys?"

"Yes," I said. "No. Well, sort of. I believe Brad and my roommate are in a relationship."

The friend scoffed at this, which I secretly delighted in. This meant that whatever Brad and Lucy had wasn't public, or perhaps not even acknowledged.

I added, more forcefully, "And my parents were killed by his dad, Dan Ellis. This is...*Brad* Ellis."

If Tommy was surprised by any of this—especially the casual mention of murder—he didn't show it. With his icy gaze on Brad, he said, "Okay. So you're saying the son of your parents' *killer* just happens to be in cahoots with that roommate of yours. The one who plants dead rats in your house and snoops through your shit."

Tommy's statements, in his thick Boston accent—*rum-mate*, *yo-ahs*—came out flat and direct, and were directed solely at Brad.

"Dead *rats*?" Brad said, glancing at his friend, who frowned.

"Yes," I said. "First in the kitchen under some floorboards, and then a couple days ago, two more in my bed, steeped in blood. A nice little Christmas present."

Brad said, "As far as I know, she's been in Pennsylvania all week." I looked at him. "So, maybe it was you."

At this, the blond friend laughed. "This from the chick who's been stalking the kid for months, maybe years. I recognize you. From being out at the bar. Always drinking alone and, like, *lurking* nearby."

I recognized him, too—Brad's roommate and consummate wingman, though lately I hadn't seen much of him, and wasn't sure if they still lived together.

I felt my whole face flame red. I thought I'd been so *invisible*.

Brad held up his hand. "Look. Things are crazy enough. We're just gonna get what we came for and be on our way."

"For a long time I was fixated on you," I blurted, omitting the better word: *obsessed*.

He turned to look at me.

"I know it's complicated," I went on, "but I was hoping one day we might talk about everything—about our parents and how hard it was to lose them, to be dragged through all that...*shit*. But I could never draw up the courage. So, yeah." I narrowed my eyes at the blond guy. "I *lurked*."

"Well, your first mistake is, I *never* considered that guy my dad," Brad said. "He abandoned me and my mom when I was a baby."

The blond friend piped up now. "I hate to break up this therapy session, but it's New Year's Eve, and we have places to be. Can we grab the trunk and get outta here or what?"

I nodded, fighting the urge to lunge for Brad's coat sleeve and tell him everything—tell him I was sorry and I could have stopped it, that I knew it was twisted and fucked up, but he and I were linked forever, if only I could just explain everything...

But I didn't. I kept my arms by my sides and my mouth shut. I'd rehearsed what I would say to Brad one day so many times, and now I'd ruined it. I simply looked crazy. Thanks to Lucy.

"Yeah, let's go," Brad said, and he and the friend moved toward the stairs. Brad was only on the second step when I couldn't hold it in anymore.

"Listen, I don't know what Lucy's game is, but I know she *plotted* to live here. I think she's *after* you, Brad. She's the one who's obsessed."

The friend snorted.

Brad sighed. "Listen. I've had a few stalkers. This isn't new."

"How humble," Tommy said. I had almost forgotten he was there.

The friend said, "It's true. Guy attracts lunatics like a fly to shit."

Brad turned all the way to look at me, leaning a bit on the railing.

"Look. What Dan did to your folks? It's *really* fucked, the whole thing. But I can't dwell on the fact that I share DNA with such a monster. And I'll tell you right now. You and I, Margo, or *Maggie*—we're not going to bond over our parents, shady alcoholics who got themselves entangled in some messed-up love triangle. So, no offense, but you should move on. And, like, stop Photoshopping pictures of you and me together, and following me around and shit."

My cheeks reddened again, deeper and hotter than they'd ever blazed before. I thought again of the Brad I'd conjured in my fantasies. I felt completely foolish, childish. Tricked by my own mind.

Tommy remained silent as the real Brad, unfriendly and disgruntled and...*mean*, climbed the stairs and with his friend hauled the trunk out of Lucy's room, down the hallway, and back down the stairs.

They were almost out the door when I called after them, hugging my arms to my chest. It was completely masochistic, me refusing to give up like this.

"Brad—that girl's up to something. Something bad. She scares me. And she *should* scare you."

Now Brad looked me dead in the eyes.

"Funny. She says the *exact* same thing about you."

Margo

Corinne poked her head out of her office door, right as I was striding by. "Margo? A word?"

Nose red and wet from the cold outside, I was almost at my desk, so I walked over to it and set my bag down, along with my free coffee from the first-floor kitchen. I smoothed my shirt, wondering how long I could stall. Corinne's tone had been clipped, and a first-thing meeting was never a good sign. I looked around the office, at the heads bent over laptops, spreadsheets on the screens and chat windows, and Astrid's desk, across the aisle, unoccupied.

So, this is it, I thought. Astrid told.

My mouth was dry. If I got canned, how would I pay my mortgage? After already being out seven grand? And when I managed to evict Lucy I'd be out her rent money, too.

Or would Lucy come home at all, now that her precious trunk was gone? All that remained in her room were some crappy clothes and endless boxes of red pens.

Corinne popped her head out of her office again. "Margo, please. I don't have all day."

A few heads turned. I ignored their curious stares and straightened my shoulders and strode into Corinne's office.

Astrid was already there, sitting in the chair on the left.

I flopped down on the other chair and out of the side of my mouth, hissed, "Felt real bad for me, huh? So much that you had to ruin my life even *more*?"

"What are you even *talking* about?" Astrid hissed back.

Corinne, who'd been doing something on her computer, shifted her attention and looked at the two of us over the top of her glasses.

"I'm sure you know what this meeting is about, Margo."

"I have an idea."

"Then you may be glad to know I've filed your complaint with HR. But before this gets rolling, I wanted to sit you both down and find out what the hell has been going on between you two."

"Wait, what complaint?" I said, glancing at Astrid, who refused to meet my eyes. Her face was beet red, and she appeared near tears.

Corinne stared. "Let's not play coy, Margo. In your complaint, you said...let me see"—she adjusted her glasses and cleared her throat—"that Astrid has a severe drinking problem. That Astrid, on the ski trip, got, quote, 'insanely inebriated and excessively loud, using the corporate card to pay for all her drinks.'" Corinne paused, scanning her screen. "Oh, and you also said Astrid harasses you daily with snide remarks and petty insults, to the point where you don't feel comfortable or safe working here anymore."

Astrid's arms were tight across her chest. "Lucy's right. You *are* evil."

214

"Enough," Corinne snapped at Astrid. I noticed Corinne's hair wasn't brushed, and her face was drawn, like she hadn't slept. Debbie's picture was still missing from the credenza along the wall.

My mind raced. Lucy had to have my password, or a tracker on my laptop, or the passcode to my phone.

That must be it, I thought, suddenly. She has my passcode. Mom's birthday, the last two digits transposed.

"Helen in HR will be taking over," Corinne was saying. "And while the investigation is pending, I'm taking both of your laptops—they're company-owned, remember—and IT is going to look through them. Any idea what they'll find?"

She stared at Astrid, then at me.

"And by the way, I'm not coming to any conclusions yet. Not until this is all substantiated. However," her eyes flicked to Astrid, "I have gotten confirmation of your behavior on the ski trip. Behavior you'd gone out of your way to attribute to Margo." She threw up her hands. "For all I know, you were *both* shit-faced on the trip, and you're *both* awful to one another."

"She's a liar," Astrid spat. "She's so full of it. She lied on her résumé, and she didn't even go to college—"

I spoke up, too, louder, eyes pleading. "Wait—I swear, I didn't send that complaint. I have this roommate, she's out to get me, she's out of her *mind*, and by the way, she also sent that other email, the first one, about the plane ticket, I know how to spell *plane*—"

"Don't believe a *word* Margo says," Astrid shouted, "she's pathological—"

Corinne pressed her pointer finger to her temple. "*Enough!*"

We quieted.

"Why is it I feel like I'm wrangling a couple of teenage girls? We're supposed to lift each other up and support each other. Not fall into some behind-the-back *bullshit*. This is a workplace, not your high school hallway. This is why it took me so long to rise through the

215

ranks here. It's what all the fuck-head males in upper management *said* would happen. 'Catfights.' They *literally* would say that." She shook her head.

It was quiet for several seconds.

Astrid shifted in her seat. "So are we..."

"Fired?" I croaked out.

Corinne sighed. "I have plenty of grounds to fire both of you—but I want to figure out the truth first, and I *will*. You're both on unpaid leave until we sort this out. Now get out of my office and go home."

* * *

"Astrid," I said, hurrying to catch up. She was almost at the elevator. "I swear, I didn't send that."

Astrid swiveled on her heel and opened the door to the stairwell. "Get away from me. You're *toxic*."

Lucy

Lucy sat precariously on the edge of Brad's couch cushion; there was a new stain toward the back, and she didn't know from which orifice it had originated. Brad was kneeling in front of the trunk, his coffee table shoved against the wall to make room for it.

As Lucy watched him lift the heavy lid, she tried to tamp down the thrill burning in her chest, the excitement. Before him were the materials she'd so painfully arranged for him to see: all the evidence organized by date, color-coded by severity, stacked to perfection in neat piles. If *Dirty Vines* had taught her anything, it was to leave no stone unturned. Or as Sly Stevens, the host, would say, *No vine unfurled.* (He needed to work on his metaphors, even she had to admit.)

Right now, Brad was fiddling with the old-school tape recorder Lucy had stolen from her parents' basement. She'd labeled it in red

Sharpie: *Voicemail recordings, August 2013.* Beginning with the tapes was a bit out of order, but she supposed it wasn't the end of the world.

He pressed play. Out of the speaker came Margo's voice, teen-shrill: "Stay away from us, you fat fuck. Kill yourself!"

He stopped, then fast-forwarded. "Die, you dirty pig!"

Fast-forward, play, and on and on, until he hit stop and lowered the device to the floor.

He looked up at Lucy, quizzical. "That's her? Margo?"

"Yes. There's *so* much more. Look."

He sighed and reached down further, to the stacks of photos. She leaned forward, watching, as he held the top picture, a baby swaddled in a blue blanket. He flipped it to the back. "Brad, 3 weeks old" was written in neat print, in handwriting Lucy had come to know as Dan's.

Brad moved to the next photo, this one of a woman leaning against a blue car, dark hair wild, shading her face from the sun and smiling. He flipped this one over. "Denise, '90."

"That's your mom, right?" Lucy asked, even though she knew the answer.

He looked up at her but said nothing.

"Now check out what's under *that*," she said, failing to keep the giddiness out of her voice.

He sighed and wiped his forehead with the back of his hand. He repositioned his knees, grunting. She had to resist the urge to leap off the couch, pointer finger ready—Come on! *Look!*—because she didn't have all day. Astrid would be home soon, hopefully fired, and certainly pissed from the "bullying complaint," and she wanted to hear all about it.

At this thought, she emitted a chuckle.

"What are you always laughing at?" Brad said.

"Nothing."

He turned back and pulled out the manila folder of printouts.

Finally, she thought.

His eyes scanned the top page, then he flipped to another page, and another. He shook his head, puzzled.

"So, these are all articles and...court cases? And they're all about—"

"Coerced suicide," she supplied.

"*Coerced*?" He gaped at her. "Are you trying to say some teenage girl told Dan to kill himself, and that makes everything he did before that okay?"

Lucy sprang from the couch and knelt beside him. She reached further down into the trunk and came up with a clear plastic sandwich bag, cloudy with age. Inside was a pill bottle. Lucy thrust it in front of his face, pointing to the patient's name: Daniel Ellis. Then she pointed at the drug name, a long one she couldn't pronounce, so didn't.

"What I'm *saying* is that this was what Dan needed to control his bipolar disorder and depression and...all of his issues that he'd had since he was a kid—you knew that."

Brad screwed up his face and said nothing.

"But," she said, soaking up the moment, "*someone* messed with the pills. *Someone* caused him to have wildly paranoid thoughts, leading to unspeakable acts. Acts that were not his *fault*."

"And that someone was Maggie," he said, slowly.

Lucy poked the inside of her cheek with her tongue to keep from smiling, to subdue her self-congratulatory mood.

"Yes. And there's more."

She reached for the last of it, down at the bottom of the trunk, another stack of papers clipped together. She handed it to him.

"What you have there are tens of thousands of text messages sent from Margo to Dan within the span of a month. She instructed him to kill himself 187 times, all while swapping his meds with *laxatives*. Can you believe that? That's what's in that pill bottle. Laxatives."

Brad stared down at the trunk, saying nothing.

"Can't you see?" she pressed. "Maggie the Murderer is the reason this all happened. And we can get her for it. I have money for lawyers. I can help you *do* this. I mean, I know what you're thinking. Dan shouldn't have killed her parents, obviously. It was a tragedy, yada yada." She waved her hand in the air. "But it was a preventable tragedy. And we," she smiled, "have everything we need to send this bitch away to *rot*. There's a legal precedent for these psycho bitches taunting people, you see that in those articles—though, they taunted their *own* fucking boyfriends, not their *mom's*—but in any case, these evil she-devils sent these guys to the edge. And then, with their painted little fingernails, they gave them that last little flick off the cliff. Maggie the Maggot just thought she could change her name and dye her hair and no one would ever find out."

She stopped speaking, almost breathless. Her heart was racing. She'd planned this speech for so long, ever since the day her mother had told her everything. The day her mother told her, voice shaking, *Honey, I'm so sorry, but there's something I've kept from you for a long time.*

Brad broke Lucy from her thoughts. He was holding up the pill bottle.

"Okay. So she did all this stuff. Maggie did. Now tell me how *you* have all this. How you know."

"Dan sent it to me." It was the truth.

"He *sent* it to you? What do you mean, like, he mailed you this massive trunk?" He cocked his head at her. "Did you guys have something going on?" he pressed. "Was he some sort of pedo?"

"Are you serious? Ew. *No*."

"*So why?*" His mouth twisted in fury, in pain. His eyes were glassy. "Why do you have all my dad's stuff? Why are you living with this Margo—Maggie—girl, planting rats and shit everywhere. *Why?*"

She knew she should tell him; he deserved to know. But she needed another carrot to dangle, another excuse to set up a meeting in the future. In case he got cold feet.

She wasn't stupid. Brad didn't like her. She could sense it. He might even *hate her.* But she loved him. Oh, how she loved him. It was instant, from the moment she'd first seen him.

A buzz on her phone. Astrid. For once, she was glad for the distraction.

"I need to go," she said, rising and heading for the door. "I promise I'll tell you everything tonight. We can talk about the financial retribution, like, if we pull off a civil suit. And forget how much we could get for the story." At this, she saw his back straighten. "So. What do you say? Dinner?" She gave him a grin, one she hoped communicated trust, love, and devotion.

"Jesus. Fine."

She opened the door, energized, the burst of cold air from the outside hitting her cheeks.

It was becoming a reality. She imagined her own season five of *Dirty Vines*, titled—she'd already thought up a name—"Inconceivable: The Margo Sharpe Story," and then maybe a book: *Dirty House: A Memoir of Entrapment.* Some details she'd have to fudge, of course...

"Wait, what's this?" Brad was holding up his phone.

"Oh. Yes. I sent some money over Zenpay. Everything you need to secure the attorney is there. I'm giving it to you because, well, you can see why you're the one who has to initiate this. The emotional impact of a son going after justice for his father, especially with you being so handsome, and along with his sidekick, his loving..."

She paused. Not yet. Patience.

"I promise you," she said as she flounced down the walkway, "we'll be *heroes*. And really fucking famous."

Margo

Later that night I wandered aimlessly down Broadway with Bearie, lost as always in my thoughts and worries. Tomorrow I'd put my tail between my legs and call Izzie for a loan. A big loan, not one of the small (but still generous) loans Izzie had given me in the past.

Tomorrow, I would also have to do what I'd been dreading for the past seven years: tell my aunt everything. How I'd lied every time Izzie talked to me about Dan and my mom, plaguing over that nasty question: *Why?*

Izzie would never look at me the same again, maybe never even speak to me again. Then I would truly be alone.

I looked up. I was nearing Delaney's. Monday nights were a staple for Brad and his friends, and, at one time, a mousy slob-girl sitting at a nearby barstool, straining to hear every word, imagining she was there with him, the cool, aloof girlfriend who put up with their fantasy drafts as she sipped her IPA. (Truthfully I hated IPAs, they tasted like dog slobber, but the cool Margo, she loved them.)

The windows were still decorated in Christmas lights. It was so festive in there. It looked cozy and happy. There weren't many people inside.

Except for *them*.

I suppose, subconsciously or not, with a dash of denial, this is what I had come this way for, what I was looking for. Them, together. Brad slicing into a steak, and Lucy beside him, waving her fork around above an untouched salad, elbowing him for emphasis as she spoke.

Thankfully their backs were to me. I stood stock still, wondering if I should barge in and ask Lucy about her latest machinations: the email to Corinne. The rats. Everything. But where would that get me? I'd inevitably end up gaslit and cornered, same as what happened in front of Astrid—

I felt a tap on my shoulder and turned.

"Still at it, huh?"

It was Brad's blond friend, the one who'd come with him for the trunk. He cackled and stepped toward the door, opening it and calling, "B! Looks like your shadow is back!"

I wasn't quick enough. By the time I got the leash ready and Bearie to even budge, both Brad and Lucy were turned all the way around their stools, staring through the window at me, their mouths parted in surprise. And, on Brad's face, a look of absolute disgust, and, if I wasn't mistaken, fear.

Margo

Bearie and I went home the roundabout way, plodding along Broadway, down K Street, and finally over to East 8th. The whole while, I was thinking maybe I should simply...die.

I'd contemplated this before, a while back, after the fiasco with my parents, after I took everything too far with Dan and there was no turning back. That raw slap of realism after it was all said and done, after the bodies and the blood were out of the house and I was still alive, unsullied, at least on the outside—that it was my fault, and out of everyone, it was *me* who should be dead.

I'd moved past that familiar despair long ago and graduated to numbness. Like all the pain I was supposed to feel had eroded into...nothing.

These thoughts of death, for instance, came almost casually, with little fanfare, without tears or grief or distress attached. I wanted—needed—to die. It was that simple.

But first, I had to return Bearie.

I pressed Owen's doorbell. Shortly after, Tawna opened the door. She took the leash, muttering, "Thank you." Tawna still didn't take to me like Owen or Tommy had, and this used to bother me, but it didn't now. Nothing bothered me. People *should* hate me.

Back at home on the couch I picked at the loose wisps of fabric. I could have cleaned the filth in the kitchen—my own filth, now—but I left it there. What was another day? The house was so quiet—would Brad and Lucy come back here? Would they ask me questions, would they taunt me—because if they did, I'd deserve it. I was a waste. A nothing.

My desired method—I'd thought of this many times before—would be pills. I imagined meeting someone in an alley. Or under the West Broadway bridge. Who would this *someone* be? Maybe I could go back through the Craigslist castoffs. I remembered "Betsey S," the accountant who assured me she would "throw away needles in trash. Very tidy."

Betsey would be perfect. And what would I ask for? Fentanyl was all the rage these days, wasn't it? It'd certainly be quick.

I stared at her phone number for a long time before drifting off into a dreamless sleep.

* * *

The doorbell. That blaring buzz. It was a fussy button, fickle, in that it worked about thirty percent of the time. People often tried it once and gave up. But not this person.

I lifted my head from the arm of the couch and wiped the drool from my cheek. I climbed over the back of the couch to see out the window. I expected to see Brad and Lucy bundled up together, snickering, punching the doorbell again and again.

But it wasn't either of them. It was a man I did not know.

I went to the door and opened it partway. "Yes?"

The man, middle-aged, was partially bald and dressed in a puffy coat three sizes too big. He was tall and lean with thin legs, swimming in his jeans. "Umm, hello," he said.

I narrowed my eyes; I recognized the voice, and the association was not pleasant. Still, I asked, "Who are you?"

"I'm looking for Lucy Somers. I'm her father, Gary. Gary Somers? I'm sorry to come unannounced like this, but she's not answering my wife's calls—or mine—and we're just so worried. Is she here?"

"She hasn't been back in a couple weeks," I said. I wanted to let him in; it was very cold, but I knew I shouldn't trust any person related to or associated with Lucy Somers.

"Oh, God," he said, his eyes widening. "She left our Christmas dinner *very* angry, and that was weeks ago. She's thirty years old, so we can't really force her to do anything, but..."

"She's thirty, huh?" I said in a monotone. Nothing surprised me anymore. "She said she was in her mid-twenties."

He grimaced. "I can imagine she—she may have told you a lot of things. Our Lucy is—" He stopped. "I think I need to file a missing persons report...Look, if you hear from her—"

"She's not missing," I cut in. "She's here. In South Boston. With a guy. I just saw them, less than two hours ago. At the bar."

"Oh," he said, looking slightly less panicked. "She told us she had a new boyfriend, but we thought she was—anyway, do you know where he lives? Or how to get ahold of him?"

I nodded and rattled off the address like it was my own. It turned my stomach, thinking of the two going back to his apartment afterward, going into his bedroom...

I noticed now that Gary's gloved hands were empty as he nodded along, uncomprehending.

"Sir, do you want to put the address in your phone? Or, do you want a pen?"

"Right," he said, shaking his head. "I was trying to memorize. My mobile is dead." He looked at me desperately. "You wouldn't mind if I came in a moment and charged it, would you? I left in a hurry—my wife, she's beside herself, and Lucy's doctor—"

I sighed and opened the door. I didn't even feel fear. Maybe death would come for me in the form of this norm-core Pennsylvania dad. Maybe he had a knife in that puffy coat and he'd shank me right in the neck. That would take care of it, really.

He stepped inside. "Nice place you got here," he said, politely.

"That's not what your daughter thinks," I said, allowing him to follow me to the living room. "Want a tea or a coffee or something—a water?"

"Water would be great. And an outlet."

He waved his phone. It used the same charger as mine. I took it, then walked it to the kitchen and plugged it into an outlet there, having to shove aside the plates and dirty water glasses to get to it.

When I came back with a glass of water his hands were resting on his long, Ichabod Crane legs. He was too tall for the chair he was sitting in.

"You know this fella? This boyfriend? Do you think she's safe?" he asked, before taking a sip of his water.

"I think she's probably safe," I said. Then I remembered something. "You know what? If you find her, you can give this to her." I reached for the paperwork, which was sitting on the end table. "I'm evicting her. If she ever comes back."

"Evicting..." He trailed off, then cleared his throat. He took the envelope but set it down on the table. "Can you tell me, ah, how it's been? With Lucy here. Has she been...nice?" He shook his head. "That's not the proper word. Has she been, ah, well?"

"Not really," I said, tiredly. "I'd appreciate it if you'd give her those and get her shit out of my house. That would be fantastic, actually."

"Of course. I will absolutely help in whatever way I can. Sorry to keep pressing you, but she may not be forthcoming with me, so I'd love to hear it from you. Did she cause any damage? Has she been paying her rent? We looked up the school she claimed to work at and it doesn't exist. We know she has plenty of her *own* money, so it's not that we're worried about that..."

"She was paying her rent until she stole from me," I said. "And she was sweet until she started being a rancid slob. And she was seemingly *well* until she started systematically ruining my life, after which it became very clear she was not."

He stared at me, helpless. "I'm sorry."

"Is she a true crime nut?" I asked.

"True crime? Umm, yes, she is, actually. Loves all those *Dateline* shows, all that awful morbid and sordid nonsense." He waved his hand and smiled nervously. "Always listening to those podcast what-chamacallits. I swear those earbuds are part of her ears." He rubbed the side of his head.

"You guys look alike," I said, watching him. "And act alike."

He hesitated. "I'm guessing she hasn't told you why she's so mad at us, at me and Judy, her mother?"

"No," I said. "Never mentioned it."

He sipped his water, then set it down.

"My wife divulged something earlier this year, a long-kept secret. Something that really sent Lucy reeling."

I opened my mouth to ask what the secret was, then thought better of it. Did I even care? I just wanted her out of my life, forever.

And this guy could do that. He just had to go get her, give her the paperwork, and get her away from me.

Turned out Gary was going to tell me, regardless.

"It's funny you—and everyone—say we look alike. Because Judy finally told Lucy that I'm not her birth father."

"What?" Suddenly, I felt sick.

"Afraid so," he said. He went into how he still considered himself Lucy's father—that he was a father in every sense other than blood— but I could scarcely hear him, my heart was beating so hard. No more numbness; something worse was penetrating it. Fear.

Gary kept on as he shook his head.

"Judy had been on summer break with her girlfriends down on Cape Cod, shortly before she met me, and dated this creep, as she called him. They went out for a while, but...let's just say that the last time she tried to break up with him, he didn't take it too well, and he...well, they had relations that weren't consensual. It was a sort of date rape situation, I think you'd call it now." He shook his head and smiled. "It was a lifetime ago, more than thirty years. Judy's fine now, and the creep's dead, anyway, so—"

"Who?" I cut in, trying to keep the quavering from my voice. "Who is Lucy's father? What's his *name*?"

Gary raised his eyebrows, suddenly wary. "I'm sure you wouldn't know him. A man by the name of Daniel Ellis."

PART III

Lucy

Lucy stabbed at her salad with her fork. "And so, I was like, 'Astrid, shut the fuck up. You won't be fired.' " She rolled her eyes, waving her fork as she added, "I don't even know why I involved her at all. Well, I do know. It's because I needed help, and wasn't sure you—"

"Enough," Brad growled, pushing his plate away from him. "We've been sitting on these stools for *hours*. And in that time, you've given me none of the additional information you promised me. So, if you don't tell me how the fuck you have all that stuff about my dad, I'm walking right out that door. You're drawing this out on purpose, wasting my time. This isn't some *date*, okay?"

"I know it's not a date," Lucy said, laughing.

Brad hailed the bartender and made a motion for the check. "Spill it, or it's time to go."

Lucy heart hammered in her chest. "Okay, okay, fine. I'll tell you. The reason I have all his stuff is that...Dan, he was..."

Brad raised his palms in supplication and jutted his head forward. "He was...?"

"He was my dad."

"Who was your dad?" Brad asked.

"Dan. Your dad is also *my* dad."

Brad said nothing for a moment. Then, stone-faced, he said, "He didn't have a daughter. He was single. A bachelor."

"Not true. Shortly before Dan died, he looked up my mom on Facebook and found out she had a daughter. He saw her pictures of me and...See, right before my mom met Gary, the guy I *thought* was my dad, she'd hooked up with Dan down on the Cape, but she never saw him again. She raised me as Gary's daughter. Shortly before Dan died, he saw the resemblance between us, in the Facebook pictures. He did the math, and I don't know, started, like, getting sad about it, or reflective, I guess—that he'd never known me. He wrote me a bunch of letters and put them in the trunk, along with the other stuff I showed you, and mailed the whole thing to my mom's address, with explicit instructions for only me to open it.

"But my parents got to it first. My mom freaked and hid the trunk from me for *seven years*. Can you believe that? My own mother, keeping that from me. I'm thirty years old. It's my *right* to know my birth father. What a fucking liar, right?" A loud bang sounded out, and she realized it was her own knife on her plate.

She set her knife down gently and squeezed her napkin in her lap to dry her wet palms. Brad's expression was so hard to read!

She cleared her throat and picked up her fork, even though the thought of eating made her want to vomit all over the bar.

She felt his hand on her arm. She looked up at him, suddenly fearful. Fearful that he wouldn't believe her, or worse, that he wouldn't consider her family in any way, shape, or form. She'd shoved these fears aside, telling herself it would all work out, but they were coming to the surface, now that he was so angry and fed up with her. She had dragged it out too long.

His hand continued to grip her forearm.

With a quavering voice, she asked, "What?"

"You're saying I have a sister? You're my *sister*?"

Lucy nodded, and fought through the choke in her throat to say, "Half. But yes."

He blinked, like he was trying to absorb it all. "He sent you that trunk and left you...all that information. What did he want you to do with it?"

"The letters were a little manic—he was a wreck when he was off his pills, *as you know*, and Maggie was harassing him and making his life hell. He wanted me to intervene, if anything were to happen to him, and to expose Maggie. To tell the world what she did. But my moron mother sat on that trunk for over seven years, never even told me he'd sent me anything at all. Never even told me he was my real father until a few months ago."

Her face darkened.

"I'll deal with her later. What we need to do is keep our eye on the prize and make sure Maggie Nevins rots for what she did to Daddy. We'll sue the shit out of her and put her on blast on every true crime show in America, for the diseased vermin she is. We'll get revenge for Daddy, and we'll be rich, too. You just have to trust me. I have it all figured out."

She forced herself to stop rambling. She was going to scare him away, just like she scared everyone away.

Finally, she looked up and met Brad's eyes.

"I have a sister," Brad whispered, and a tear fell down his cheek. He wrapped her in a tight embrace. "We'll address the other stuff, soon. I'm still trying to wrap my head around this. I have a *sister*."

Margo

"You honestly don't know what was in it?" I asked. "She never said?"

Gary shook his head.

We were standing in Lucy's barren room. All that remained were one white sock, a couple shirts hanging in the closet, and a prominent indent on the carpet, where the four corners of the trunk had dug in.

"When it first came to the house, Judy kind of sat on it for a few days, unsure of whether to open it, whether she should show Lucy and be transparent about who her blood father was. She even considered burning it. She did not have fond memories of this Dan character, and didn't like that Dan knew where we lived.

"Poor Judy. Her conscience was eating at her, and, it proved to be too much. So one day, she decided to come clean and show Lucy the trunk. But right before she does, she googles Dan's name. She hoped to find out where he lived, get a phone number. Thinking that she could talk to him first, ask what was in the trunk, and what had spurred this sudden desire for contact after more than thirty years? At the very least, maybe they could break the news to Lucy together. Frankly, she was angry; she wanted to give him a piece of her mind, too." Gary rubbed his face.

I stood still, listening. Waiting. Trying not to hyperventilate.

"Anyway, lo and behold, when Judy googles Dan's name, he's all over the local news in Massachusetts for a double homicide. She saw what Dan had done to that poor couple on Cape Cod, and she was beside herself. With him dead, and with that news, it's a miracle she didn't burn that trunk right then and there."

"What did she do with it all this time?" I asked.

"She kept it in a storage unit." Gary looked up helplessly, shaking his head. "She wanted to tell Lucy one day. But not then. It was too raw."

"Then what prompted your wife to show the trunk to Lucy all these years later?" I tried to keep the panic and anger from my voice. This Judy woman, if she had any brains, should have burned it. I could only imagine what Dan had put in that trunk—what relics from my abuse that would implicate me in the events leading up to my parents' deaths. And I could only imagine what conspiracy theories he'd peddled, in his addled, suicidal mind (*Because of the pills, Margo—don't forget about those pills—it's ALL YOUR FAULT*).

"A few months ago," Gary explained, "Lucy was doing all this DNA stuff—you know, when you mail it out and they send it back and all that. She was always threatening Judy with claims she wasn't her real mother, especially when she got mad at her. As you can imagine, when the results came back, everything went to hell in a handbasket. Judy was forced to tell her the whole story. She got the trunk out of the storage unit, and Lucy opened it in private. Then she refused to tell us anything about what was inside.

"But she began to act strange after that. Mighty strange. There were some incidents. We, miraculously, got her to agree to go to a facility, but she hated it there, and at home, that's when she really started to..."

Gary trailed off, catching my intense gaze.

"You don't need to know all of this. I realize I'm rambling. My apologies. My phone must be charged by now, yeah? I really think it's time I headed off to find her. I'm just so very glad she's okay. That's she's not missing, I mean."

When he went downstairs I didn't budge for a minute or so.

I was picturing Brad and his friend carrying the trunk out of the house. Right under my nose. And I was picturing Owen coming to my door with handcuffs—even though he wasn't actually a cop, it's who I pictured—leading me away after realizing what I really was.

I've never figured out where my rare—but explosive—anger episodes come from. Maggie the Mood. My parents had always laughed it off, too absorbed in themselves to really look too closely at it. Once I got old enough to be self-sufficient, and got good-enough grades and had friends, like Jessie, to keep me occupied, they could go on with their partying, their fun.

Maybe that was part of it. Maybe their obstinate lack of awareness helped to make me who I am.

Gary had taken his phone off the charger and was waiting by the door. He asked me to repeat Brad's address so he could enter it into Google Maps.

"Thank you kindly," he said. Then he looked at me. "This boyfriend of hers, Brad—he's not the volatile sort, is he?"

"Brad—he's not—"

Gary looked up from his phone. "He's not what?"

The full realization came, delayed, as I spoke the words. And it was accompanied by the sickening knowledge that I was not only alarmed and frightened by what this meant—*What was Lucy putting him up to? What exactly does she have on me?*—but part of me was actually

239

glad. Lucy and Brad were not dating. Out of all the information I'd learned today, this is what I was *glad* about.

Something was wrong with me. Very wrong.

"He's not her boyfriend, Mr. Somers. If what you're telling me is true, about her real father, that makes Brad...Lucy's *brother*."

50

Lucy

Brad paid the tab and they hopped off their stools. With a punch on the shoulder he said good-bye to the blond roommate, whom Lucy had just learned was named Peter. He *looked* like a Peter—a little sniveling shithead who'd spent most of the evening smirking at Lucy from where he sat, two stools down. She knew he assumed Lucy was just one of Brad's conquests, some *uggo* he was using as a plaything.

As they were leaving Lucy smiled at Peter as she linked her arm through her brother's. He glared back at her. On second glance, actually, she thought he was glaring at Brad. Maybe it was because Brad had asked for a separate check so he'd only have to pay for his and Lucy's tab and not Peter's.

Or maybe Peter was simply jealous, Lucy surmised. Jealous of how much better-looking Brad was, how Brad was so beloved by everyone who met him. It must be tough to live with an Adonis when you're an average-looking loser.

"You should *see* the way girls look at him!" Lucy had written in her Decomposition Notebook the other day. "People bend over backwards for him. He has POWER. And when I'm by his side, I have power, too."

When they got outside Delaney's Lucy looked one more time through the glass at Peter, who was shaking his head into his phone, texting furiously.

Let Peter think whatever he wants, she thought. When she and her brother were plastered on every podcast—and for old people, newspapers—across the country, he'd wish he'd been more welcoming and respectful.

Brad let Lucy lead him down the street. It was cold.

He pulled his phone out and muttered at whatever he saw there. She craned her neck to see it, but couldn't. He slipped it back into his pocket, and said something about Peter being a "dickhead" and a "pain in the ass," and how he wished he could afford to live alone so he could have some fucking *peace*.

Lucy nodded understandingly and said, "Peter seems like a jerk."

"He's all right," Brad said absently. "Roommates are just a pain sometimes."

"Tell me about it!" she shouted, laughing.

He gave a small smile, though it seemed mixed with a slight wince as his eyes darted to the turned heads on the street.

It had started to snow, lightly, and when she looked up, the green lettered street signs were partially covered in white flakes. At East 8th, she steered him to the right.

"I thought you said your car was on K," he said, stopping.

"It is," she said, trying to tug at his sleeve. "But I just have to check something."

"Check what?" He pulled his arm back, not budging.

She grinned and shrugged, glancing down the street, in the direction of Margo's house.

He huffed into the cold air and shook his head. "If this is gonna work, Lucy, you need to stay away from her. Let the attorneys do their job."

"I *know*," she said. "*God*, I'm not stupid." Then, just as quickly as she'd snapped at him, she smiled. "Brother–sister fights. We're already doing it, huh?"

"Looks like it. Though, haven't we been fighting since the get-go? Honestly, I couldn't fucking stand you."

"On some level I bet you knew we were related," she said. "And now you love me. Because you have to." Then she punched his arm, like she figured sisters did to brothers.

He smiled and rolled his eyes.

Lucy took stock of how she felt. Now that she'd come completely clean to her brother—her brother!—she felt buoyant, confident, invincible. She not only had a brother, she had a co-conspirator. Someone who would help her finally make things right for Daddy.

"If you won't go with me, I'll spy on her myself. But I'll be careful. I promise."

He sighed. "Fine. Just don't let her see you."

* * *

From outside the house, Lucy spotted a shadow figure through her own bedroom window. No, two shadows. Margo must be going through my things, she thought. Not that there's anything left. Suckers. Brad has the trunk now. You're *fucked*.

Lucy crossed the street and stood behind a car, pulling her hat low and her jacket tight. She waited to see more, but the light in the bedroom window had flicked off and the downstairs shades were drawn. She waited and waited, watching the cold air escape her lips. Forget it, she thought. Maybe that chubby aunt was over, and what did she care anyway. Her brother was right. She couldn't risk what Margo would do if she saw here there. She couldn't take any chances, not after all the work she'd put in to get to this point.

Suddenly there was noise behind her head, the tapping of a window. She turned quickly.

Two faces stared out at her from behind the glass: one was that squat little brunette from the apartment tour—what a horrendous human!—and the other was the pretty blonde, Stephanie, who'd invited Lucy for a roommate interview that hot August day, the one with Pottery Barn everything and a patronizing attitude, but who was so pretty Lucy kept getting distracted, babbling up a storm and betraying way too much information about herself.

Stephanie's place had been the backup plan, but Lucy had blown it. Asked too many questions, set off alarm bells. At least that off-putting behavior had taught Lucy how *not* to act around Margo during their interview. To merely keep her trap shut and smile.

Now, Lucy lifted her middle finger and then turned and headed back to Brad's. He'd agreed, begrudgingly, to let her stay at his place while she "figured things out," so long as she helped pay his exorbitant rent. He told her how strapped for cash he was lately. School loans and credit card debt. She told him he shouldn't go on so many dates; it was bleeding him dry. But in the end, he was family. She didn't mind.

As she ambled along, she saw a red smart car illegally double-parked with a fluorescent orange ticket tucked under the wiper. It looked familiar. She knew that car.

Lucy shrieked into the night air, because now she knew precisely who was poking around her room. The plates on the car were from Pennsylvania.

Fucking Gary.

* * *

Lucy hid in Brad's bedroom, in the likely event Margo gave Gary Brad's address. "He'll come looking for me," she told Brad. "Trust me."

She wondered if Margo had the guts—the gall—to go with Gary, to confront her at Brad's house. No, she would never, Lucy told herself. And, on the off chance she did—well, she was in for quite the show. Lucy had her cornered.

Lucy looked around Brad's room. A basketball. A random kettle-bell. A mattress on the floor and rumpled sheets on top of it, which, in keeping with the rest of the apartment, were stained and stinky. A rat trap sat in the corner. He had real rats. Maybe she could ask for a spare to leave at Miss Margo's.

She moved over to his dresser. Riffling through the top drawer, she found condoms, lube, a small tube of face cream. There was also a cheap-looking bracelet from some poor soul who would surely never get it back.

As she swiped aside a golf scoresheet, beneath it she found a different sort of item. She raised her eyebrows as she peered down at it.

It was a picture of Dan. He'd taken it from the trunk. It was the one of a grinning Dan holding the bundle that was baby Brad in his arms.

Lucy's heart heaved. She was happy for Brad to have that memory of his father, even if her own mother had ripped that experience away from her. Worse, so had Margo. Dan never got to know Lucy, his own daughter. Never got to hold her in his arms. He missed out—and Lucy missed out—on so many firsts, so many experiences.

She realized in that moment that she was gripping a large chunk of hair in her right hand. She took a deep breath in and out and relaxed her fist.

She tried conjuring comforting thoughts. At least the current phase of her plan was under way, meaning, the lawyers. But they would take a very long time, and she didn't know if she could wait that long. She didn't know if that would be enough punishment.

When she'd floated a couple ideas to Brad—minor stuff, like tampering with Margo's mail or putting dog shit in her shoes, or filling an eye-dropper bottle with some sort of insidious chemical—his eyes had blazed with alarm. He'd asked her if she was "nuts."

"Oh my God, Brad," she'd said. "I was *kidding*."

Brad's doorbell rang, and just in time, Lucy shut the drawer, right as Brad poked his head in.

"Where do I say you are again?" he asked.

"Shopping. And be sure to tell him I'm not interested in seeing him. And you know," she waved her hand, "all the rest of the stuff we talked about."

He sighed and shut the door.

Lucy put her ear to it to listen.

Brad answered the door. Soon she heard Gary's voice rise. "Listen, buddy, I need you to tell me the truth. Because I've got a very concerned young woman over there on East Eighth who says that Lucy—"

"Sir," Brad cut in, "Lucy and I—"

"Yes, I already know. You're half *siblings*. We put it together when I told her about Lucy's issues. And yes, Lucy has been quite distraught ever since discovering the identity of her real father, and it has affected her mental state, and we've been attempting to...Anyway, that's not so important right now. Most pressing is that Margo, that poor girl, told me Lucy has been *terrorizing* her for months. Lying and stealing and planting dead animals everywhere—"

At this, Lucy burst out of Brad's bedroom and into the living room, almost tripping over her feet.

"You *idiot*!" she screamed. "You're ruining *everything*!"

Lucy

Brad stiff-armed Lucy, who'd flown like a bat out of hell straight at the door. He'd managed to stop her before she got close enough to clock Gary in the jaw.

Gary called over Brad's head, "Young lady, why haven't you been answering our calls?"

"Because I'm thirty!" she shrieked, her voice muffled by Brad's upper arm. "And because you are not my father—and as far I'm concerned, that *liar* is not my mother." Tears had sprung from her eyes, despite herself.

"Come inside, we need to discuss this like adults," Brad commanded Gary, while still holding Lucy with one arm. He pointed to a broken-looking wicker chair.

Gary obeyed, lowering himself gingerly into it, causing a cracking sound.

Brad clutched Lucy's upper arm and hissed, "Will you calm the fuck down? You're not helping the situation."

She wrenched her arm away and leaned her back against the wall, crossing her arms over her chest. Gary was a good person, not that she'd ever admit it aloud, and a good father. He was *too* decent—and this was precisely why she hadn't been truthful about why she'd moved to South Boston. He would've gotten all saccharine about everything, wanting to mediate and involve her mother, and *of course*, Dr. Reject Reynolds...

Suddenly she realized Gary was talking.

"*Rats*, Lucy? Hacking into that poor girl's phone?"

This. This was why.

Brad tossed Lucy a warning look and raked his hair back from his forehead. Then he turned to Gary. "Did Margo happen to tell you who *she* is?"

Gary shook his head, nonplussed. "It doesn't matter who she is, quite frankly. What matters, and thank your lucky stars, Lucy, is that she won't press charges so long as we can get Lucy the help she needs and move her out for good. I said I thought that was a fine idea. I think we need to get you back home and see if there are any spots available at Serenity Meadows—"

Brad spoke up before Lucy lost it. "Sir, this Margo Sharpe person—her real name is Maggie Nevins."

"Am I supposed to know who that is?"

"Margo is the daughter of the Nevins couple, from the Cape," Brad said. "The ones my—our—father...killed."

Gary paled and sat back in the chair, which creaked under his weight. "That poor girl. Lucy—that makes this even worse. Why are you terrorizing her? She's been through *enough*!"

Lucy walked slowly to the couch and sat. She could do this. She could stay in control. She had to.

"Gary," she said, leaning forward.

248

Brad shot her another look.

She corrected herself. "*Dad*," she said, more sweetly. "Let me tell you what happened. The *whole* story. Will you promise to listen and not interrupt?"

Gary nodded. "As long as you're telling me the truth, I won't say a peep."

She glanced first at Brad, and then back at Gary.

"Okay. After I found out Dan was my dad—no thanks to Mom, thirty years too late"—she glared at Gary, but then relaxed her face. *Not now*. She went on. "I found out through my research online that Dan had a son from a previous marriage. I found him on Instagram and on all these volunteer websites—he does a lot of charity work." She smiled proudly at Brad. "He's generous. Caring. I couldn't wait to meet him."

Brad, sitting on the opposite end of the couch, shifted uncomfortably.

"Naturally, I wanted to find my brother. It's why I chose to look at jobs and grad schools in Boston."

Gary winced. "Gosh, Lucy, all those times we came up here to visit—why didn't you just *tell* me? We could have looked for him together."

She ignored him and kept going.

"After I found out where Brad lived, I didn't have the courage to approach him. It's...heavy, finding out you have a brother on top of finding out what happened to Daddy—Dan—and I didn't..." She trailed off, thinking. Calculating. "Anyway, I focused on grad school. I told myself I'd contact him when I was ready.

"Then one day I got a message, online, from a recruiter for a grad school here. Telling me that there was an opening—affordable, and right near the train and the bus and all that—and to check out this listing on Craigslist. Little did I know, it was Margo—*luring* me here. And, little did I know," she wiped a tear away and sniffled, "she was plotting something. I don't know how she found out who I was—it's

249

possible maybe Dan told her, before he died, that he'd just discovered he had a daughter, so she's been searching for *me*."

Gary said, "Well, that doesn't make all that much sense—"

"No, it doesn't," Brad said, glaring at her. After checking that Gary wasn't looking, he mouthed, *What are you doing?*

Lucy held up a finger. She wasn't done. Truth was, she was coming up with this bullshit completely on the fly, and needed a second to think of what to say next. She thought she was doing pretty well so far.

"So I get to this apartment of hers and find out that she has mold—and *rats*. Those weren't rats that I planted there, that's silly—you would have to be *insane* to believe that. She would also poison my food—that's probably why I would get so sick, because of all the vermin in the place—why I was always too tired to call you back, too weak to hold a job..."

Gary, it appeared, was sufficiently horrified. "Is *this* why you lied about that job? Because we looked up that Montessori School—"

Lucy nodded sadly, hoping her expression was sufficiently forlorn and pitiful. "I was ashamed. I'd made such a big deal about it to you and Mom, that I could make it on my own, that I was well again. I didn't want to disappoint you guys, or worry you. But truth be told, I was terrified. Did she tell you she changed the locks on the front door? That's illegal, you know, and I've filed a complaint with the city housing board, and the health inspector. She's awful. She's deceitful and ugly. She's just like her parents."

At this, Gary frowned. "The people who were *killed*?"

Lucy, attempting to keep the excitement out of her voice, informed Gary, in a shortened version, what was in Dan's letters and the other evidence in the trunk.

"She gave him the idea, to use the garden hose as a noose." This, at least, was the truth. Brad knew it, too—he'd seen the text. Lucy suspected that was the nail in the coffin for Brad—the impetus to *get this bitch*.

250

She forced some more tears and turned now to Brad.

"Tell him about the attorneys. Your buddies who went to Suffolk Law—how you have a meeting, next week."

Brad gave a weary nod. "Yeah, we're seeking legal counsel."

He looked very tired. Lucy's heart swelled. This was a lot on him, too. It was a lot on both of them. Now if only annoying-ass Gary would get out of here and let them get back to it.

Gary leaned forward in his chair, his long thin fingers stretched over his kneecaps.

"We need to keep you safe from this maniac. Mold and rats and such, and this diabolical plot to get you to live with her? Lucy, we need to get a restraining order, immediately. You, too, Brad."

Lucy shook her head. "We're perfectly fine and safe. And in the meantime, while we sort things out on the legal end, I'm staying here, with Brad. He's letting me pay a little rent to help out."

Gary looked unconvinced.

She walked over and crouched beside him, resting her chin on the arm of the wicker chair. "I'm safe, and I'm happy, and I'm doing good in the world. I'm focused and have a reason to get up in the morning. My mind has never been sharper. If the courts decide she's not guilty, then fine. But maybe it'll give her a little scare, you know? Maybe it'll make her realize you can't treat people the way she treated our dad."

Gary said nothing, but she knew from the look on his kind, dumb face that he was acquiescing. At least for now. She knew it would be another story once he got home to Judge Judy.

"Give me your phone," she said, holding out her hand.

"Why?" Gary asked, leery.

Lucy forced herself to create more tears. She thought of the most awful things imaginable—Brad dying; Margo living a long, healthy life. "Please, I just have to see something. Make sure she doesn't contact you again."

She held out her hand, palm up, and wiggled her fingers.

251

Gary shook his head. "I can handle it if she contacts me."

It took everything in her not to leap on top of him and wrench the phone from his hand.

"If you love me like a real daughter, you'll let me see your phone."

"Of course I love you like my real daughter. You *are* my daughter. I've told you this."

He slowly held up the phone. Lucy snatched it and punched in his passcode.

"Hey, how do you know my code?"

She navigated to Margo's contact and crafted a message: "Found her. We are going back to Pennsylvania, to get help. Thank you for telling me where she was. I'm forever indebted to you. —Gary Somers."

"What are you typing," Gary said. "Do not—"

Margo immediately started typing back; Lucy could tell by the dots.

Brad, for his part, distracted Gary by asking him where he'd parked, telling him he may have been towed; should they go check? It's a bear to recover your car from the tow lot; it's pretty far...

Lucy quickly typed another message: "Lucy knows my passcode. Need to delete your number or else you'll invite her wrath. She's very angry right now. Let's not rock the boat. Good luck in your endeavors. I'm happy we can get Lucy the help she sorely needs. And I'm so very sorry about your parents. —Gary Somers."

Gary turned back to Lucy and craned his neck to see what she was typing.

Lucy hurried to delete any past messages to and from Margo, then blocked Margo's contact. Lastly, she created a new contact under the same name, "Margo Sharpe," and changed the last digit of the phone number, in case he ever tried to contact her himself. It would at least buy her some time if it appeared as if Margo's number was still stored in the phone. At least the real Margo could never contact him again. Thankfully, imbecile Gary barely knew how to work a phone, so he wouldn't be able to figure any of this out.

She smiled up at Gary and handed back the phone.

"I was just checking something. I thought maybe she'd texted you while you were here, but she didn't. If she does, we'll want to enter it into our court evidence. That's harassment. You'll let me know, right?"

He took the phone back, frowning. "Okay."

"And you'll go back to Mom and tell her I'm good?"

"I will tell her you're doing...fine. That you're reconnecting with your brother. I may leave out the rest. She's a ball of nerves lately—and when I go back there empty-handed—"

"That's a fantastic idea," Lucy said, grinning.

Brad stood up. Gary, out of propriety, stood as well. Brad put a hand on Gary's back and gently led him to the door.

"We'll let you know how everything shakes out," Brad said, gruffly. "I'm glad Lucy has you in her corner. In our corner."

Gary was shuffled outside.

Lucy was pleased. Sure, she'd freaked out in the beginning, tearing out of Brad's room; she'd been forced to intervene. She couldn't just let Gary wander around Southie looking for her and calling the cops with wellness checks or whatever else he had up his sleeve.

In fact, Lucy should have banked on this dazed acceptance all along. Gary got overwhelmed sometimes when faced with too many inexplicable (to him) details and stressful situations. Like when Lucy had told him perfect Savannah was off her face on molly at her school dance, even though Savannah made Lucy swear not to tell their naive father.

"She's...what?" he'd said, horrified. "Are you saying she has a... girlfriend, some Molly person? Oh, dear. Well, best to let Savvy experiment, I say. She's a beautiful girl. Anyone would be lucky to have her, whatever gender. I'm a very understanding person, I hope you know."

"Oh, for fuck's sake, Dad," Lucy had screamed. "She's on drugs!"

Now Lucy walked him to the car, which did indeed have a ticket on it.

In case Margo was lurking somewhere, watching, Lucy put on a show, wiping her eyes, a whole performance. She even got into the car with Gary, saying she wanted to grab a coffee with him before he hit the road. He was so glad.

Afterward, she made him drop her off down the road "at a friend's house." She promised to come home for Easter, and to call home once a week.

Tearfully, off went Gary Somers, back to Pennsylvania, and hopefully out of her hair long enough that she could finish what she'd started.

* * *

Lucy practically skipped back to Brad's, feeling that she'd been getting sharper, wiser, more attuned to her surroundings, and to controlling others.

When she got there, Brad was sitting on the couch, his face stony.

"What's wrong?" she said.

"All that stuff about the grad school recruiter...was any of that true? Because for a few seconds there, I thought..."

She beamed back at him. "Nah, none of it was true."

He shifted uneasily on the couch. "You're a really good liar."

"Thank you."

"He seemed like a nice guy. He obviously cares about you. I'm starting to feel weird about this whole...operation, to be honest."

Lucy bristled at this, but right then the front door opened and Peter entered.

"Ellis," he said, as he passed through the living room. He didn't acknowledge Lucy. "Rent's a week late."

Brad ran his fingers through his hair. "Shit, yeah—I'll get it to you."

"Like, tonight," Peter called from the kitchen.

"Yeah, tonight." Brad looked at Lucy. "Make yourself scarce for a while, yeah? Because I've got a date. Two, actually. Drinks with one, dinner with another."

"Where am I supposed to go?"

Brad shrugged. "It doesn't matter. Just out. Oh, and if you could get me your share of the rent money. Zenpay it over. Then we're square, yeah?"

52

Margo

A knock sounded at the front door. I shot up from bed, bleary-eyed, and then stood in the center of the room, frozen and disoriented. I listened for a moment in the dark. It could have been a dream. Also, I wasn't sure whether it was early in the morning or late at night.

The knock came again; I hadn't dreamt it.

Reaching into the closet, I snatched an old field hockey stick and raced downstairs to the kitchen, lifting the eviction envelope from the counter, clutching it in my sweaty palm.

I'd tried one last time to pawn it off on Gary, but he'd refused to take it, convinced we would sort this all out like civilized people; once he got Lucy the help she needed, everything would be hunky-dory. *You're delusional*! I'd wanted to scream, but his eyes were so kind, his intentions, so pure—just one of those people that melt you without even trying—that I didn't say anything. I sent him on his way, to Brad's.

I knew when he got there the Bobbsey Twins would tell him about whatever was in the trunk—which was nothing good, *it couldn't be good*—and worst of all, they'd tell him who I was. Because clearly, Lucy knew.

Another three knocks came hard, insistent.

I strode down the hallway, the field hockey stick feeling foolish in my hand, and at the front door, checked the peephole.

At the sight of who it was, I drew back. A mixture of emotions: relief, because it was Jessie. Dread, because it wasn't Lucy, and we were once again delaying the inevitable. I couldn't legally evict someone who wouldn't come home. Especially someone who'd decided to torment me and ruin my life from afar.

* * *

Jessie wore a ski parka and a smile, and in her hand, she brandished two tickets.

"Call out sick. We're going skiing."

I rubbed my eyes, as if I was still groggy from sleeping and not completely wired and freaked. I led Jessie inside and down the hallway toward the kitchen to make coffee, where the clock said it was six a.m.

"I called you last night," Jessie said. "And again, on my way up. But your phone went to voicemail, and the mailbox was full."

I rinsed the coffee pot at the sink, keeping my eyes forward, facing the sauce-stained backsplash. I'd cleaned up a little since Gary had gone, but not that well. I still hadn't had the energy.

"I don't need to call out sick. I'm off today." And every other day, I thought. "Let's do it."

"Great," Jessie said, tapping her fingers on the table and looking around at the water glasses scattered about, the bills on the counter.

I knew I would need to clean this place, for real, at some point. The only reason would be so when someone came upon my body after I killed myself (When? Soon), the state of the house wouldn't be too embarrassing. Also, I didn't want poor Izzie to have to clean up the remains of yet another family member. I couldn't bear the thought of her having to scrape old egg pans on top of it all.

I poured Jessie some coffee when it was ready and then went upstairs to pack. As I threw thick socks and undershirts into my duffel bag, I set aside my worry over leaving the house unmanned. Clearly, from the camera footage, someone had made copies of the keys. What could they steal, after all? I had nothing of real value. They could torch the place. It would be doing me a favor, really.

What's the alternative, I wondered. Stay here, in the only place where Lucy knows to look?

* * *

The chairlift floated up and up, eventually dropping us at Black Hole, a double black diamond, the most difficult trail on the mountain. I was grateful we were able to simply strap on our boots and get right to the chairlift. No sitting around, talking, catching up. That would come later.

Earlier in the car, as I was pulling out of my street, Jessie had said, "You look off. Is everything okay?"

"Everything's fine," I said. "I just *really* need to get out of the city."

Once we got on the highway, I noticed Jessie wasn't talking much either; she kept checking her phone, then returning it to her lap and staring out the window. About midway through the trip I turned the dial down on the radio and sucked in my breath before asking, "How's your mom?"

Jessie kept her gaze out the window, saying nothing at first. "I found her a decent hospice facility. It was tough getting her to agree to go. She was taken there, yesterday."

"Oh, Jessie, I'm so sorry."

Jessie nodded, and then there was silence for several exits. I put on some Leon Bridges, Jessie's favorite, or at least he used to be, and Jessie turned the volume up. After a while, Jessie fell asleep, face pressed against the glass. I hadn't exactly been eager to tell Jessie about Lucy and the madness trailing me like a shadow, but now, I was certain: The last thing I wanted to do was worry her—not with everything she had going on with her mother.

What would Jessie think of me, anyway, knowing how awful I'd been to Dan—how I'd pushed him to the edge until he fell off, taking my parents with him? Jessie would think me a monster. I couldn't afford to lose her. Not again.

Now, the two of us peered down the steep pitch, turning back to review the trail and condition signs: "Caution: Ungroomed terrain. Packed powder. Continuous pitch."

"I'm rusty," Jessie said. "You go, and I'll follow."

"I'll take it slow," I promised.

We threaded down, taking wide turns where we could, navigating the capillary-thin alleys where we couldn't. The gorgeous glade of evergreens surrounding us went nearly unnoticed, nerves and focus superseding all other senses.

Suddenly, Jessie, close behind, shouted, "Wait, stop."

I heeded her call. I looked down, absorbing the severity of the slope before us, the darkness of the glade beneath.

Jessie pulled up beside me and stood up straight, gripping her poles.

"Follow me." Jessie was the more technical skier; it was better that she led. I was faster, more daredevilish, often getting myself into trouble.

Jessie got us down safely, and after a few more runs, we went inside the lodge for lunch.

There was a slim opening at the end of a long wooden table, set against a row of cubbies, where I stuffed our backpacks and gloves. The rest of the table was taken up by a hodgepodge of families, with small children eating home-brought lunches. The kids sprayed Goldfish all over the table and floor, their puffy winterized bodies lined up on the bench like little ducklings.

"You on the wagon or something?" Jessie said, eyeing my water.

"Trying to save money."

Jessie got up, strode to the bar, and came back with two beers.

"You drove," she reminded me after I protested, and then said, "So. You haven't said a word about the roommate. Lucy, right? How are things going?"

I squirmed a little on the hard bench and scrunched my napkin into a ball. "Things are fine."

"Uh-uh. You forget I *know* you. Something's up. You haven't answered Izzie's calls in over a week. She said you text her one-word answers, or not at all. She's worried."

I shot up from the table, blinking hard, chest hot with anxiety.

"Is that the only reason you're here? Because Izzie sent you?"

Jessie opened her mouth to protest, but I pointed to the bathroom sign and said, "Be right back."

Jessie called after me but I pretended not to hear, and headed for the stairs that led down to the ladies' room, on the lower level. As I looked down, a figure came into view at the base of the steps. Blonde. Goggles down. Gray coat. The woman looked up and seemed to catch my eye, though I couldn't be sure, through her goggles. She looked quickly away and took off toward the bathroom, her black rental boots loud and unwieldy.

I rushed to follow, but a group of boys in neon-colored coats and snowboard boots cut in front of me, roughhousing and taking their sweet time plodding down the steps. When I finally reached the bottom, the bathroom door was slowly swinging shut. But before it did, there was that gray jacket, that wiry blonde hair. I jostled a woman with a small child to get by, then burst through the door.

"Lucy?" I called. I looked beneath every stall door, clomping past the women at the sinks. Nothing. I tried the other side, identical with matching stalls. At the very last stall at the far end, finally, were the scratched black rental boots. I pounded on the door.

"Come out, Lucy. Now."

The door unlatched, slowly, then opened.

"Fuck," I said, slowly backing away. "I'm sorry, I thought you were—"

A wide-eyed, blonde stranger gaped back at me. "Can I *help* you?"

* * *

"Margo—you in here?" Jessie's words echoed off the bathroom walls. It had been fifteen minutes.

She drew closer and stopped at the last stall.

I undid the latch and opened the door. "Jessie, I think I need help."

Margo

"I remember being so mad at you that summer." Jessie, sitting on the couch, adjusted her legs beneath a blanket. She had a faraway look on her face.

I'd just finished telling her everything.

We'd decided to stay overnight at the mountain. A four-hundred-square-foot "cozy ski chalet" was the cheapest thing we could find to rent, an obscure Airbnb with a low satisfaction rating ("Unless you're the size of my left foot, the place is CRAMPED.").

Jessie had paid the lion's share. It was directly above the kitchen of a restaurant, and the sounds of barked orders and clanging dishes seeped through the floor.

"I missed your mom's charity walk," I said, quietly. I was sitting cross-legged on the floor. "That was my first strike."

It was a Relay for Life walk, down at the high school track, right after Jessie's mom was first diagnosed, which back then was accompanied by lots of pink and hope. I didn't go because I'd become so absorbed in my texts to Dan, infatuated with my own cruelty, and I also feared leaving my mother home alone. The cancer walk came and went, and it was dark by the time I realized how much time had passed, how much time I'd spent beneath my covers, leaving voicemails, my voice raw, and sending text messages, leaving me with stiff fingers.

"Yeah, that was one of the major things," Jessie said. "But you were so distracted and flighty, in general. I thought you didn't care about my mom or me—about anyone but yourself, really. I remember thinking you had a secret boyfriend, because you were shadily texting all the time. I think I called you selfish. And self-absorbed." Jessie looked down.

"You did, and I was," I said. "I was nasty and angry at the world."

Jessie pondered this a moment. "I've run it over and over in my mind, wondering if I did something wrong to make you never speak to me again. Now, it's worse, because what if I'd sat you down back then and really talked to you—pressed you to tell me what was going on."

I was shaking even though I was wrapped in a blanket, and not just because the apartment was frigid.

"You couldn't have done anything, Jessie. And Izzie couldn't have either." I was quiet for a few seconds, allowing, for once, the memories to prick through. "I started to realize things had gotten out of control when he started calling me back, because for a while he'd ignored me, which would just make me madder. He'd leave me voicemails where he'd say he believed my mother was undercover, and that my father was in witness protection, and not really her husband, and that they'd been secretly married in Vegas in 1974. My mom would have been like, two years old. It was bonkers, and it got worse and worse, him spewing all kinds of shit. He thought he was carrying out a government coup."

264

I looked up, imploringly, at Jessie. "I *made* him that way. Because before, sure, he had a crush on my mom, and he'd follow her around all the time and stuff, flirt with her—and maybe he was deluded about how she felt about him—but he wasn't, like, spewing conspiracy theories. You have to understand," my eyes were misty, "that I truly just thought the laxatives would make him shit his pants so bad that he'd stop coming over for a while. That if I kept telling him what a piece of shit he was, he'd be embarrassed and angry enough to move away. It was so stupid but honestly, that's all. I swear I meant to swap the pills back, but I couldn't get back into his house. He'd started to deadbolt the doors.

"I didn't even know what medication he was taking, or how badly he needed it to keep it together. I figured it was, like, Xanax or something, and it wouldn't matter if I swapped his pills for the laxatives. All I wanted was for him to stay away. In the end, all it took was a week, two weeks, tops, of him being off his meds, and it was enough for him to completely lose it." My responsibility for what happened had now been recast in my mind as a given, a bald fact. "I messed with his brain, Jessie. If I hadn't switched the pills, he wouldn't have killed my parents."

Jessie waited to be sure I finished, and then finally spoke.

"Margo, you're explaining things to me as if I won't believe you, which is nonsense. I do believe you. What happened was tragic, and you made some awful, immature mistakes, but you need to stop blaming yourself. I don't know how in the world you think what *he* did is *your* fault. You've been stewing in this for years, torturing yourself. You need to lean on people like me and Izzie. And that Owen guy—he works in security, right? Regardless, you said he has Southie connections, so let him help you stay safe, and I'm not just talking about cameras. Don't face this Lucy girl alone. She sounds just as malevolent as Dirty Fucking Dan."

My throat thick and my face drenched in tears, I thanked her for believing me. Thanked her for being here. I told her she was right about everything.

The wine bottle sat empty on the table. Our glasses, too.

Jessie yawned, said she was going to bed.

I stayed on the floor and looked up at her. "What I need to do next is warn Brad. God knows what she's been telling him, probably acting all sweet and innocent. She's dangerous. He needs to know."

Jessie sat back on the couch and frowned. "I'm sorry, what? *Warn* Brad? Come on. He's on team Lucy, and he sounds like an asshole. Margo, after everything that's happened, you're still stuck on this guy?"

After a moment I shook my head. "Forget I said that. You're right. It's like a habit, like I'm addicted to the idea of him. The real him isn't so nice, I guess."

"Promise me one thing," Jessie said as she stood up again. "The second you dip your toe into the *real* dating world, you'll please, for the love of God, go back to your natural hair color. It looks like..."

I examined a few strands between my first and middle finger. "Like what?"

"I don't know. Like you're Lydia from *Beetlejuice* or something. It's terrible. And your bangs—Jesus. The second you get home, make a hair appointment. Tell them you're a *blonde*."

I grinned, despite myself. "Deal."

* * *

We decided to ski for another half-day before heading home. The morning cloud cover was so thick it almost looked like it was nighttime. The chairlifts were mostly empty, too, except for a few snowboarders hooting into the crisp air.

I wanted to squeeze every moment out of being away from home, of not facing my problems. It made me a little reckless on the trails. I sped up and careened into the woods, finding makeshift paths, until I took a turn into what I thought was the same trail as Jessie, who'd shot ahead. But it wasn't a trail at all.

I stopped and tried to get my bearings. I pulled out my phone to bring up the trail map on SKIngle. No service. Still, I tried sending a text to Jessie. "LOST! I think I'm near the Brave Brothers trail?" It wouldn't deliver.

Eventually, I shot out of a little clearing and found myself back on a main trail. But the drop had grown more precipitous, the path narrower.

I jerked a little, my right ski slipping on some ice. I was going too fast. As I attempted a sharp turn to slow down, I heard someone approaching from behind, on the left, foretold by a whooshing sound.

I turned my head slightly to the left.

It was a snowboarder, coming fast: a flash of neon-yellow, heading straight at me. There was a small spray of ice and then, *wham!* The force sent me flying into the woods. As I skidded and crashed into the branches, my left ski snapped off, a release, as it was designed to do. But the right ski didn't. That knee twisted, and I impelled my body to keep moving, keep tumbling so as not to make a hard stop, so as not to break any bones, if I hadn't already.

My sight cleared right as I torpedoed into a pine. I thought I heard a snap. Something in my body, but where? Next I was on the ground, unable to move.

Then, a quick succession of sounds: the scraping of snow beneath a board, the weight of a body hopping back on, a couple snaps, and then a prepubescent voice fading as he pushed off, "Watch it, bitch!"

I howled in pain, into the snow. I tried to get up, but the left side—where the snowboarder had struck—exploded in pain. My knee wasn't as bad as I'd suspected; at least I could move it. My head was another story. I could barely lift it off the ground.

Breathing sounds, huffing. The crunching of snow. Breaking sticks. A figure approached from deeper in the woods. A woman, it looked like, hair tucked inside a helmet, goggles masking her eyes. A gaiter covering her from neck to nose. Black rental boots, a jacket too large, pants too large. No poles or skis. If only I could run, walk, crawl, anything, because on the woman's hands—Lucy's hands—were my mother's old, bright pink gloves.

Lucy drew nearer and stood over me, wordless.

I didn't see the boot coming at my head; I was barely conscious of it, barely felt the ringing blow.

My whole body fell limp.

My cheek was resting on the snow. The cold felt so good against my face, as did the snowflakes that had started to fall.

I closed my eyes.

* * *

When I opened them, I was in a hospital. There were cards and balloons everywhere—one with a paw on it, from Owen/Bearie no doubt—and Jessie was sitting at my side, adjusting my blanket.

"We found you underneath a steep ridge," Jessie explained, handing me an apple juice carton and adjusting the straw so I could sip it.

I leaned my head toward the straw. The pain was almost blinding.

"It's a miracle you ended up with only a cervical fracture and a sprained knee."

I looked up at Jessie, suddenly remembering those final moments.

"I saw Lucy. She did this."

Jessie tilted her head and grimaced. "You woke up a couple of times, saying that already. I'm sorry, Margo, but I don't think that's possible. You got hit by a kid on a snowboard."

"I know that, but...she was there. She kicked me in the head—"

Jessie shook her head. "The kid who hit you called Ski Patrol and stayed with you the whole time. He didn't see anyone else there. He was certain of it."

"The boy called them?" I said. Everything was muddled. "No, he left me there."

"Well, he did, but then he felt bad—or rather, his friends made him feel bad for leaving you. After he found cell service, he called Ski Patrol and then went to wait with you. He's the reason we found you so quick. You were out cold. He's a real sweetie, stayed by your side. He and his mom left you that card over there." Jessie pointed to the windowsill. It was a homemade card that said, "Get well, Margo—I am sorry!"

"I must have been dreaming," I said.

"Must have," Jessie agreed.

But Lucy had seemed so real.

And if she hadn't been there, the truly terrifying was this: How much of all this was in my head? Suddenly I felt like my brain wasn't working properly, like everything that had been happening thus far with Lucy wasn't real, or at the very least, wasn't as horrible as I'd worked myself up to think it was.

But then again, *No*, I thought. Those *were* real rats in my bed. Dan's trunk—it was real. I'd helped carry it up the stairs. Lucy *had* plotted to live with me. Stephanie from across the street had witnessed her bizarre behavior. Then there was Astrid, and all the madness with my job and Corinne. It was all real. It couldn't be denied.

While Jessie nattered on, trying to keep my spirits up, I doubled down on what I believed I'd seen: Lucy. She'd been out there on that mountain, wearing the same bright pink gloves—my mom's old pair—that she'd borrowed the day of my work trip. I was certain of it. And next time, I might not be so lucky.

Next time, I might end up dead.

54

Margo

I hung up with the insurance agent and let out a sigh of relief. I was at least covered until the end of the month. Still no word from Corinne about my job, and I was afraid to ask. All I knew was I was blocked from work email and my paychecks had stalled. All else was a mystery.

Sitting on a high stool in a coffee shop, I faced the window and stared straight ahead. I had to, because it hurt to look down, wearing the neck brace. Texting was most painful; craning my neck and hunching over the phone was out of the question. I was abstaining from taking the pain medication as prescribed. Instead, I'd been stockpiling the pills. Just in case I needed them for something more major.

As the minutes dragged on I stared and stared, dead-eyed, at Brad's apartment. I had a direct view through the window. No activity, no lights, no comings or goings.

I had nothing else to do, so I ordered coffee after coffee until, as chance would have it, I saw the door opening and Brad hopping down his steps. My chest throbbed as he crossed the street and walked right into the coffee shop.

I was two seats in from the door. He hadn't seen me through the window, and didn't look over at me now as he strode past. He ordered at the counter, large banana hazelnut, black. The girl at the counter rang him up. "BHaz for Brad," she called to the person behind her making the coffee, and then rang him up.

I'd swiveled around on my stool to watch him, but after he got his change and took his coffee, I swiveled back to face the window. I stared at the reflection and watched his tall, dark form approach the door. He was leaving. This brought on both immense relief and disappointment.

But then, a slight hesitation. His free hand patted his jacket pocket. He stopped completely, turned, and came right up to the stool beside me and sat. He set his coffee cup down and took out his phone from his pocket. Out of the corner of my eye I could see the screen, some sort of betting app with football logos—Giants, Falcons, Panthers. A few seconds later, when he went to sip his coffee, he brushed my arm. "Sorry," he murmured, not looking up.

I remained erect, wooden, barely breathing. I knew I looked different now, newly blonde and in a neck brace, but did he truly not *know*? Was he pretending? Was this some sick little game?

I rotated to the right, expecting to see Lucy in some cartoonish disguise, low-brimmed hat or face-swallowing sunglasses, further down at another window stool. But the shop was small. There was no one of the sort.

Finally, I cleared my throat. "Brad."

His head jerked up. He stared at me blankly, his eyes traveling to the neck brace, then back up to my face.

"It's me. Margo." I almost said Maggie, because what was the difference?

"Jesus. What happened to you?"

"Someone hit me from behind when I was skiing. Knocked me out." My tone was cool.

"Huh," he said, hopping off the stool. He reached for his coffee and put his phone in his pocket. His eyes were on the door. He was leaving, and fast.

"Wait," I said, lightly touching his sleeve, which he drew back, as if I was poisonous. "Will you give Lucy this eviction notice?" I'd pulled the envelope from my pocket and now held it out to him. "She won. She fucked me over, humiliated me, made my life hell. So, it's over. Please, make it be over."

He didn't take the envelope and instead, started to back away, scowling. "Leave me out of it."

"She was at the mountain," I blurted. I had to keep him here. He had to hear this. Even if my strained voice made me sound manic, out of control. "She—I don't know how, but she did this." I pointed to the brace.

Brad sighed, exasperated. "I don't track her every move. I've been busy with...guests."

Girls, I knew. I'd been watching.

"That trunk you took," I said. "I have some idea what might be inside. The police never recovered your dad's phone, so..." I looked down, ashamed. "I know how awful I look. It's horrible, what I did to him. But trust me, I've been sorry every day since, and will be for the rest of my life. I mean, look at what I've done. Would you want to live with that? Would you ever forgive yourself?"

His eye twitched. He'd stopped moving, at least, and stood very, very still.

I pressed on.

"But Dan wasn't some saint, okay? He was a *bad* guy. Gary told you, right? How Lucy was conceived? Why Lucy's mother kept his identity secret? She was *raped*, Brad. And I know for a fact you had zero relationship with him. I remember my mom telling me, a long time ago, about the little she knew about you. Dan told her he never got to see you, because your mom didn't want you around him. He played the victim in that situation, but if I had to bet"—I stared deep into his eyes, pleading—"he didn't treat your mom so well, either."

"This is too much. I shouldn't be talking to you. My lawyer advised against it."

"Lawyer?" I said. "For *what*?"

He'd already made for the door. But his last words, over his shoulder, rang out in his wake. "You should know she has the pill bottle. And all the transcripts. It doesn't look good for you. You need to stop watching me. Stop *stalking* me."

The pill bottle. So that was it. She knew everything.

One small mercy: As I watched Brad head down the sidewalk, I saw that his face was red, eyes glassy. As soon as I'd mentioned his mom, what Dan might have done to her, Brad had looked visibly upset. Disturbed.

At least I'd struck a nerve.

55

Lucy

Lucy watched as he strode out of the coffee shop, watched as Margo mooned at him through the window like some abandoned shelter animal.

He rounded the corner and almost walked right into her.

"What the hell, Lucy?" he snarled. "You're watching me, too?"

"What did she say?"

"Move!"

She crossed her arms and widened her stance. There were garbage bins on one side and a car parked hubcap-to-curb on the other. He would have to bulldoze his way past, or double back to get by.

"She's all banged up," she said, her tongue pressing into her bottom lip to keep from smiling. "Wonder how that happened."

"Did you do that? You and Astrid?"

She took a small step back. "No," she said carefully. "I *wish* I did, though."

He rubbed his eyes. "She said she thought she saw you on the mountain. If that was you, you could have killed her. What were you thinking?"

She put her hands on her hips. "Oh, come on. You think I hauled ass to some random mountain just to push her around? How would I know she was even there? I can't even fucking *ski*." She stared at him a moment. "See, Brad, look at what she's doing. Oh, poor battered Margo, crying wolf. I bet she's faking that injury. Don't you see how she's a *lying sneak?*"

Brad's eyes lasered into hers. "Did Dan rape your mom?"

Her face darkened. *Fucking Gary!*

"Of course not. My mom *cried* rape. She was lying."

"How could you say something like that about your own mom? And how do you even know that for sure?"

"It's all in Daddy's letters to me, dumb-dumb."

"What are you, twelve? Why didn't you show me those letters?"

"He wrote them to me, not you."

"What did the letters say?"

She rolled her eyes. "Jesus, calm down. I told you, he left me instructions. He told me all about the trunk, how he'd been scared of Margo—*Maggie*—and that she was driving him to think and do bad things." She hesitated. "There *may* have been a few things about aliens and government cover-ups, but that's because he wasn't taking his meds." Then she said, with nonchalance, "He also added me to his will or whatever."

Brad gaped at her. "Dan left you his *money?* You never told me that. How much?"

"I don't know," she said, shrugging. "Everything? The money had just been *sitting* in an account tied up in his estate, for *years*. My mom ignored all the notices from his lawyers when they'd been trying to

276

sort everything out and identify his heirs. She was spooked. Little did that bitch know, she was sitting on his entire estate."

"He named you his sole heir," Brad said, flatly. "Unbelievable."

She nodded and smiled sweetly. "Uh-huh."

She stepped aside now and gave an affected bow. He was beginning to irritate her, and she had work to do, anyway.

He stayed put, though, and crossed his arms. The empty coffee cup was still in his hand.

"I don't know if I want to do this anymore. I have a bad feeling."

Lucy's smile fell. "Are you kidding me?"

"No. I'm dead serious. I think it's time you cool it and stay away from me for a while. Hey—stop pulling at your hair like that—*stop*." He reached out and yanked her hand down.

"Ow," she cried, clasping her wrist.

"Oh, come on," he scoffed, "I barely touched you."

Suddenly, Lucy noticed a man watching from across the street. He was around her age with a big beard. With him, on a leash, was a massive black dog.

The name came to her: *Bearie.* The nasty drool-factory Margo would walk for chump change. Afterward, without fail, Margo would trail in layers of fur on her pant legs, making Lucy's allergies act up. One time, Lucy asked Margo, *politely,* to stop walking him and said that the excess dander was endangering her health. Margo had looked at her like she'd asked her to slit the dog's throat. "No," Margo had answered, glowering at her. Then again, more firmly, "*No.*"

Now, Lucy tilted her head back, twisted her face into the biggest grin she could manage, and laughed loudly. "Brad! You're *so* funny."

Brad looked at her incredulously. "What is *wrong* with you?"

Through gritted teeth she said, in a singsong voice, "There's a spy, over there, but don't look."

Of course he looked, and then turned immediately back to Lucy. "That's the guy—"

"Who was there when you got the trunk," Lucy finished. "His name is Tommy, and he is Southie trash. He and his fat old dad are all protective of poor little orphan Margo because she went yapping to them about the rats, and whatever else. She's such a baby." She rolled her eyes. Then, remembering, she smiled and said, "Just to piss her off, I told her I thought he was cute. It was *great*."

Brad stared at her. Then he drew in a breath. "That's it. I'm calling my attorney and putting everything on hold."

"*What*?" Lucy drew out the word. "You have to be joking. After everything I showed you that she did to Daddy?"

Brad looked back in the direction of Tommy, and Lucy followed his gaze. But Tommy was gone.

Brad patted his pocket, his phone. "I need to talk to my mom. She's always shielded me from the real reason she got sole custody, why she never wanted me to see him. And if what Gary says is true about how *you* were conceived—"

"No, no, no. Daddy and my mom were in *love*—a 'Cape Cod love affair,' he called it, on the *dunes of the cape*—he wrote those lyrics in his letters, included pictures of them, happy. I have proof, Brad. And then what does my mom do? Hides her pregnancy from him, jumps ship, and pawns me off on *Gary*. It's all in Daddy's letters. Take the red pill, Brad; don't believe everything you hear."

But Brad was already walking away.

* * *

Lucy was self-aware enough to know that she was not an attractive person, inside or out. It wasn't something she ruminated over; it was simply a fact. But charm and good looks were what drove the listenability, the *salability*, of any good crime story, any story with

278

legs that led to book deals and TV spinoffs and everything else she'd pinned to her vision board.

Without Brad, there was no story.

Worse, what if she got Brad to take part in the interviews, and Brad painted Daddy in a bad light? Margo's crime would then be seen as a favor to society.

Lucy couldn't have that.

If she lost Brad—she hadn't, not yet; but if worse came to worse, and she did—she would have to pivot. And do something big.

She texted Astrid, thankfully away visiting family while on unpaid leave: "I'm staying at your place again this week."

Margo

Downstairs, I tossed and turned on the couch, half dreaming of Brad running his fingers through my hair, newly blonde. *The lawyers told me not to speak to you.*

The soft caresses turned, progressively, to hard tugs. And his whispers grew crueler.

You killed my father. Prepare to die.

He began to yank my hair with violent force, bashing my head on the arm of the couch, again and again and again.

Prepare to die.

My eyes shot open. But the taunts from my dream resumed, on a loop. It wasn't coming from my dream anymore. No. It was real. The sound was coming from somewhere.

Heart pounding, I stood up. I flipped on the hall light and checked the front door. Dead-bolted. The kitchen was empty.

But the familiar male voice persisted. Like it was coming out of a speaker.

I walked back to the living room and pressed my ear to the TV, feeling idiotic. It was off, of course. No sound.

I returned to the hallway and walked toward the kitchen.

Now the audio grew stronger, echoing off the walls.

Prepare to die.

It was so close.

The camera. I looked up at the small black bulb above my head, at the blinking red light. That's where the sound was coming from. The cameras.

Suddenly, the audio recording cut out. Now, it was Lucy's voice: "Just do it already, you miserable bitch. Do the world a favor and kill yourself."

57

Lucy

Lucy lolled around in Astrid's bed, sleeping in after her late night.

At some point early in the afternoon, Astrid's gleeful voice rang out in the hallway. "*I'm not fired!*"

Lucy covered her ears with a pillow and groaned.

Astrid pounded down the hall toward the bedroom and flopped onto the bed beside Lucy, yanking the pillow off her head.

"Corinne called. She put me on probation. All I have to do is take a stupid workplace bullying seminar." She snorted. "But whatever—I still have my job." She squealed and shook Lucy by the shoulders. "Isn't that fucking amazing?"

Lucy wriggled away and sat up. "What'd she say about fuck-face?"

Astrid winced. "We had a long talk about her. Like, Corinne knows she lied on her résumé about college and stuff, but she also said

Margo's been through a lot. She feels terrible for her, and I couldn't argue with that—"

"Does she have a job or not?"

"It's not decided, like, officially? But I *think* Corinne wants to give her another chance."

Lucy whipped a pillow at Astrid's face. "Great job."

"Sorry, but I was more concerned about myself. Like, I'm not rich off some dead dude like you. My parents told me I need to be more independent. They're even making me pay my own *rent* now." She twisted up her face at this, then added, "As long as I have a job, that's all I care about—"

"That dead dude was my *dad*, you bitch." She regretted ever telling Astrid about her inheritance. She regretted involving her at all.

"Yeah," Astrid scoffed, "but you didn't know him. Like, how sad could you be?"

"Really fucking sad," Lucy snarled.

She got up from the bed and sat at Astrid's vanity. Her hair was pressed flat on one side, frizzed out on the other. She took her phone out. When she saw what had come into her email, she gasped.

"What?" Astrid asked, leaning forward, attempting to see.

"I got a reply from <u>Dirty Vines</u>. *Took* them long enough."

"What does it say?"

The subject line said, "Re: Crime Tip," and the email was long. A good sign.

Lucy began to read, excitedly. But the further down she scanned, the wider her eyes got.

"No," she said, violently shaking her head. "No, they're not *getting* it!"

> *We are so stoked to have you as such an avid fan! Unfortunately we get hundreds of tips a year for crimes to investigate or revisit, and while yours sounds compelling, we looked into it and just can't really get on board with your angle—a*

redemption story for a man who murdered two innocent people...

She scanned further down, her vision off kilter.

> We would appreciate it if you'd stop sending so many requests—on the hotline, over email, in our DMs. We are aware they are all from you, despite the different usernames.

Her eyes shot down to the last paragraph:

> However, if you happen to have a line on Margo, we were thinking she would make a great get, if she'd be willing to talk to us. We think our listeners would be fascinated by her compelling story...

Lucy chucked her phone across the room. It hit the wall and bounced to the floor.

"Hey, you'll scratch the paint," Astrid said, reaching down and handing it back to Lucy. "I take it they said no."

Lucy seethed, her mind going a mile a minute. She was barely aware of Astrid, shifting from foot to foot, chewing her nails and staring at her.

Finally, Lucy yelled, "Would you quit that? *What?*"

"I have to tell you something."

Astrid turned to fluff the pillows and took a deep breath.

"I can't be messing with Margo anymore. Not if I want to keep my job. It was hilarious, like, at first? But it's gotten out of hand. I mean, I saw her walking around the other day in that neck brace. You can't miss her. Her eyes are all dead looking, and her face all bruised."

She thought a moment.

"You know what's weird, though? She has that blonde hair now, and her bangs are all grown out. She looks kinda pretty—"

"What are you saying?"

"I'm *saying* that I think our friendship has come to an end. I mean, I definitely can't have you staying here anymore. Raj asked if you were going to start paying rent. He wasn't a fan of your, like, racist comments about his curry."

Lucy jerked her thumb to the wall. "I'm not being racist. It *stinks*!"

"You know what I think? I think you should call Brad, and go back to his place. I know he tends to kick you out a lot, 'cause of all his girls—which I can see would be annoying. Hey, maybe you could, like, go back to Pennsylvania? 'Cause you're done, right? Like, all those pranks. You can't go on *forever* like that. I'd say you had a successful run. You got your message across. And honestly, Lucy? Be glad you're done and you don't have to answer to anyone. At least you don't have to apologize to her in front of HR. Corinne said if she keeps Margo on, I'll have to do that. Part of the terms of keeping me employed. That's gonna be so mortifying."

Astrid was out of breath by the time she finished.

As she smiled her dumb, pig-faced smile, it took everything Lucy had not to skin her alive, just claw her ruddy, fat-sleeve of a face right off.

Instead, Lucy stood and attempted to smooth her unruly hair. She kept her tone steady, neutral. "Fine. Consider it done."

Astrid raised her eyebrows. "That's it? You're not mad?"

"What's done is done. This was all kinda crazy, anyway. You're so right." She stepped toward Astrid with her arms out.

Astrid took a wary step back.

Lucy continued to hold out her arms. "What, you scared of me or something?"

"No...of course not."

"Okay, then, hug me good-bye, *bestie*."

After a slight hesitation, Astrid extended her arms. Lucy leaned in and squeezed. Hard.

Lucy stepped back and smiled as Astrid, face pale, let out an audible breath.

"See you around, Ass Turd."

Lucy slammed the door so hard it rattled.

Margo

"Have you filed another police report?" Owen asked. He was standing in the corner, arms crossed. "This is harassment. Especially if she had something to do with your ski accident. I wouldn't put it past her."

Tommy was on the couch, fiddling around on his laptop. "You see this with baby monitors, people hacking in to use the talk feature and saying creepy shit to kids."

I sat beside him, staring into space, thinking.

I was thinking about yesterday, when the city health inspector had come by, responding to Lucy's "tenant complaint" over the mold and the plumbing; it turned out someone had been flushing feminine pads, along with reams of toilet paper, down the bottom-floor toilet. I was slapped with seven health code violations, accompanied by a stain on my record and fines I couldn't afford to pay.

289

"I saw her the other day, by the way," Tommy said, eyes still on the laptop screen. "She was talking to that pretty boy. The one who came for the trunk that day." He peered over at me. "They were fighting on the sidewalk, over on M Street. They were going at it pretty hard about something."

I could only nod. Surely, a sibling spat Lucy would twist around and slither out of.

"Haven't seen ya down at The Sham lately," Owen said. He was watching me intently. "Bearie misses you."

I tried to smile but found tears were imminent. "It hurts to walk down there." What I didn't say was that it hurt to do anything. To walk. To think. To *be*.

Tommy and Owen exchanged glances. "I'm gonna put some calls in. Some favors. To keep an eye out for this Lucy girl. Keep you safe."

I nodded wearily. "Thanks."

All I wanted to do was sleep. I leaned back on the couch. Then, right in front of the two of them, I did.

I woke in the dark, a blanket across my lap. A Styrofoam box lay on the coffee table with a clean white napkin over the top. I opened the box, and inside was a Shamwich, cold now. Owen and Tommy must have gotten it for me.

Their kindness hurt. I didn't deserve it.

I shut the box without eating, and stood shakily. I tapped my phone screen. Seven more missed calls from Izzie. Six from Jessie. Dozens of unread texts. I deleted all without reading. Then, I went to go find the pills.

* * *

I woke with my face in my pillow, arm racked with pins and needles from hanging over the side of the bed. I got up, creakily, and in the bathroom opened the bottle with a shaking hand, and peered inside.

It was all coming back now. First pouring the pills—all of them—into my hand. Then, returning them one by one to the bottle, except for the five that remained in my palm. Feeling their weight, unable to ignore the one question that kept running through my mind, the only thing stopping me from taking them all down: What would it do to Izzie?

So, I'd compromised: I wouldn't die tonight. I'd just erase the pain. The five pills I washed down with a cheap bottle of red Lucy had left behind, a bottle I now recalled spiking onto the floor in the living room while deep into a hazy, depressing playlist of Pink Floyd, a favorite of my dad's.

I left my bedroom, all my muscles aching, slowly descending the stairs. Through the slats of the bannister, I saw the destruction.

Crystalline pieces spread down the hallway, in the living room, the kitchen. Black plastic and wiring and drywall. The small cuts and dried blood on my hands and feet made sense. I must have ripped the cameras from the wall, smashing them to pieces.

Now, I tiptoed around the shards, waves of anxiety undulating in my chest. I was thinking very hard and trying to remember where I kept the broom when a single, hard knock came at the front door.

"Honey? You need to let me in." My aunt. "I've been calling you nonstop. You're giving me a permanent heart attack. I'm serious." Pause. "Jessie said the two of you had a talk. She filled me in on Lucy to a point, but said you had more to tell me. Something about a trunk? Maggie—Margo, sorry. I'm just worried about you."

I scanned the broken pieces of plastic and glass in the hallway, and the smashed wine bottle out in the living room, the crimson spillage that had further stained the table and the rug. Then I looked at Izzie's forlorn, frightened face through the peephole.

"Please come back in twenty minutes. I have to clean up."

"Don't be ridiculous. You don't need to clean up for me. I'm not waiting out in the cold—"

"Twenty minutes."

* * *

I cleaned up the best I could and set out an air freshener—the wine smell in the living room was overpowering. In my periphery were the sparkles of shards I'd missed, under the kitchen table. I didn't bother cleaning them up. Instead I showered, which took me a while; it was still quite painful. I blow-dried my hair, even more painful. The whole process took far longer than twenty minutes.

Still, when I opened the door, Izzie was sitting on the front steps, waiting.

In the kitchen we settled in at the table.

"So—"

"I—"

"You talk," Izzie said, nodding me on.

"Izzie," I said, shaking my head, tears nearly blinding me. "I did something horrible. You'll never forgive me. If it wasn't for me, he wouldn't have done it." I covered my face in my hands.

"Who, Dan? That's insane, honey. Don't think like that."

"I know I need to tell you the rest, but I...can't." I felt like I might hyperventilate. I tried to take slow, deep breaths.

Izzie scooted her chair closer to me and started rubbing my back. I was faced with the familiar sensation of déjà vu, of the times Izzie comforted me by rubbing my back. It was after my parents were killed, but before their delayed joint funeral, too depressing and expensive to arrange right away, and we'd had to wait until the investigation wrapped up.

Every night, Izzie would come into the guest room at her house, where I was staying. This was when I was having my night terrors—horrific dreams, sweaty screams—and Izzie would climb in with me and run her fingers through my hair and rub her warm hands on my back. "I promise to protect you," she would whisper. "That's my job from here on out. I need to make sure you end up okay, and someday, happy. I owe it to my sister, and I owe it to you."

Then, when she thought I'd drifted off, Izzie would talk to herself—or rather, she would talk to Patty, whispering quietly, each word suffused with emotion. With raw hurt. "Why did you have to be such an *attention* hound, Patty? All our lives you just had to be the brightest and best. You always had to be—God. I suppose it doesn't matter. None of it matters now. It's too late. I should have seen the warning signs. He was a nuisance. It was a harmless crush. I should have paid more attention, and oh God, I'll never, *ever* forgive myself."

This memory—this scene, so starkly drawn in my memory—was what spurred me to speak up now, to tell Izzie once and for all what I'd done.

I started with the voicemails and text messages. The relentless taunts, the threats, the insults. Day after day, week after week.

Izzie didn't say anything, just listened, even when I got to the part about last night, and the pills. She was catatonic, staring at a spot on the table, and facing this silence I found I finally wanted to discuss *everything* now—not just what I did, but what would happen if Lucy exposed me. What would happen to me now.

Could Lucy make it so that I'd be tried for murder? Manslaughter? I followed all these stories in the news about girls who would taunt their boyfriends over text, telling them to kill themselves. I could picture the young women's hollow eyes, their drawn, pale faces beside lawyers in courtrooms, then later in their prison jumpsuits. At the coffee shop, Brad had mentioned lawyers...

Izzie stood up from the table. "I need to leave."

"Izzie—" I said, faltering. "I'm sorry. I'm scared. Will you stay with me? We can keep talking? Please?"

Until this moment, I'd had no idea how immense my desire for companionship really was, how fervently I needed someone who loved me, who knew me.

"Please," I said again. "Stay with me. I need you."

Izzie stared at me a moment. Her expression was hard to read, though her eyes were wet and her fists, clenched.

"You have lied to me so many times, Maggie. And that's your name, by the way. The name *my sister* gave you, right there in the hospital, when she looked into your tiny face." Her voice broke. "Your name is *Maggie*. You insist on calling yourself by another name, and you insist on being this other person. A slap in the face to your mother. And you lie to me. Again and again and again. That's what hurts the most. Not what you did; it's the lies. It's you shutting me out and making me worry and trying to fix things on your own. I asked you, back then, do you remember? Whether you thought Dan was a problem. I know you were a teenager, but you said no."

I shook my head, confused. "You asked me that?" It was entirely possible, though I didn't remember it. There was a lot about those weeks I'd blocked out.

Izzie's expression was cold. Colder than I'd ever seen it. Like she hated the sight of me.

"Yes. I did."

She stood, looped her purse strap over her shoulder, and strode toward the hallway without looking back.

"Where are you going?" I called. "Can't you stay? Please?"

She didn't answer, shutting the door behind her.

Lucy

BROTHER BRAD. Send.

    BROTHER BRAD. Send.

    BROTHER BRAD. Send.

    Fifty-one outgoing calls, and counting.

    Lucy had been outside Margo's for hours watching from her new car, a trade-in for that beige shit-box. (She didn't know why she hadn't been traveling around in luxury sooner. She certainly had the money for it. So, she'd settled on a brand-new BMW. Thank you, Daddy.)

    The aunt had come out an hour ago, her several chins bouncing as she flopped down the front steps, wiping tears from her eyes while Margo stood in the door with a pathetic, pleading look on her face. They'd had some sort of tiff, it seemed.

    But that's not what interested Lucy. Not really.

What interested her was the handsome visitor who'd arrived shortly after the aunt, hands stuffed in his pockets, looking sheepish. That *fucker*.

BROTHER BRAD. Send.

Fifty-two outgoing calls.

Finally, several minutes later—several agonizing minutes later—Margo's door opened.

Brad hopped down the steps and stepped into his truck, double-parked out front. The red chrome shone in the sun, as did the rims on the lifted tires. A brand-new truck. He'd talked Lucy into paying his rent and now he was buying a new *truck*.

A face shadowed in the window, watching him. Margo's. Her expression was inscrutable.

Lucy tailed him home. He found a street space directly out front. *Of course* he had that sort of luck, she thought. She double-parked across the street.

When he jumped out of the driver's seat, he turned right toward her and caught her eye. He rushed into his apartment, slamming and locking the door behind him, then drawing the curtains.

Lucy marched up and rapped on the door until her knuckles started to bleed. When it was clear he wasn't going to answer the door—and her hand couldn't take any more abuse—she got back into her car.

BROTHER BRAD. Send.

His voice mailbox was full. She'd left as many messages as it would hold.

It was starting to get dark. She pulled the visor down and looked at herself in the mirror. Her face was wet, but she hadn't felt herself crying. Tufts of hair lay on her lap, on the console, draped over the steering wheel. She hadn't felt any pain as the hair was ripped from her scalp, but as she touched the crown of her head, she supposed it did hurt. A little.

She stared down at her phone, willing him to pick up.

As for incoming calls, Brad hadn't called *her* in days.

She decided to take a break from calling Brad. For a while, she stared blankly ahead, into space.

Her phone began to ring in her hand. She picked it up, realizing too late that it was not Brad calling, but her parents. How had they gotten her new number?

Her mother crowed into the phone—she was in the kitchen; Lucy could hear dishes clattering in the sink: "Lucy, you picked up! I didn't expect—how are you? I'm calling because...well, *we're* calling—"

Gary, passive, obsequious Gary, piped up: "Luce, we'd love a visit. Bring your brother, even! The more the merrier."

Silence.

Her mother: "Hon? You there?"

"I'll ask him," Lucy said, absently—she thought she saw movement behind Brad's front window curtain. She pressed her nose into the cold car window and squinted.

Gary: "So whaddya say we secure a date? How 'bout next weekend."

"Can't," she said.

"The next?"

"Can't. I'll let you know."

Silence. Then, Gary again: "I'm curious—have you spoken with Dr. Reynolds?"

"Yeah. A couple times."

Her mother: "When?"

"I don't know. I've talked to him; that's all you need to know."

Someone on the line cleared their throat. A third person, whose phlegmy voice she knew too well. "I don't think you're telling the truth, Lucy."

Dr. Reject.

Now, they had her full attention.

"You *assholes*!" Lucy screeched. "You sneaky fucking assholes."

297

"Your brother is very worried about you—" started her mother.

Lucy, in shock, at first said nothing, and then cut her off.

"He would *never*. He would never call you and betray me like that."

"Well, he did," said Gary. "He gave me his number when I was there. When you were in the bathroom. I begged him. He's a nice fella, that Brad. I'm happy you found him. However, he's extremely concerned about your...behavior, so he called us. We've just been trying to get you to come home..."

Right then, Brad's front door opened. Lucy sat up straight.

A female emerged, blonde, like all the rest. Had she been there the whole time? Had he left her there while he went to Margo's? It was one of his Tinder dates. Lucy had seen messages on his phone the last time they were together. Her name was Taliaah or Everlyn or something stupid like that. It was an endless string of these robots.

The blonde shut the door behind her. Brad wasn't seeing her out— that would require decorum and respect. She wondered what he'd told the blonde about all the knocking and yelling. It didn't matter.

Lucy was forced to turn her attention back to the phone call, where all three of them—her mom, Gary, Dr. Reynolds—were still babbling, her mother's shrill voice against Gary's timid one, and Dr. Reynold's commanding.

Lucy began to talk.

Gary: "Judy, *shush*. Hon, could you repeat that?"

"I said, great job, dummies. You've done it. Now I'm never coming home. And Reynolds, you unethical prick, family friend or not, this is *so* against HIPAA. I could *ruin* you. And you all know how much money I have from my real father. It's why you're so nice to me, isn't it? It's why you're always trying to get me 'help'—all so you can get your hands on my money. Well, I'm not Britney Fuckin' Spears, you morons. That's *my* money. You will *never* get your hick hands on it. I will repeat for the zillionth time: I am thirty years old. I am as sane as your left tits. And I will not—ever—voluntarily check myself in *anywhere* again."

The three started to talk over each other again, but Lucy shouted even louder.

"As of today, I no longer consider myself your daughter. Burn my things and tell Savannah she sucks. Good-*bye*."

The car, and the night itself, turned very quiet.

She found, as she sat there, that she was not upset or sad, even if a few more chunks of hair had found their way to her lap. A load had been lifted. She'd needed that closure; she had needed to let them know they were the snakes she always knew they were. To fully and officially communicate her defection.

Brad's living room light turned off. Then the red home-alarm light turned on by the door.

It was at that moment she got an idea.

* * *

She chose a red wig and a profile name: Darlene. She liked Kurt Vonnegut, and Asian fusion was her "fave thing to nosh." She jacked a couple photos off Instagram, some aspiring model with big boobs and a decent nose. It took all of twenty minutes to create the profile and lure Brad out of bed for his latest conquest. She just had to say she was new in town, looking for company. *Boston is so big compared to my tiny wittle town in Iowa!* she messaged through the app. *I'm so bored!*

She now sat in the corner of the restaurant facing the wall.

"Here," was the gallant text she'd received, announcing his arrival. He was ten minutes late.

"Back left corner," she responded.

When he slid into the booth and met her eyes, he immediately shook his head and slid right back out.

"Stay, or I scream rape," she said. "I'll make a whole scene."

He sneered down at her. "You're nuts."

"This man brought me here by *force!*" Lucy's words echoed off the cavernous restaurant walls. Despite the late hour, it was crowded. Heads turned.

He practically dove back into the booth. "What is wrong with you?"

"Why haven't you been taking my calls," she asked, itching her hairline and taking care not to push the wig askew.

"Because...you're crazy?"

Lucy flinched at the word. "I saw you leave Maggot's apartment today."

He sat back and crossed his arms. "Following me. Catfishing. Again. And wearing a *wig*? You're going off the deep end."

"And you called Gary," she blurted, suddenly unable to control the tears springing from her eyes. "I trusted you. I thought we were a team."

Brad sighed. "Look, I thought maybe he could try to get you some help. Because I'm done with all this madness. I had a long talk with my mom about Dan. My mom never wanted to tell me the details, but when I asked her directly, she broke down and told me. They were married for all of about five minutes. Dan was a fucking creep, both on *and* off his meds. You should feel lucky you were raised by someone else. I know I do.

"I don't know what I was thinking, anyway. You tricked me into believing we were seeking justice for something awful, but when I went to see Margo today, I realized that she's really not that bad—she's just kind of pitiful. She made a mistake when she was sixteen. She wanted to keep him away from her family. She knows she went about it in a terrible way..."

He trailed off, staring intently into Lucy's eyes.

"But let's never mind all that for now. Because it's clear, Lucy. You are *not* okay—"

"So, Daddy wasn't a saint," Lucy said, waving her hand dismissively. "You don't think I know that? Even so, he didn't deserve to be messed with like that. He didn't deserve to be humiliated by that whore Patty, and certainly not harassed by his vile daughter, who sent him to the brink. We've got a way to punish Margo, litigiously. You said yourself it could work; you said your attorney friend thought we had a chance. And even if that *doesn't* work out and we lose, or it doesn't go to trial or whatever, fine. We've still got a *story*. But without you, the handsome fuck-face son," Lucy rolled her eyes, "you know I'll never be able to get anyone to even notice the story—"

"You're crazy."

"Crazy, crazy, crazy," she shouted, banging her fist on the table, rattling the silverware and almost knocking over a water glass. She could sense dozens of eyes on them. A hush had fallen over the restaurant. She didn't care.

"I've been called 'crazy' and 'stupid' my whole life. And you know what I think? I think it's a cheap way to shut down smart people who might think differently than everyone else. People who go against the grain. You may not want to accept this, *Brother* Brad, but I am *smart*."

She wiped the snot that was trickling from her nose. She felt her false eyelashes dangling from her eyelids, so she tugged them off.

"Jesus," he said, holding his palm up, "*look* at you."

"Look at *you*," she hissed. "You're an opportunist, you snake-fuck. I don't know why you just won't stick to the motherfucking plan." She banged on the table again with the palm of her hand. This time even Brad jumped. An approaching male waiter changed course and scampered off.

Brad stood up.

"Where do you think you're going?"

He addressed the surrounding tables, his voice loud and clear.

"Everyone, I apologize for this. This is my sister, and for the record, she needs help. But first, she needs to help herself. And apparently,

I'm unfit to do that. Mental health is important. I urge anyone who needs it, to get the help they need. There are resources out there."

A nearby table of twenty-something females tittered, and one called out, "You can check *my* mental health anytime."

Lucy whirled around, her wig shifting on her head. "Shut up, slut!"

Brad shook his head sorrowfully.

"Shaming other females, when you should be lifting each other up. That's what people do when they're rotten inside. Look, I wanted a sister." She noticed he wasn't even looking at her; he was looking at his audience. "Truly. As an only child, I'd begged for a sibling. But this isn't healthy. I don't need this drama in my life. Good-bye, Lucy."

The sound of clapping followed him out of the restaurant.

After he'd left, the eyeballs shifted to her; she could sense them.

She turned back to the wall. She sat there, very still, for a very long while. Finally, the waiter crept up to the table. "You good, or...?"

"No, I'm not good."

She stood and tossed her napkin, smeared with eyelashes and black, makeup-tinged tears, onto the table. Then she wrenched the wig off, causing gasps and more titters, and threw it at the waiter. It hit him in the chest and dropped to the floor.

"Not good at all."

Margo

Owen had sent a strange, cryptic text about how he was coming over, right now. And how his hands would be full, so if I could please wait by the door to let him in, that would be ideal because, "I've got a surprise."

I watched for movement out the window, taking care not to twist my neck, which was slowly getting better, but still sore.

Walking up the sidewalk was Owen, holding a box. There was no Tommy, whose absence disappointed me. There was also no Bearie at his hip, panting expectantly with his snout upturned, memories of my generous treats manifesting in a puddle of drool. Then I remembered I'd texted a couple of days before, in a bout of intense loneliness, to see if I could walk Bearie, and Owen had said that Bearie's breathing had been labored, and that the dog wouldn't leave Owen's side...

I whipped open the door. "Is Bearie okay?"

There was a trace of a smile as Owen studied my face. "The old boy's fine. You gonna have a conniption, or something?"

I shook my head and gestured for him to come in, a little embarrassed that my mind still went straight to death and loss and worst-case scenarios.

Owen struggled with the box, which was hugged to his chest. "This is for you," he grunted, slowly setting it down.

A small sound rang out from inside the box, then, scratching. And what I thought sounded like a hiss. My eyes went wide.

"You didn't bring me a cat, did you? 'Cause while I very much appreciate the gesture, I don't really care for—"

"Open it, will ya? For fuck's sake."

He threw his hands up and shook his head. He was grinning, though.

I opened the flap. A black nose breached the side, tickling the edge of my hand. Then came the brown eyes, fluffy ears, and black fur. Last, a waggling tail.

"Oh!" A yelp escaped my throat and tears sprang forth as I searched Owen's face. "Mine?" was all I could manage to croak out.

"Yup, all yours." *Yo-ahs.* "My buddy's bitch got knocked up, and he can't keep more than one. You know these things grow to Godzilla size. She's distantly related to Bearie, by the way."

I scooped up the puppy and inhaled his—no, *her*—sweet, soft puppy fur.

She gnawed on my fingertip with her needle-sharp teeth until I set her down and assaulted Owen with my own "Bearie" hug.

"Thank you, thank you, thank you." I wasn't even going to posture about how this was too big of a gift, that I couldn't accept it. That's how lonely I was. That's how much I needed this.

He told me it was nothing major, then launched into what house-training regimen worked well for Bearie, and what brand of vacuum worked best for the ridiculous amount of fur that came with a Newfoundland.

When we heard a rustling noise and the sound of scratching claws on the hardwood, we rushed into the living room. There she was, in the far corner, looking up at us guiltily.

"I'd keep a close eye on her at this age," Owen warned.

A cardigan—Lucy's, one I'd kept meaning to throw out—had been folded beneath the side table. Now, it lay on the floor by the puppy's feet. I guess I'd finally have to throw it out, seeing as this darling new pup had decided to take an inaugural piss right on top of it.

* * *

As soon as Owen left, I began to dial Izzie, feeling a strong urge to hop in the car and drive down to Marshside so that Ray and Damon could play with the pup (her name would be Little Bear, I'd decided, "LB" for short). But then I remembered, with a sinking in my chest, that Izzie still wasn't speaking to me. She hadn't returned any of my texts or calls.

Slowly, I set the phone down on the table.

I couldn't call Jessie, either, who was currently at her mother's bedside, watching her ragged breaths, wondering—and to her horror, hoping—for the last to come, to grant her mother some peace. I wanted nothing more than to be there for her.

In both cases, it was a moot point, at least logistically. I had no way to get down there after selling my car, and no money for an Uber. I could have borrowed Owen or Tommy's car, but they'd already done so much for me—Owen had not only gifted me a purebred dog that usually costs at least two grand, he'd supplied me with everything else I'd need: food, a crate, dog training book. I couldn't bear to ask anything else of him. The sale of my car helped make a dent in overdue bills, but I was still in the hole from the Zenpay theft. The funds still hadn't been recovered, and probably never would be, along with all the rent Lucy owed me.

My misery was compounding.

You're useless. You don't deserve to be here.

The next step would have to be either selling my place or going into foreclosure. I had no idea what the process was—if someone would just show up and rip the keys from my hand and kick me out. And then where would I—and now LB, whom I could barely afford to feed, let alone myself—go?

I stared down at LB, whose chest rose and fell against my stomach. I picked up the puppy and stared into her big, brown eyes.

Little Bear—what do I do?

And then, because I knew it was coming—I could feel it in my bones: *When is she coming back?*

61

Margo

This was familiar, this feeling of being hunted. Or rather, my mother being hunted.

One day, late that summer, close to the end, I'd been up in my room when he came over and began to pound on the front door. I'd sat frozen, cross-legged on my bed.

"Patty! Open the fucking door!"

Mom, who'd begun to lock every door and window that summer, had holed herself up in her bedroom, pretending not to hear any of this. I knew because I'd texted her from my room, too afraid to have the conversation in person, too afraid to look her in the eye and divulge what I'd been doing to Dan to fuel this unbridled fury.

"Mom," I texted now. "Should I call the cops?"

"No," she texted back. "He'll go away. Just ignore him. He's upset with me."

"BUT HE'S BEING A PSYCHO!" I texted back.

"I promise, it'll blow over. It always does."

Eventually, after half an hour of pounding and bellowing and swearing, he did go away.

My dad wasn't home to ask why Mom wouldn't let him in the house, why there seemed to be some issue with his "buddy," Dan Ellis. Of course, at the time, I thought this was a blessing. Mom wouldn't have to explain and get caught "cheating," when in reality, Dad could have put a stop to it.

I understood now that Mom was ashamed for what she'd gotten herself into—Patty the Party Girl Nevins, the swinger, all fun and games, pretty and clinging to her youth, getting caught up with her frumpy neighbor, ensnared by flattery. And shame, as I understood fully now, can be crippling. Shame can be deadly.

Later that same night, I left Dan a voicemail. My voice was low and gravelly. "Stop coming here. My mother doesn't want you. She hates you. She loves my dad more than anything. You should be embarrassed. You should move away to another town so you can be a lonely, forever-single, bald loser. You should take that garden hose you're always pretending to use while you're spying on my mom and choke yourself with it. Die, you fat fuck. *Die—*"

"Mags? Who are you yelling at?"

Dad had just come up from the basement and was watching me at the kitchen table, my hand shaking, my mouth up to the phone. I pulled it away from my face and hit "end."

"No one," I said.

"Well, you sound like you're possessed. Cut it out." Then he ruffled my hair and said, before going off to bed, "You're too old for prank calls."

* * *

The following night I went to bed early. I knew LB would need to pee a million times, and sure enough, she whined all night long in the metal crate beside my bed, restless, jamming her small body against the sides, waking me up anytime my eyes started to feel a little heavy. The dog training book Owen had given me said to shake the crate a little to get her to stop.

When LB and I did finally fall asleep, I dreamt of Brad out in Dan's yard, kicking the soccer ball. Boom, boom, against the side of the house. Boom, Boom.

Boom.

The sound, the force of it, was so vivid in my dream that it woke me. It was 2:30 a.m.

I fumbled with the light. LB was crying now, trembling, and no amount of shaking the crate would make her stop.

I carried her down to the kitchen and from the drawer beside the fridge, grabbed a pee pad, so she could do her business on the deck. When I went to open the glass slider, the lock was halfway down, stuck. Putting LB down on the floor, I pressed hard with my thumb and it gave way.

We stepped outside. "Come on, little one," I said, coaxing LB to follow by patting my knees. The puppy bopped affectionately against my leg, then stepped onto the pad and did her business. I handed her a treat. "Good girl."

My words echoed into the night, into the empty chamber between the surrounding buildings, across the neighbors' gardens and "backyards," cramped little plots of dead grass and clotheslines.

LB yipped; she was finished.

I leaned down to pick up the pad, and as I did, something slipped over my head and around my neck. Something cold and thin and strong, some sort of *wire*.

My hands flew to my throat. I fought for breath, digging under the wire with my fingers as I was jerked backwards. The more I resisted, the tighter it got, so I allowed myself to be led inside. Except that while they were dragging me, I tripped on the groove of the sliding door.

This was a good thing; the sudden imbalance, and then my fall, caused the wire to loosen; the sudden force must have released their grip. But that only lasted a second. It was still around my neck, so with another horrid yank I continued to be pulled backward, this time on the floor. A kick to the ribs followed, then to my head.

The last thing I saw before losing consciousness was what had fallen to the ground beside me, what the person had used to wrap around my neck. It was the wooden sign that had been nailed, by the wire, to my living room wall. INCONCEIVABLE!

* * *

When I came to—woken by LB licking my face and my throbbing neck—Lucy stood before me, her back to the still-open glass door, a knife clasped in her right hand. She'd dyed her hair black, just like mine had been, and it fell almost to her shoulders. I thought first it was a wig, but then I saw pale patches of scalp—bald spots.

LB licked me in the eye and I blinked.

Lucy swiftly leaned down and wrenched LB away from me, gripping the scruff of her neck and shaking her roughly in the air.

"Please," I gasped. "Don't hurt her."

Lucy laughed. Red striations on her eyes were growing more and more pronounced. She sniffed up a clear droplet of snot while grinning at LB, who whined in response.

"You make me sick," she said to the dog, "and I can't be having that, so..."

Before I could register what was happening, Lucy backed onto the deck and dangled the puppy over the edge. LB cried out. Then Lucy tossed her, all fifteen pounds of her, over the edge as if she were a sack of trash. There was one last cry into the night air, and then a thump, and then, nothing.

"No," I whimpered, imagining LB's fragile neck snapping as it hit the ground.

Crumpled on the floor, helpless, my entire head vibrating in blinding pain, I could only weep.

"Oh, shut up you *baby*," Lucy barked.

So, this is how it ends for me. Maybe it's all I deserve.

Lucy's right eye had begun to water, forming more spidery threads.

I tipped my head up. I supposed now was as good a time as any to get my questions answered. As I spoke, my voice rasped. Even if I'd tried to scream, not much would have come out.

"How did you know where to find me, when you first came looking?"

Lucy picked under her nail with the knife.

"What do you want, story time or something? You want to delay the inevitable? Okay. Let's see. How did I find you?" She chuckled. "Like it was hard. Your aunt should really lock her doors more. What I needed wasn't even inside; it was right in her mailbox. An outgoing card addressed to Margo Sharpe in South Boston. I opened it up, and voila! 'Happy housewarming to my favorite niece!' Thanks for the cash, by the way."

She'd been to Izzie's house. My little nephews could have been home. And after this, she could easily go back and finish them off, too.

Lucy wiped her nose.

"How did you know I would be looking for a roommate?"

"Kismet," Lucy said, cackling. "Honestly? I just waited. Daddy told me in his letters that your father was an idiot with money. The handsome Andrew Nevins was a *loser*, and put your family in the hole. It's why your mother, Patty the Slut, was attracted to my daddy.

He was more of a man. Turns out you're just as terrible with money as your parents were. How could you ever think that as a pathetic orphan with a shit-pay job you could afford your own place in South Fucking Boston? It's one of the most expensive cities on the East Coast. I did my research. I'm not stupid." She stared at me a moment, as if to challenge me. I said nothing.

"So," she continued, "I snuck through your slider a few times early in the summer and messed with your plumbing. Flushed some gifts down your toilet. Oh, and I fed your little mold aquarium there, over by the fridge. All it needed was a steady diet of good ol' H-two-oh. I knew the bills would mount up—that you'd need help. You'd be forced to find someone.

"I created about fifteen different email addresses and sent in some glorious applications, ones that would make you beg to live with someone like me. That Kangaroo idiot was just the icing on the cake. Now, *that* was kismet."

Another trickle of clear snot rolled down Lucy's upper lip. She wiped it quickly with her knife hand and then hunched over, her eyes narrowed.

"You're a monster," I said, a flood of anger and shame washing over me. "I can't believe Brad's even related to you."

At this she locked eyes with me. "Even in your pathetic misery you can't stay away from him, can you? Still stalking him, after all this time."

"I'm not stalking him," I sneered. The anger and helplessness and sadness, I found, were quickly alchemizing into what I knew best, rage, and this sudden burst of sentience was proof, I realized, that I did *not* want to die. Not by the pills I'd refrained from using last night, and not by Lucy's hand. Not today. Not ever. I would not allow this person to step one foot onto my aunt's property ever again.

So, folded up on the floor, neck throbbing, I kept on, hoping to goad Lucy into making a mistake. Into losing her cool.

"Brad's done with you," I said. "He came here to tell me that. He told me he knows Dan was an asshole, and that you're crazy—"

"*Shut up!*" Lucy shouted. "That's not true. And I am *not* crazy. I'm so sick of hearing that word—"

"That was you on the mountain," I said. "I know I saw you there."

"Of *course* you saw me, you idiot!" Lucy shrieked, waving the knife in the air. "You and your stupid friend had SKIngle on the whole time. You were *asking* for it. Give any kid twenty bucks and a Snickers and they'll do anything. He pushed you, then I paid another kid to stay with you and say he'd been there the whole time. Made him lie to his stupid mom, too. Brad underestimates me, but I'm smart as *shit*."

"So, you admit it," I spat. "It doesn't matter now anyway. You've got nothing and nobody. You've pushed everyone away. Brad hates you. Even Gary; all he wants is for you—"

"Shut up about Gary," she screamed. "Shut up, shut up, shut up! Look who's talking, you loser. *You've* got nobody." She shook her head violently, and then stopped and became very still. Her stare, though directed at me, seemed a mile off. "Brad doesn't hate me. He hates *you*. He was just putting on an act when he came here that day." But then Lucy turned to me, eyeing me in a way that reminded me of when I'd caught her snooping—with uncertainty, and a trace of fear.

Lucy sneezed. Her eyes were watering more, and her cheeks were flushed.

Slowly, I shifted my legs; the right one was aching like crazy, while the other had fallen asleep. I tried to scoot out, just slightly, from under the table.

"Ah-ah-ah," Lucy warned, hunching over, thrusting the knife at me. "Do not move an inch. I'm not done with story time. Do you know what Daddy said about you and your mom in his letters to me?"

Daddy. That word again. It sounded strange in her mouth. I hated it.

"He said everyone in town thought your mother was the world's biggest lying slut. Everyone talked about her. And your stupid dad, just thinking everything was hunky-dory. And you—the evil beast who wouldn't leave Daddy alone. He said he couldn't take it anymore. That he was going to do something drastic. That he was sorry that he'd never get to meet me."

Her voice broke at this, but she quickly recovered, drawing herself up to full height.

"But he said it was for the best, and that he'd make sure I was set for life, so long as I fulfilled his dying wish: to make everything you did to him public. Sure, he was losing it, at the end, the letters made that clear. But whose fault was that? I see those old news articles, pictures of the scene: cops, ambulances...and then there's you! Poor little Maggot Nevins. Wrapped up in a blanket, everyone hovering all around you. Like *you* were the victim. Like it hadn't been all *your* doing."

Lucy's next intake of breath was labored, junky-sounding. She cleared her throat and blinked, lifting her free hand quickly to wipe the tears away.

Now.

I grasped the legs of a kitchen chair and flung it in Lucy's direction, then scrambled to my feet and fled into the living room. Lucy knocked the chair to the side. She was on my tail in an instant, screeching.

I went straight to the side table to the left of the TV, gripping the glass vase that sat on top, and in one swift movement chucked it at Lucy's head. It only grazed her. The glass remained intact, even after it dropped to the floor. Water spilled down Lucy's chest, and so did the stems of the daisies and wispy white baby's breath that had been contained within.

Lucy burst forward with the knife and jabbed at my abdomen. I lurched backward just in time. Lucy tipped her head back, squeezing her eyes shut, and I used this split second—while her face was scrunched for an imminent sneeze—to leap to the other end of the couch. On that table: daffodils. Raising this vase overhead with both hands like a tomahawk, I heaved it down as hard as I could. This time, it knocked Lucy in the temple. The blood in its wake was instantaneous.

The moonlight through the front window revealed the hives—blotchy, red bumps—on Lucy's neck, arms, and face. That gash now, too, beside her left eye. Rooting her feet in a wide stance, Lucy stood to block my path to the front door. I thrust forward, feinting toward the door, toward Lucy. But at the last moment I pivoted and went right, down the hallway and into the bathroom. Inside, behind the door, was the tallest vase in the whole house, and inside it were sunflower stalks, garden hose–thick. They were nearly five feet tall, their burnt orange heads framed by brilliant yellow. I pulled them out and emerged from the bathroom, water dripping from the stalks onto the floor.

Lucy stood in the hallway, wiping furiously at her pooled-with-blood eyes, trying to hold firm the knife in her hand and make sense of the giant flowers in my grip.

I didn't give her much time to think. Instead I took a giant back-swing and walloped Lucy across the face with the flower heads. The knife clanked to the ground. I kicked it down the hallway and clouted Lucy again. *Whap. Whap.*

"Stop!" Lucy puled, swatting them away, her knees buckling.

But I didn't relent, shoving the heads into Lucy's nose, creaming them into her face like a pie.

Lucy finally slumped to the ground, gasping for air, immobilized. For now.

That's when I flew up the stairs to my bedroom, the pain in my neck—from the wire and from my old injury—masked by adrenaline. I dialed 911.

"Intruder," I panted into the phone. "Armed. Need ambulance." Then I hung up and texted Owen and Tommy at once: SOS. LUCY HERE.

When I clambered down the stairs, there was a knock at the front door. Were they here already?

I rushed down, unbolted the door, and whipped it open. Standing there on the stoop was Carmen Kangaroo, a baseball bat in one hand.

"Are you *okay*?" she said.

I froze. "I'm—"

Suddenly Carmen shoved me. I fell into the coatrack. Carmen raised the bat over her head and I didn't have time to scream.

62

Margo

I removed my arm from my face and looked up. Carmen hadn't hit me with the bat. She'd hit Lucy, who'd somehow death-crawled up the hallway and had been right behind me.

Carmen gently pulled me up by the elbow.

The two of us looked down at Lucy as she lay on the ground, blood pooling on the floor beneath her head. Lucy's neck, like her face, had ballooned to resemble a flesh-filled donut. She was still alive and breathing. Barely.

Carmen's whole body shook as tears streamed down her full cheeks. She looked very small.

"I didn't mean to—I just saw commotion through the window, and I'd seen her creeping around your place lately. I tried to call you, but it wouldn't go through, so I just came over...I didn't mean to hurt anyone." The tears rained down.

I placed my hand on her shoulder. "She was trying to kill me. You saved me."

From the ground, Lucy gurgled, "I was doing what he told me."

I looked down at her. It was true. Lucy was just doing what that heinous beast had told her to do, from beyond the grave.

I wondered if the ambulance would get here in time. There shouldn't be any more death, any more heartache, for anyone, I thought. There's been enough.

Lucy took another long gasp. Her red eyes shot up to meet mine, and her lips contorted with rage. "You took him from me. You're a dirty whore, just like your mother. She deserved to die, and so do you."

My short-lived pity vanished. Without thinking, I blasted Lucy in the ear with my bare foot. A repulsive screech escaped Lucy's lips. Poised to kick again, I caught sight of Carmen, who stood beside me, gaping.

I looked over and saw myself in the hall mirror: red-faced, almost unrecognizable, and yet, familiar. It was the Maggie underneath the covers, snickering as she taunted Dan over text, night after night, never dreaming what it could lead to. The Maggie who'd walked by his house on the way to the lake, shouting things like "Limp dick!" as he watered his roses and glared back, his pebble-eyes cold and gray, locked on me like quarry.

Oh, God, I thought. *I'm still her.*

There was the sound of a radio. Voices. Blue lights reflecting on the wall.

I stared down at my foot, big toe throbbing from striking Lucy so hard in the head. Then, I remembered what I had to do—praying it wasn't too late—and turned and opened the front door. I almost knocked foreheads with a male police officer, middle-aged, with kind brown eyes.

"She attacked me," I cried, pointing to Lucy, on the floor. "She needs help. She needs an epi pen."

Then I pointed to Carmen, who'd retreated further down the hallway and was standing there in apparent shock, swaying. "And she was protecting me. That's my neighbor."

The officer craned his neck to look beyond me. He said something into his radio, brushed by, and knelt next to Lucy, who was still lying prostrate, the rise and fall of her chest now nearly imperceptible. On the floor was a small white object. I saw him raise it up to the light. A tooth.

I stumbled outside. There was Owen, waving his arms at me from the sidewalk, with a concerned Tommy beside him. I cried out, "The puppy, I have to find her! Lucy—"

But a uniformed arm held me back. A female voice said something about having to ask me a few questions, that I wasn't going anywhere right now...

I heard Owen call something out, but my ears felt blocked, like I was underwater. Not to mention the tears were coming so fast that they blinded me, and the revived pain in my neck was unbearable.

Wiping my eyes, I saw Owen talking to the female officer. After a minute, she nodded, walked up to me, and took me gently by the arm. "Okay. Show me where the puppy is."

"LB!" I called, rushing down the alleyway to the back of the house. I turned my phone flashlight on, pointed it left, right. I called her name again and again. "LB!"

The officer's flashlight aided in the search, but it revealed only candy wrappers, an old tennis ball, a beer can. I almost didn't want to find the puppy, because this stillness, the quiet, probably meant she hadn't survived the fall.

Or maybe LB had toddled over to a neighbor's. Or she'd found her way to the street, which wouldn't be good either—

"Over there," said the officer, pointing the beam of her flashlight.

I rushed over to the lump of black fur and reached down and scooped up the pup. She was still. Too still. And bloody.

"Little Bear," I sobbed, pressing my cheek into the pup's back. I deserve this, I thought. I deserve everything.

Carrying her like an infant, I stumbled to the front of the house. The officer allowed me a little more space. Red lights occluded the blue now, and there lay Lucy, on a stretcher, her head and neck blown up like a tick. She had on an oxygen mask; she wasn't dead. Not yet.

Owen had appeared at my side. Tommy was hanging back, chatting with the female officer. I noticed how pretty she was. Stupidly, I found I was jealous.

I turned to Owen. "She's dead."

"Is she?" he said, his eyes flicking to street, to the rear lights of the ambulance as it drove off. "She looked pretty bad."

"I meant..." I looked down. "The puppy." I stroked LB's fur. "But I kicked her. Lucy, I mean. I kicked her when she was down. I'm evil."

Owen looked me square in the eye. "Listen to me, Margo." His thick Boston accent made it sound like *Mahgo*. "Did you illegally enter her home and attack her? No. Other way around. She threatened someone's life in the dead of the night and tossed an innocent little puppy off a fucking deck. Okay? Don't beat yourself up. You didn't do this. She did. You're safe. That's all that matters. You got that, Margo? Tell me you got that."

Tearfully, I nodded, and then bowed my head, finding solace in stroking LB's fur. Time seemed to stop. When I became aware of my surroundings again, Owen was gone, replaced by a pair of new officers.

Voices buzzed all around—questions, which I couldn't hear, let alone understand.

Someone led me back inside. Every light had been turned on. Upended on the floor in the living room were the vases I'd hurled at Lucy, their wet stains soaking the carpet. There were sprigs of baby's breath. Yellow daffodils. Daisies. And, in the hallway, my last resort: sunflowers.

Outside, neighbors had gathered on the sidewalk, watching with their phones out. I stared dumbly back at them. Suddenly, I felt something beneath my finger. I'd refused to put LB down, and now I was glad, because that was her pulse. A faint pulse. Her eyes were open now, and she was breathing lightly, tongue lolling out of her mouth.

"Oh," I whispered, nuzzling my face into hers.

I looked up at the sky. For seven years, I'd hated looking up at the stars, acknowledging the nebulous place in which my parents may or may not have resided. But I did it now, knowing they were there, knowing they'd been there all along.

"Thank you," I whispered.

Margo

Two months later

Jessie called me after the open house, breathless.

"We've got twenty offers for your parents' house—all over asking. The photographer did an amazing job. The new flooring, fresh black paint on the front door, new plantings out front—the house looks gorgeous. Cars were lined up down the street. I ran out of business cards. It was in*sane*."

"Izzie told me she drove by," I said. "Said it was a complete zoo."

"Does that mean things are okay between you guys now?"

I told Jessie that Izzie had driven up as soon as she could after the night Lucy attacked. There were a lot of tears. A lot of laughter, too. Neither of us slept. We stayed in my bed, holding each other, and she told me stories about my mom and dad I'd never heard before, from when they were young and happy, and even after they'd had me unexpectedly—how much they loved me.

"It was a terrible couple of days, obviously," I told Jessie now, "but she made it so much better."

I just needed time, honey, Izzie had said. *To wrap my mind around everything. I'd blamed myself for so much. You're not the only one who still needs to do work on herself. Because listen to me, Maggie. You were a* child. *The real evil was Dan. Never forget that.*

"Margo?" Jessie said now, "we're getting way more for the house than I'd ever hoped. You're going to be okay. You'll pay her back, easy, and still have a lot left for yourself."

"For you, too," I said. "Hopefully the commission will help you out."

"It will," Jessie said. "I was looking at urns and headstones this morning? That shit's expensive. A complete racket. He tried upselling me on this bougie urn. Like, seriously? Talk about the most depressing shopping trip ever."

"Tell me about it," I said. "They got me and Izzie on this stupid princess-looking thing, and after we bought it, we were like, what the hell? Mom wouldn't be caught *dead* in that." Jessie and I laughed, and then she said, "Guess if we can't laugh, we'll never get through any of this."

"That's why I love you," I told her. "And always will."

* * *

Everything was happening all at once.

Later that same day, Corinne called.

"I'm hoping enough time has passed, since your...incident. You know, for you to come back in and discuss your future at this company. If you still want one."

"Will I have to report to Astrid?" I asked.

"No," Corinne said. "We'll discuss all that, okay? But no."

"That's all I needed to hear. I'll head in now."

When I got to the Events wing, trudging down the row of cubicles, no one looked me in the eye.

Except for Shanna. As I passed her desk, Shanna whispered, "Hey."

"Hey," I said, but continued to walk on.

"Come here a sec?" Shanna said.

I stopped and turned.

She rolled her chair closer to me, into the aisle. "Please don't think any of us took part in any of Astrid's bullshit. We all wanted you to know that. We feel terrible. Like, it makes me sick she still has a job, to be honest. Corinne's heart is too big." She lowered her voice. "She took Debbie back, even. After she cheated."

"Okay," I said, uninterested in Corinne and Debbie. What they did was their business, and if Corinne believed in the power of redemption, was that so bad? If people don't believe in that kind of thing, what does that say about the world we live in? It wouldn't be one that would accept me, that's for sure.

I started back toward my desk.

"I heard you offed that Lucy girl with a sunflower."

I turned. "Partly true," I said, "I used a sunflower. But she's still in the ICU, hanging on."

"Badass," Shanna said, eyes shining, not seeming to hear that last part. "Was all that planned—having those flowers in the house?"

I allowed a smile. "It was a backup plan."

* * *

Jackie's Flower Shop, off East 3rd, was run by a buxom, no-nonsense woman who'd lived in Southie her whole life. I had never met

325

her in person—every order in the past had been online, back when I used to send myself flowers from "Brad," and back before Lucy had made me throw those flowers in the trash.

But it turned out Jackie was incredibly kind, and helpful. Especially in identifying for me the most allergenic types of flowers, which I would return for and purchase week after week, like daffodils, daisies, baby's breath, and—most deadly for hay fever—sunflowers.

One day Jackie finally asked, "What's all this for, anyway?" She'd been standing at the register, her breasts spilling out of her tight black blouse.

"Self-defense," I said, handing her the last of my dog-walking money.

Jackie gave me an odd look and rang me up. When she was finished, she said, "I always found daffodils fascinating. You know that myth about Narcissus, the guy in love with himself, who'd stare at himself in the lake all day?"

I nodded.

"Well, the flower is from the genus, *Narcissus*. And get this: The gods believed Narcissus would die of hunger from staring at himself so long. Rather than have him starve, they turned him into a flower." Her accent was like Owen's. *Nahcissus*, and *flowah*. "Some accounts say he killed himself," she added, "but either way, whaddya think they planted in his place?"

I paused, following Jackie's gaze. "Daffodils?"

"Uh-huh. They're supposed to symbolize vanity. Unrequited love. Whenever a guy comes in here asking for daffodils—and let's be real, most of them are cheap-asses; I mean, might as well pick 'em off the side of the road—anyway, I tell them not to do it. Not just 'cause it's cheap, but 'cause they're considered bad luck." She grinned. "Who knew, right?"

I thought of those sad, droopy daffodils in my mother's kitchen, unsolicited gifts from Dan, rotting in the water my mom never bothered to freshen. I thought of the yellow petals he'd placed over the sockets of their eyes, after coring them out with his garden shears.

Bad luck, indeed.

* * *

Later, in the meeting room, Corinne made me sit through Astrid's forced-apology tour. I wasn't alone with her, at least; both Corinne and a woman named Lynda from HR—cropped-short hair, furiously typing notes—were there, too. I did my best to sit quietly and nod and not look at the clock during Astrid's tearful whining, even when Astrid had to excuse herself, because she'd gotten so worked up.

When that was done Corinne outlined all the anti-workplace-bullying workshops they'd put in place. She told me it would never happen again, and that if it did, Corinne wanted to know immediately. ("I don't want you suffering in silence.")

None of this made me feel better. None of it *mattered*, as far as I was concerned. All that mattered was that I was steadily employed—at least, until after my parents' house had sold, and I could find something better, a job where I wouldn't have to see Astrid every day. At that point I'd finally be able to see my way out of the tunnel of debt and renovate my own house. I'd never need a roommate again.

Finally, HR Lynda wrapped up her notes and concluded the meeting.

Corinne apologized three more times, and I stayed a few extra minutes alone in the room, letting it all sink in. Everything would be okay.

Especially because now, I had something else to look forward to.

I peered down in my lap at the Decomposition Notebook, turned past the last of Lucy's private scribbles and scrawls.

These new pages were mine. These new pages would contain my *own* plan.

* * *

Brad walked into the dark bar. Sean, behind the bar, didn't greet him. Neither did the men lined up down the end, swiveled halfway around their stools to look at him. Owen was one of those men, and so was Tommy. Tommy, I noticed, wore the biggest scowl of them all.

No matter. To my shock, and my happiness, Brad had been answering my texts, my invitations.

Brad looked around the bar, spotted me, and walked over.

"You look really good," he said, sliding into his seat. His tone was kind. Kinder than it had ever been.

"You do, too," I said, and meant it. His hair was freshly cut and his under-eye circles were gone. I knew he meant it about me, too; Carmen and Stephanie, from across the street, finally approved of my new highlights after seeing the first attempt, a rusty orange, and insisting I visit their stylist, instead. I had also put on some weight, my skin was clear and tanned, and my bangs had grown out. I looked like Maggie again.

The two of us sat for a while, staring at one another, saying nothing.

Finally Brad set his elbows on the table. "So is this about you getting harassed by those podcast people, too? The ones she was obsessed with?"

"You know perfectly well that I have."

Brad raised his eyebrows. "What do you mean?"

"You called them," I said. "You initiated it."

"No, I didn't." He said this weakly, without conviction. Then he shifted in his seat. "Okay. Technically, I called them *back*. Said I'd do an interview."

328

"I take it they offered you money, too, for the interviews?" I said.

He gave a sheepish smile. "I'm going in to the studio tomorrow," he said. "I could use the cash."

"I'm surprised you do, after everything."

He cocked his head. "Why do you say that?"

"Well," I said, pausing, "how much did you get out of her?" Then I bit into my Shamwich, which Sean had just brought over, without a word.

Brad watched as the mustard dripped down my chin. I quickly drew up a napkin and wiped.

"I don't know what you're talking about," he said.

"Money for the 'attorneys,'" I said, making air quotes. "Come on, Brad. I know. Lucy told Astrid enough shit to fill a book."

He crossed his arms. "I wouldn't listen to that train wreck."

"Brad. Don't worry. I really don't care. In fact, I'm glad you bled her dry."

He smiled, relieved. "Good."

"I did ask you here for something else. There's one more thing I wanted to ask you. Something I want to hear from you."

"Okay."

I turned on my phone, navigated to the picture, and showed him my screen. "Know who this is?"

"No."

"Look a little closer."

"Some small, skinny person with a ski mask on. I don't know. Why? What's that from?"

"It's a still-shot of the person who broke into my house and planted dead rats in my bed."

"Well, it sucks that that happened, but I don't know who it is. Is it Lucy?" He looked at it again, squinting. "No, I guess that person's too...short."

I swiped to a different picture. This time Brad was in the frame, next to a preteen boy, in front of a basketball hoop. "What about him?"

Brad frowned. "That's Corey. My Little Brother."

"Right. He's about the same size and frame of that scrawny thing who dumped rats in my bed. He also happened to be at Triton Mountain, the day I got wiped out by a snowboarder."

I waited. Brad stared at me blankly.

"Did you know he was involved with Lucy, that she was paying him to do shit for her?"

Brad's face flushed. "I swear to God, *no*. I didn't. Look, let's lay it all out. The truth. Yes. I took money from Lucy. But that money was owed to me. I was the kid that asshole abandoned. Not some bastard child with a dad of her own already. A nice dad, too. A good dad. Anyway, Lucy started dumping money into my accounts. Some of it was for the lawyers, some to chip in for my rent. She was staying with me, annoying me, eating all my food, so I kept it. She gave it to me, fair and square. It was legal. What I did with it was my business. Maybe that makes me look like a piece of shit, but, whatever." Then he held up a finger. "Corey, on the other hand, I'm gonna fucking kill. No wonder she asked me all those questions about my charity work." He shook his head in disgust.

My eyes slid over to Owen and the rest who were watching from their stools. I gave them a tiny nod, then looked back at Brad. "I believe you. About Corey, your Little Brother."

"You do?"

"I questioned Corey earlier, with Owen over there." I pointed at Owen, who was glaring at Brad from his barstool, his foot resting on Bearie. "He knows Corey's dad from high school. Owen and Corey's dad put the fear of God in the poor kid, and he still swore you didn't know anything." I smiled. "Lucy had made him promise not to tell you. He said Lucy practically had him on salary."

"Okay," Brad said. "Why'd you ask me here and question me, then, if you knew the answer already?"

"Guess I wanted to hear it from you. And, I wanted to see if you'd admit to keeping her money."

"Well, I admit it. And I give zero fucks about it."

"Same. Honestly." I laughed and sat back. "Serves her right. They're pulling the plug tomorrow, I hear. Not much else they can do."

"Well, that's a shame."

We smiled at one another, and Brad didn't get up to leave, to be rid of me. Instead, he gestured to Sean for a beer.

And this is when I knew it was the beginning of something beautiful.

Margo

"Welcome to *Dirty Vines*. I'm your host, Sly Stevens."

"And I'm Skye Stevens!"

"We're true crime's number-one podcast in America, and today we're on episode 145. Can you believe it, Skye?

"Can't believe it, Sly."

Brad sat beside me in the booth, headphones on. The thrill of being beside him, less than a foot away—the thrill of his very presence—was as electric as it was before, back when I didn't truly know him. Maybe even more electric.

Because then, I didn't know the bad parts. Didn't know the real him. That was when the idea of him—that foolish idea of him, that positive, happy-go-lucky version, with the fake number in my phone—eclipsed the real person.

Izzie, Owen, and practically everyone else were still telling me to stay away from Brad. But I couldn't. We were tied together forever, just as I'd known all along. No one else would understand the impact of Lucy Somers, of what she had put us through.

At the moment, Brad was recounting his very first "date" with Lucy.

"Here she is, looking like she got electrocuted five minutes ago. I mean, her hair was, like, sticking straight off her head. I got cat-fished big-time, was all I could think about. I gave some excuse that I had to go, to work or something. But she wouldn't take no for an answer. She was *dragging* me around this pizza shop, then dropped the bomb: 'Hey, by the way, I've got information about your dad, information *from* your dad.' And I'm, like, holy shit, *what*? *How*? But she wouldn't tell me.

"She got me to see her again the next day, and the next, and the next. She was pretty good at that. I was about to bail when she finally revealed she was my sister. Then, I was so happy to have a sibling that I forgave a lot of her extreme behavior. At least, for a while. Until I realized how dangerous she was. How *crazy*."

My thoughts floated to lunch in less than an hour, after this was all done. A long overdue lunch date. My stomach fluttered in antici-pation, as well as hunger; I hadn't eaten anything all day, having been too apprehensive.

Up until this point, Sly and Skye had preferred that Brad and I record separately. Brad had gone on at least five times, me once. But today, I'd insisted we do it together. Today was going to be special.

"I remember when I saw you through the pizza shop window," I cut in, softly.

Skye turned up the volume on the soundboard and nodded for me to keep going, gesturing toward the mic so I'd get closer.

"When I saw them together, I knew it was over," I went on. "My crush on you"—I smiled ruefully at Brad—"had come back to bite me in the ass. It was pathetic."

334

"Honey," Skye purred, "you can't beat yourself up. We've all done embarrassing things like this at some point in our lives." She laughed. "And look at him—I mean, any girl would be obsessed."

Sly said, "Hey. I'm sitting two feet away."

Skye laughed and so did Brad. Again, he didn't appear to be disgusted or annoyed by my adoration, but rather, flattered. Happy, even.

"I don't know if your listeners know this," Brad said, "but Margo is a *total* babe now. Like, you guys have the pics from before, with her, like, pasty skin and black hair and shit? Now, she's, like, transformed." He shrugged and smiled. "I'd bang her."

Skye and Sly whooped into the microphone. "Is he asking you out?" Skye asked.

I smiled absently as I looked down and checked my phone. A text had come through.

The text.

I looked up. "Hey, guys—I have a fan, I guess you could say, who wanted to call in and chat with us. Is that all right?"

"Right on," said Sly. He hit a button, whispering, "We'll edit for placement, but let's hear it. Always love to hear from fans."

"You can call in now," I texted.

Thirty seconds later, he did.

"Umm, hey," he said, his voice piping through our earphones.

"Hey, Peter," I said.

"Peter?" Brad said, furrowing his brows.

"Who's Peter, again?" Sly said, looking at his notes.

Peter spoke louder and clearer into the phone.

"I'm Brad's old roommate. Thanks to Margo for arranging this, by the way, but I wanted to call in after hearing some episodes and seeing all this...*adulation* for Brad. Guess I felt compelled to tell everyone, like, this dude? He's a piece of *shit*. Like, not just your run-of-the-mill, womanizer piece of shit, but a really bad guy. Did you know he owes me thousands of dollars in rent? And that he doesn't even have a job? He's legit, like, a white-collar criminal after embezzling money from his last company—"

"What the fuck, Peter," Brad snarled into the mic. His eyes were slits, directed at me. "What the actual fuck?"

Skye and Sly kept turning knobs, exchanging gleeful glances.

"Go on, Peter," I said.

"Yeah, so, like, all that charity work he does is actually community service, as part of his punishment. Somehow he was able to get it expunged from his record. And dude, don't ask me how he managed to get placed around kids doing the Little Brother thing, 'cause again, he's a criminal. Wait. Did I say that already?" A pause. "Sorry, I took some edibles earlier.

"Anyway, all the guy does is lie. He's good-looking, so he gets away with it. And man, that sister of his had problems, and he played into that so hard. It was sad, man. Really fucking sad. I mean, yeah, I thought it was funny at first, because she was like a cartoon. But Brad didn't even tell me she was his *sister* for the longest time, so I was thinking she's this stalker. But then, she's showing up at all hours, banging on the door, screeching about their father and their 'plan' or whatever.

"That's when I told Brad not to encourage her. Like, clearly she had *legitimate* mental health problems. But he didn't listen. I'd officially had enough when I heard him telling Lucy to go over to Margo's place and scare her a little, that it 'couldn't hurt.' Then I hear that she actually went there and tried *killing* Margo, and I was just, like, holyyyyy—"

Brad stood and ripped his headphones off.

"I didn't agree to this. You can't use any of this. You can't prove it."

I took out the Decomposition Notebook from my bag and flipped to Lucy's last entry. I began to read it out loud:

Brad did a complete 360. Wait. 180. Or 360?
I don't know, but HE IS ON BOARD. I repeat, my
LOVING BROTHER IS ON BOARD. He told me

he'd changed his mind and called the lawyer
back and everything is STILL in place. He said
he was sorry, and that Margo was dangerous. A
threat. That she had plans for me, just like what
she did to Daddy, and I should be on guard. He
told me I should maybe even pay her a visit,
scare her a little. I said GLADLY, you dummy, I
would be HONORED—

"Those are all lies," Brad shouted. "You know those are lies. She was messed up, obviously. She was an absolute dumb bitch. Besides, you really think lawyers would look at that case and charge you, Margo, for taking a fucking pill bottle, seven years ago, when you were a *kid*? You think I even cared about Dan, that asshole? Like, fine, I humored her for a while. But nothing I did was illegal—and it wasn't my fault she was showering me with cash. Cash *owed* to me."

He looked beseechingly at Sly.

"Margo and I talked about this off-air, and now she's acting like this is some *revelation*. You're making me seem like a monster, when all I did was—"

"You told her to come threaten me," I said, keeping my voice calm. "You encouraged her to attack me. You knew I'd filled my house with flowers. You saw a bunch in my house that day when you came over to 'apologize' to me. You knew if she came there, she might die. You wanted to get rid of her for good, at the risk of me losing *my* life in the process. You *are* a monster."

He lunged at me, reaching for the notebook. "Give me that."

But Sly, as wiry as he was, had at least a foot on Brad, and Skye, nearing six feet herself, was surprisingly lithe and strong. They held him off and managed to push him out of the studio and into the hallway.

As for me, without another word, I walked out the other exit, which led right outside, into the fresh spring air, where I walked to the beat-up pickup truck waiting for me at the curb.

The window rolled down. "How'd it go? Need any backup in there?"

I smiled. "I think they've got it handled. Besides, I'm hungry."

"You choose the place," Tommy said. "That was the agreement."

"I'm in the mood for a Shamwich," I said, climbing into the passenger seat. I turned around to look in the back. "Right, Bearie? That's where you want to go."

Bearie poked his head over the seat and emitted a happy whine as I patted his head.

"You good with it, too, little lady?" Tommy asked, looking in the rearview.

LB gave a happy yelp as her head, encased in a lampshade cone to prevent her from licking her stitches, knocked against the back of my seat.

"The Sham it is," Tommy said, and we set off.

* * *

It hadn't taken long, after the debacle with Lucy, for me to finally put to rest the fantasy version of Brad Ellis.

The unadorned facts about Brad, removed from his shiny pedestal, were this:

Brad Ellis was the son of my parents' murderer. Brad Ellis was not the answer to my problems—a shoulder to cry on, a love-of-my-life Westley.

No. Brad Ellis was a Prince Humperdinck.

That I had ever thought otherwise was, I knew now, inconceivable.

Epilogue

There were other entries, written during lucid moments, introspective moments. And these have a startling clarity to them when I read them now:

> September 14, 2020
> Daddy. Dad. Pops.
> What would I have called him? What nickname would he have given me?
> In his letters, he kept calling me Lacy. That stung, and I wish it didn't. Mom says it's a sign he didn't really care about me. That he made, according to her, "no effort, once he found out about you, to meet you. All he cared about were his own warped schemes."
> Lacy, Lacy, Lacy. What an ugly name.
> He didn't know. It's not his fault.
> Daddy, if you're reading this, it's okay that you called me Lacy. I don't mind.

> November 1, 2020
> I'm not glad he died. But sometimes, I am glad he didn't know me, and see me for what I am. Ugly.
> If he wanted a nice daughter, it's good that he died, because he'd be disappointed.
> If he wanted a successful daughter, a smart daughter, one who doesn't feel so angry all the time, it's good he died, 'cause he'd be so disappointed.
> If he'd lived, he would have met the real Lucy Somers, who can't stop ripping her hair out. Who can't make friends. Who can't attract any men.

December 15, 2020
Daddy, I can tell from your letters—I reread
them over and over—that you had someone in your
brain—an intruder. I have one, too. He tells me I'm
worthless. He has your voice.
I'll make things right for you, Daddy.

December 25, 2020
Sometimes, I hate myself.

February 14, 2021
I look back on what I wrote in this stupid note-
book, and I don't even recognize the writing. It's as
if it's someone else. I hate that person. Why am I
that person? When will the voice stop?
When
will he stop
haunting
me?
It's not his fault. It's mine. No.
It's his. It's his.

* * *

I feel embarrassed that I have her notebook and that I've read these things.

I'm glad I'll finally be getting rid of it today.

When I get to Serenity Meadows I have it wrapped up in a gift bag, along with some other gifts: a couple of books, a new notebook, some pens—though I'm not sure those are allowed. I'll have to ask Gary.

And there he is.

"Hi, Miss Maggie!" Gary says, and he's smiling, loping toward me in shorts, with those long legs of his, even skinnier unsheathed. "They tell us she's having a good day," he says, leading me to a chair over by the window in the waiting area. "Judy and Sav went to the gift shop for a couple things. They'll be right back."

I hold out the gift bag. "I put a few things together for her, too. I'm returning her notebook—you know, her diary. I hope she's not angry that I read from it on the podcast."

"Are you kidding?" Gary says, laughing, "She's over the moon. She's getting fan mail now. Real old-fashioned letters from 'Team Lucy.'" He frowns. "Although, nothing from that *brother* of hers."

"Not surprised," I say. I don't add that Brad probably figures Lucy is dead, since I never updated him on her condition. Weeks ago, she somehow clawed out of the near-vegetative state and woke up, lucid, with no long-term damage that they could see. A near-miracle, the doctors said.

"There they are," he says, and I turn and see two tall, beautiful women: Judy, dark, curly hair streaked with gray around her face, and wearing a soft, friendly smile. And Savannah, striking, with her father's legs.

Savannah runs up to me and gives me a hug, then backs off.

"I hope that was okay, Margo. Maggie. I'm just...I'm so happy to meet you, and happy that you're such a nice person!" She hiccups. "Oops!" she says, laughing, holding her hand to her mouth. When she hiccups again she plugs her nose.

"Should we all go in?" Gary says, looking at his watch. "They said two o'clock would be a good time. She'll be rested, after taking her pills."

"Are you sure?" Savannah says to her father, narrowing her eyes. "I don't want her to throw a succulent at me again."

"All projectiles have been removed."

Savannah holds her breath and her nose, and then after another hiccup erupts anyway, she lowers her hand, breathes out, and nods.

Judy touches my arm. "At first I wasn't sure what to make of your intentions coming here, Margo, I'm afraid to say. But Gary says you've been in close contact, that you've worked hard to make your own amends. So, I suppose I should thank you. For not writing her off. For not pressing charges, or...you know, for just being here. If you'd known her before she had these mental health issues...Well, I think we're getting a little of her back, day by day."

Savannah purses her lips and looks at me guiltily. "Let's be real, though. She wasn't ever, like, a saint. She wasn't always the nicest to me." Hiccup.

"No, not a saint," Gary says. "But...her heart. It's good. We know it's good."

I think of those notebook entries. The intruder. Then I take a deep breath, clutching the gift bag.

I know there is a chance she could have a stolen knife or something under her pillow. She could stab me in the eye with it. She could be fooling everyone. She could be tossing her medication into the toilet.

Or, she could be trying. She could be accepting that it's not her fault. She could have forgiven herself, as I've forgiven myself—and, though it's been hard, as I've even forgiven her.

"Shall we?" I say.

Gary links his arm with mine. "We shall."

Also by Nicole Barrell

The Hollow: A Novel

Acknowledgments

Thank you to all who helped lift me, and this book, up to where it needed to be, especially to my early (early!) readers: Emily Dumas, Beth Perry, Mandy Darnell, and Hayley Nickerson. These later readers helped me out of some dead and loose ends: Caitlin Butler, Sarah Teczar, Casey Cormier, and Erin McGee. Much appreciation goes to my equally busy, sweet, and smart colleagues at Sturgis: Megan Briggs Magnant and Anna Botsford. All your kind and generous feedback was crucial for me to keep moving forward.

I also want to extend a massive thank you to Laura Carter, who read *countless* drafts over the years and offered her razor-sharp eye—and enthusiasm—to every one of them.

Thank you to Miranda Heyman at Woodhall Press for championing this book along with the team there, including Melissa Hayes, who showed me how painfully often I start sentences with *so*. I can't forget my lovely Cape Cod Writing Center fiction writing group: Alyssa, Harris, Jonathan, and Pam, who offered feedback, commiseration, and support on a weekly basis.

Thank you to my students at Sturgis for making me laugh, cry, and care.

Thank you to my husband, Mike, for not running for the hills as I shirked *many* responsibilities in favor of my manuscript, and shout out to my little Nolan-Noly-Noles—my little miracle blondie, my little motivator.

To say I wrote myself out of some tough times these last seven years would be an understatement. At varying points this book was an obsession, an albatross, a distraction, a balm. The first draft came before my stupid boob cancer, the last draft came after my mom died from her stupid boob cancer. In between were tormented afternoons in parking lots where I sneaked in as many words, edits, and queries as I could between my day job and daycare pickup. In effect the main character, Margo, changed from draft to draft, page to page. She was a shapeshifter, depending on my moods and whims. I finally nailed her down in this last draft. She's not me, but she's an extension of me as I moved through my own grief; I can't deny that. To claim anything else would be, well, a goddamn sham.

I want to say a final thanks to my friends and family who grew up with me on Cape Cod for their support and inspiration over the years. It's a unique spot to live in year-round. And, in my estimation, the most beautiful, with the most beautiful people. I love you all.

About the Author

Nicole Barrell is the author of the psychological suspense THE HOLLOW, called an "admirable debut...an engaging journey into a troubled mind, a promising novel (Kirkus). She was also a Kirkus Critics' Choice "Author to Watch." Nicole earned her Publishing and Writing M.A. from Emerson College and her Journalism B.A., *summa cum laude*, from the honors college at University of Massachusetts Amherst. Nicole is a native of Cape Cod, where most of her stories are set. She now teaches high school there and lives outside Boston with her husband, toddler son, and dog.